MEASURE OF A MAN

Music City Heat: 3

Marie-Nicole Ryan

RYANDALE PUBLISHING

Copyright © 2019 by Mary Varble
Cover by Mary Varble
First Ryandale Press Electronic Publication: July 2019
First Ryandale Press Print Publication: July 2019

All rights reserved, Ryandale Press.

Library of Congress registration pending

Chapter One

Showtime.

She blinked, giving her eyes time to adjust to the dim lighting in Gatsby's Jazz Bar. Mellow notes from a saxophone band drifted lazily through the air.

There.

Tamsyn Holt spied her client's fiancé sitting at the end of the bar nursing what looked like vodka rocks. The jazz bar was a nice departure from Nashville's usual country music venues where she normally found her clients' significant others.

Her mark glanced impatiently at his watch. Was he meeting someone? Better make a move before someone else showed up and spoiled her action. Weaving her way through the bar patrons, she spied an open barstool. Backup, in the form of her brother Justin, entered the bar a minute or so behind her. She could smell his Old Spice after-shave. Yes, her brother used the old-fashioned aftershave, in spite of being the family agency's information specialist aka computer nerd.

Initially, she'd been reluctant to take on Brianna Tollison as a client because of their previous friendship. As she neared the mark, one Jason St. John, she noted he was even better looking than the photo Bree had provided. Seen live and in color, this dude exuded a definite James Bond vibe. He was entirely too virile to be a mere financial consultant. His longish dark hair was expertly trimmed by someone who knew what they were doing. And his profile was movie-star perfect.

She slid onto a barstool two spots away from his and ordered a glass of white zinfandel, something she could sip slowly without becoming impaired. From the corner of her eye, she noted her brother had occupied another seat, two away from hers closer to the door.

She paid for her wine, then clumsily elbowed her purse to the floor so that everything spilled. A tube of lipstick rolled toward her mark.

Perfect.

"Drat." She hopped from the stool and scrambled for the tube. As she did, St. John eased from his seat and retrieved it.

"You lost something." His voice was low and resonant. The very sound set her senses thrumming. His steely blue, yet amused, gaze seemed to bore through her, as if he recognized her ploy but wouldn't necessarily call her on it. Or would he?

"I believe I did," she murmured when she regained her power of speech. "Thank you." She grabbed for the tube.

He held the lipstick just out of reach. "Not so fast."

"Excuse me?" What was he playing at? She held out her hand, palm open. "My lipstick..."

"It's certainly isn't my shade." He arched a dark-winged brow. And laid the cosmetic gently into her palm. The slight brush of his fingers against her hand...warm...sensual...inviting.

Her heart sped up, her mouth dried. Irrational thoughts of leading him away from the bar and screwing him blind came to mind. "Uh—" she managed to utter. She tried to swallow.

"You wanted to meet me. I'm Jason."

Her fingers closed over the lipstick. This mark wasn't responding the way she'd expected. Usually, they either made a *how-about-it* comment or else they politely ignored her. But St. John seemed to be onto her game and was intent on seducing *her*.

Maybe she should've tried a more subtle approach. He was definitely a cut above the typical good old boy she was ordinarily hired to tempt. Maybe she should get her thoughts in order. *Maybe* she should run like hell.

"Well, didn't you?"

"Want to meet *you*?" She stiffened her spine. "I merely came in for a drink before heading home."

"You're a working girl." Not even the hint of a question in his tone.

OMG. He thought she was a prostitute. "What I *am* is a woman who works, not in any sense a *working girl* as you seem to imply."

He arched a dark brow in Justin's direction. "And the blond dude who came in behind you isn't your pimp?"

She sucked in a breath. How had he pegged Justin as being with her so easily? "M-my what?" She glanced around. "In Green Hills? Seriously?" She whirled to leave.

Dammit. She'd screwed up. Now she'd have to return Brianna's retainer and recommend another firm to see if her fiancé could be tempted. Still grasping the lipstick, she shoved it inside her purse and headed for the door.

Dammit. Failure sucked. Especially failing an old friend.

Outside on the street, she headed for the lot where she'd parked her new—okay, gently-used—Porsche Boxter. Her cell phone rang. Justin.

"Screwed the pooch on that one, didn't you, sis? Losing your touch?"

"*You* gave it away," she growled, knowing full well the fault was hers. "See you at home."

Jason St. John watched the small brunette leave, followed half a minute later by her blond pimp. Her outrage seemed real enough. Was she a hooker or not? Who could tell these days?

But if she wasn't, what *was* her game? Some sort of deception or honey trap?

Relocating to Nashville's field office might've been a mistake. He hadn't counted on staying in Music City this long. His career aim was New York City or DC, even better. But when his superiors discovered he'd met a young interior designer by the name of Brianna Tollison at a charity fundraiser, they'd suggested he initiate a relationship in order to get closer to her father, the man at the center of the Bureau's current investigation. Hopefully, he wouldn't need to go through an actual marriage ceremony. *Some* assignment.

Bree's father, Randall Clay Tollison III, had some very suspicious characters in his circle of business associates, not to mention his listed profession as an importer of foreign goods. And it was imperative Jason be accepted into that circle. As Tollison's future son-in-law, he stood an excellent chance.

But his physical reaction to the wannabe hooker had stunned him. Her dark eyes had flashed with fire when he'd called her on her moves. She was a tidy bundle of sex appeal all right. Under normal circumstances, he wouldn't have hesitated to hookup. Frankly though, he couldn't afford the distraction of juggling two women in the midst of an undercover op.

He left a tip on the bar. The jazz would have to wait

until another time.

He made it to the street just in time to see the dark beauty nip into a small red Porsche.

Fortunately, his vehicle was nearby. He waited just long enough for her to clear the parking lot and sprinted for his black Range Rover. By the time he made it to the street, she was already heading toward downtown on Hillsboro.

He followed her until she reached Woodmont, then turned left. He hung back about a half block. The bright color of her sports car made it easy to keep in sight. She continued making her circuitous way through the upscale neighborhoods, obviously knowing where she was headed and avoiding more highly trafficked streets.

Keeping an eye on her vehicle, he shook his head. Technically, he was engaging in stalking behavior, but she intrigued him. Yes, his curiosity had gotten the better of him.

A block ahead, she crossed West End Avenue, heading into Richland Park, an area renowned for its Victorian and turn of the century houses. She turned into an alley running behind a row of houses. He slowed long enough to see her stop and pull in behind the third house.

Gotcha. He circled the block, then noted the address of the large Mission Style house, third from the end.

Finding who owned the house would be a breeze. Didn't appear to be a house of ill repute. Indeed, the Richland Park residents association wouldn't sanction such a business in their midst. He circled the block once more and chuckled when he observed a boxy, 1950s puke green vehicle, the same one that had dogged him all the way from Green Hills, park in front of the dark beauty's house.

Was the blond dude her husband or her pimp? Was she a hooker or were they a free-loving couple on the prowl for some threesome activity? A *ménage à trois?* He smiled. The possibilities were endless. Unfortunately, none of them were on his agenda.

Back at his condo located in the Gulch, Jason booted up his Bureau-encrypted laptop and accessed public records. Entering the Richland Avenue street address, he quickly located the names of the inhabitants: three with the surname of Lackey and one with that of Holt. A blended family? He'd been in Nashville a mere three months—long enough to meet and sweep Tollison's daughter off her feet, but the name Holt—now that had a familiar ring. He Googled the names and found the family business, Holt Investigations. According to the agency's web site, the head of the agency was listed as an Andrew Scott Holt, providing full-service investigations serving professional and private clients. So was the brunette one of the family or one of their investigators? Or both?

Had Bree actually gone so far as to hire someone to see if he could be tempted? So much for earning the trust of his *true love.* He really must do a better job of convincing her of his devotion. Blowing his first undercover assignment wasn't an option. He had a lot to prove to himself. To the Bureau. And especially to his father, Supervisory Special Agent Marcus Stone.

He spent the next hour researching the family-run, private detective agency. It turned out that Andrew Scott Holt was married to a Metro Nashville homicide detective, one Tess O'Malley Holt. As for the hot tamale investigator... She could prove to be a damned nuisance. If so, then he'd just have to find a way to deal with her

Chapter Two

Tamsyn entered the house through the French doors, slinging her Coach hobo bag onto the kitchen island. She ran her hand over the purse's pebbled texture. Got a nice deal on it. Yes, she had. Walking over to the fridge, she stopped with one hand on the handle.

"You're home early," Scott yelled from the man cave.

Damn it. Why wasn't he at home with Tess? "And what are *you* doing here?" Now, she'd have to report her failure, as well as endure endless jibes from Justin, who at this very moment, was traipsing into the house through the front door.

Scott, her eldest brother and head of the family's P.I. agency, moseyed into the kitchen. He leaned against the doorjamb. "Tess was just called to a homicide on Music Row so I thought I'd come over to watch the game with Justin. From your expression, I'd say things didn't go well with Brianna Tollison's fiancé."

"You'd say right," offered Justin. "She—"

"Just so y"I can speak for myself," Tamsyn interrupted. "Okay, I blew it. He took me for a *working girl*. As if." She opened the fridge and took out a wine cooler. "I *need* this," she said through clenched teeth, daring either brother to say a word.

ou know, Tam, you're getting sloppy. You were followed."

Whoa. A frisson of unease slithered through her. "Followed? Are you sure?"

"Your target left right after you did. I tailed him, and he tailed *you* all the way home. I can't believe you didn't notice that big-ass Range Rover behind you. He was pretty cagey though, not getting too close. He circled the block and checked out the address."

"That's not good." She chewed her lower lip. Great, not only had she screwed up the job but also let frustration get the better of her and hadn't paid attention to her surroundings. Good thing she always had Justin for backup. Still, she'd never been so careless before.

"Well, that settles it," Scott said. "We'll have to refund Ms. Tollison's retainer and recommend another firm. But if this guy was suspicious enough to follow you home from Green Hills, he'll be on the alert. He won't be easy for anyone else to catch out."

Scott's expression grew concerned. "Again, we should reconsider whether you, or rather the firm, ought to be taking cases like these." He shook his head. "I don't like them. I've never liked them. Except for your cases, we're taking fewer and fewer domestic clients. Corporate security is the direction we're pursuing."

Not again. Tamsyn took a deep breath. "I bring the firm a substantial amount of revenue with *these cases*," she said with a touch more heat than she intended. But damn, she got so tired of hearing the same old thing. Dammit. Her clients had a right to know what kind of men they were involved with.

"What's going on?" Her older sister Carrie, who acted at the agency's office manager, came downstairs, carrying an empty bottle of water. She chucked it into the recycle basket, then leaned her elbows on the counter. "I could hear y'all, even with my door closed."

"You can settle this tiresome argument once more, Carrie. Tell Scott the agency can't make it without my client caseload."

"It was true," Carrie said with a wide smile, "to a point. In the past, Tam's cases brought in a full thirty-eight percent of our revenue. Quick cases. Fast turnover. Word of mouth brought us more."

"I hear a *but* coming."

"You are correct." Carrie leveled her no-nonsense gaze on Tamsyn. "*But* as Scott says, we are actively pursuing corporate clients, and over the last quarter, revenue from your cases dropped to twenty percent."

"Twenty?" She couldn't hold back a gasp. How could that be? "But I have as many clients as ever."

"Correct. Bottom line: corporate security pays more— pure and simple."

"And we're a business. We have to be about the bottom line." Honestly, she couldn't imagine doing anything else but working for the family business. What other career could provide her with such an interesting job? Even though her cases followed the same basic format: meet the guy, see if he can be seduced, and report to the client. What made it exciting was she never knew for sure how the mark would react. Needless to say, over three-quarters of the marks tried to take her home or to a room or wherever. True, the job and previous life experiences had given her a jaundiced view of men in general. Until tonight, she'd never, repeat never, been attracted to any of her client's significant others.

Until tonight.

There was just *something* about him. Something dangerous. And, even though she hated to admit it, something exciting.

Yeah, he was dangerous all right. He'd actually had the balls to follow her home. Not only had her carelessness endangered herself, but possibly her entire family. If he was a financial consultant, she was a prima ballerina.

"I said 'to a point,'" Carried interjected. "Our base of security clients is growing rapidly, up thirty-six percent last quarter. And up to sixty percent overall."

"Thank you. The sooner we can dispense with divorce and honey trap cases, the better." Scott held his hands up. "Just going on record."

"Yeah. We all know you don't like my clientele, but they've been the bread and butter of most P.I. agencies."

"We're aiming higher than 'most'. Honey traps smack of entrapment," Scott said. "Whatever happened to trust in relationships?"

"Aren't you sweet and idealistic?" she said, unable to keep the derision from her voice. "You're newly married and still starry-eyed. But believe you me, there aren't many men out there like you—I should know. And besides, Tess would shoot your ass if you dared to play around."

Scott patted Tamsyn on the head. "So cynical, as well as profane, for one so young."

"Whatever..." She waved him away.

"She's not cynical." Justin shrugged, then grabbed a beer from the fridge. "Just realistic. And don't forget I'm on her six for these assignments."

"And, in my opinion, that is a waste of resources."

"Ugh! Thank you for the impromptu board meeting." Tamsyn's stomach growled. "Anyway, what's for dinner? I'm starved."

"I'm going to surprise you," Carrie said, pouring herself a glass of Chablis. "I didn't feel like cooking."

"That means probably Cajun. Perfect. Paper plates okay?" Tamsyn asked. "Are we eating here or in the den?"

"Den," Scott suggested. "There's a game on."

"Den it is," Carrie declared.

"Has anyone heard from Allie and Nick?" Tamsyn

asked. "Or are they still in their honeymoon lockdown phase?" Allie was their younger sister who'd just moved out after marrying one of the agency's investigators, Nick Vitelli.

Carrie gave a broad smile. "I have it on good authority—meaning Allie called me this morning—they're back from Gatlinburg. Judging from all the sighs and giggles when questioned about said honeymoon, they had a *wonderful* time." She paused long enough to fan her cheeks dramatically. "She starts her legal nurse consultant courses next week. And Nick will be back in the office tomorrow." She heaved a sigh. "I can't believe little Allison got married before I did."

"We'll grow old and alone together, then," Tamsyn said with a smile and set her empty wine cooler down with a thump. "Because I'm *never* getting married." She'd seen too many men ready to jump at the chance to be unfaithful.

"Uh-oh. Never say never," Justin warned, wagging his finger.

Tamsyn gave him the eye roll of all eye rolls. Nevertheless, she couldn't quite forget her intense reaction to Jason St. John's touch. A shiver zipped up her spine. He'd actually followed her home. She wouldn't be caught out like that again. No way.

Detective Tess O'Malley Holt showed her badge to the uniform officer who stood at the elevator of the Music Row high-rise condo.

"Sixth floor. Unit 612," he said.

"Got it." She stepped into the elevator, punched the sixth-floor button. The elevator car rose swiftly and smoothly. When it stopped, the doors opened and she stepped out, noting two surveillance cameras, one at each end of the hall.

Good.

She strode down the hall to unit 612. She badged the officer at the door and entered the condo, stopping long enough to pull on a pair of gloves while she surveyed the scene. The living room was a disaster with two lamps on the floor and a tipped-over occasional chair. Apparently, the original attack started here, then moved into the bedroom.

She spotted the medical examiner, ginger-haired Derek Jacobs, kneeling beside the body. Rob Irby and Malik Samson, two young detectives from her team, were already present. She acknowledged their presence with a nod. "What've we got?"

"Neighbor in unit 611 reported hearing a disturbance around five," Samson said. "Things quieted down, so she didn't report it. When 611's roommate came home, she insisted they call."

Irby held up a heavy brass statuette, already bagged and tagged. "Looks like the murder weapon. Really did a number on her."

She swallowed hard and then turned from the body. Whoever had murdered this young woman had been full of rage. The victim's face was a bloody pulp. Probably not random. No, this was personal. Very personal.

"Do we have a TOD yet?" she asked the M.E.

Jacobs glanced up, his pale gray eyes shuttered at half-mast. "No more than a couple of hours."

Tess nodded. "Certainly fits with when the neighbor heard the disturbance."

Blood spatter could be found on almost every surface of the stylish bedroom in the condo. Yet in spite of his rage, the killer had taken time after battering her to death to pose her partially clad body with palms outstretched as if in supplication. She crossed to the bureau, picked up the victim's red YSL clutch, and opened it.

"According to her Tennessee driver's license, this is Brianna Tollison. Description fits, but the photo's useless." Tess shivered. Rest of the contents were about what she expected to find in any young woman's purse, except no cell phone. Plus, one thing she hadn't expected to find—a business card from Holt Investigations, belonging to her sister-in-law Tamsyn. Ought to make for an interesting interview.

She turned to Irby and Samson. "Let crime scene finish in here. I've seen enough. Irby, interview the neighbors. Look around for her cell phone. It wasn't in her purse. Samson, interview any employees, also any contract workers if they use outside janitorial or landscaping services. Also, check with the office for any surveillance tapes. I noticed the CCTV when I arrived."

They nodded and departed. She pulled out her phone. Now to deal with Tamsyn.

Tamsyn pushed away from the table. "I can't eat another bite. Well, maybe one more." She speared a fat piece of shrimp from the bowl of gumbo and ate it. "Can't let it go to waste."

Her phone rang and she answered, noting Tess's number, "Hey there. What's up?

"I'm at a murder scene. Found one of your business cards in the victim's purse. Can you come down to the precinct tomorrow morning?"

"Are you sure she's even my client. She could've just had the card."

"You'll have to keep it quiet. We haven't notified her next of kin yet. The victim's name is Brianna Tollison."

"Oh, crap! She *is* my client—or was. Whatever I can do." A sense of dread skittered through her. She'd never had a client murdered before, much less a friend—even a former friend. And what did her smooth fiancé have to do with her murder?

Or was it related to something that had happened a long time ago? Something Tamsyn would've preferred to forget. But now...

"Am I right in assuming you were checking someone out for her?"

"Yes, her fiancé." Damn. She'd been stupid to take Bree's case—definitely against her better judgment. But Bree had begged to put the past aside and do one more favor. "Just tonight, in fact," she said, lowering her tone. "I should say something to Scott. He needs to know what's happened since a client is involved."

"He's there?"

"Yeah. We just had Cajun and were about to watch the game."

"I'll be over as soon as I notify the next of kin. I'll need to know everything you know about this fiancé of hers."

"Right. We'll be here."

Scott pushed away from the table. "Was that Tess? What's going on?"

Tamsyn took a deep breath. "My client, Brianna Tollison, is dead. That's the homicide Tess is working."

Chapter Three

Jason tried Bree's number for the fourth time and was ready to toss the damned phone against the wall. Insufferable. First, she'd hired a P.I. to test his fidelity, and now she couldn't be bothered to return his calls. What had the investigator told her? Lies?

He'd have to work hard to heal this breach. If he were truly in love, she'd be the one who needed to come up with a reasonable explanation. True, his feelings were a sham, and he'd damned well have to do a better job of convincing her he was deeply in love. Too much riding on this op to screw it up now.

His father had tried to talk him out of taking this assignment. Said he was too inexperienced. Not ready for such a high profile case. But the Nashville field office Special Agent in Charge, Michael Chase, believed in Jason where his father didn't. So much for family support.

More than anything, he regretted the necessity of using Bree as a way to get close to Tollison and his coterie of arms and weapons dealers. It was a lousy way to treat a nice gal. But it was a perfect plan. Otherwise, it would've taken weeks, maybe months to gain an introduction any other way. This way, he and Tollison would soon be family. Tollison had already had Jason investigated, triggering alerts with the Bureau. Needless to say, his cover had held up to Tollison's deep scrutiny.

Might as well face Bree and find out what the sexy

investigator had told her. He slipped his phone into his inner jacket pocket, ready to leave when someone knocked.

He opened the door and discovered his future father-in-law, leaning against the wall. His features drawn, his skin ashen, he appeared to have aged ten years. Yes, he was in a hell of a state.

"Jase, it's bad." The older man's shoulders started shaking. "Brianna's dead. Murdered. My baby girl..." He fell into Jason's arms.

Stunned, Jason tried to process the news, even as he staggered backward with the weight of his hefty future father-in-law. He maneuvered the man to a chair. "Let me get you a drink." Tollison drank Jack Black, neat.

"I'll kill the son of a bitch who did this. I'll kill him." He pounded the chair arm with his fist.

Jason didn't doubt him for a moment. "What happened? How? When?" he asked while he poured Tollison's drink. Hell, make it a double. He handed it over.

Tollison's hand shook as he grasped the glass. "Few hours ago." He gulped the whiskey in one go. Wiping his mouth with the back of his hand, he gasped, his face growing red, "Why weren't *you* with her? How could you let this happen?"

Jason poured himself one, then took a seat opposite Tollison. He leaned forward. "Here's the thing. We *were* supposed to meet at Gatsby's, but she called at the last minute and canceled. So I stayed for a while, had a drink and listened—"

"Never mind that!" Tollison shouted, his face in a contorted mask of grief. "My baby girl's *dead*. Someone beat her face to a bloody pulp. Her mother's had to be sedated. And the police want to know if *I* know why anyone would want to kill her."

Beat her face to a pulp? Sounded like rage. And that

degree of rage was typically personal. Images of Bree flooded his mind. Her dark flashing eyes. Her ready wit. "*Do* you?" He leveled his gaze at Tollison.

Even though Jason hadn't been in love, he'd enjoyed getting to know Bree. He certainly never wished her any harm. And once his undercover investigation was over, he would've made their future divorce, if it came to that, as painless as possible. But now she was dead. How could this have happened? Why would someone have killed her? Who?

The assignment was over before it'd barely begun. He'd have to notify the SAC of this turn of affairs. Even so, his thoughts were callous and unworthy.

"Of course not!" Tollison's eyes widened. He clenched his fists, started to rise, but sagged back into the chair. "What kind of stupid question is that?"

"I'm sure they meant an old boyfriend or someone like that. Bree mentioned someone she dumped recently—for the life of me, I can't remember his name. And you, you're extremely successful. Perhaps, you've made enemies along the way who might want to punish you by killing Brianna."

"You want to blame this on *me*? What about *you*? Did *you* beat my daughter to death, Jason? *Did* you?" He got to his feet, his physical presence immense and threatening.

Jason took a step back. He could take Tollison in a fight, but having an altercation with Bree's father, who was in the depths of grief, wasn't what Jason wanted. "Of course not. I *loved* her." His words rang hollow, even to him. "We were getting married. What reason would *I* have to kill her? I tell you we were in love. We hadn't had so much as a spat. She was the love of my life. Surely this was a random attack." No. Not random. Either someone had been stalking her, or it was someone she knew. And he would be suspect number one.

Tollison staggered back, collapsed, burying his face in his hands. "I couldn't tell who she was. My beautiful girl. Her face was..." He shook his head unable to continue.

It took another hour and two more whiskeys before Tollison could regain his composure. Jason offered to take him home, but Tollison had a driver waiting.

Thank God.

As soon as Tollison had left, Jason placed a call to Special Agent in Charge Chase.

"This operation is in the crapper, and it's bad," Jason said, then proceeded to update Chase about Tollison's daughter. "Thing is I don't know the TOD. I was alone all afternoon. I need a digital trail created for those hours."

"Worry about your alibi later," Chase said. "You can salvage this operation. Stay close to Tollison. Support him like the son-in-law you'll never be."

"Right." At least, Jason hoped his superior was right. He really needed to score a result. Yes, he was a selfish bastard, but Bree was dead, and there wasn't a damned thing he could do to change it. Nonetheless, he had a mission to complete.

The ballgame forgotten, Tamsyn paced from the den to the foyer and back again while waiting for Tess's arrival. "Go to bed, guys. I can handle this."

"No way," Scott said. "I'll wait with you. Besides, I don't live here anymore."

"Thanks." Comfort and support—that's what the Holt-Lackey family did best. The blended family, first united by the marriage of their widowed parents, Tom Holt and Jan Lackey, the bond further cemented by Tom and Jan's deaths in a car crash over ten years ago, was again united and supportive.

Like always.

No matter what.

Scott turned to Carrie and Justin. "Why don't you two get some rest? Someone needs to be awake enough to open the office in the morning."

After some back-and-forth discussion, Carrie and Justin reluctantly headed upstairs.

Tamsyn continued pacing, her mind racing with possibilities. If only Brianna's murder was something random and not related to anything at the agency...or the past. If it was, Scott was bound to use the incident as a reason to jump on the no-more-of-these-cases bandwagon again. And what would she do without her cases?

After hanging up from Chase, Jason opened his laptop and dug into backgrounds on Holt Investigations as well as the Holt-Lackey family. He found numerous mentions of the Metro Nashville homicide detective, Tess O'Malley Holt. Her father was an MNPD captain. From the society page write up of their wedding, he discovered her mother was a renowned painter. From a much older source, he noted the death notices of Tom and Janice Lackey Holt, who left behind a blended family of six children: Scott and Tamsyn Holt, Caroline, Justin, Allison, and Kim Lackey.

Which one of the four women had he run into at Gatsby's?

His curiosity heightened, he left his rented condo in the Gulch and drove back to Richland Avenue. He parked across the street, one house down. His line of sight was perfect. It was late, but lights were remained on in the front of the house and on the upper story as well.

At eleven, two of the upper floor windows went dark. Only one remained. But the porch light and the first floor were still lit. He settled down for a boring night of surveillance. Damn, he should've thought to bring a thermos of coffee.

Not a stalker. Not at all. He was merely curious. And he definitely meant no harm.

In spite of his best intentions, he dozed off, only awakened by the lights of a passing vehicle. No. Not a passing vehicle. It stopped, then parked in front of the Holt-Lackey house. Hoping he hadn't been spotted, he ducked. A tall woman emerged from the SUV and strode up the sidewalk toward the house. Her purposeful confident body language had law enforcement written all over it. This had to be the homicide detective. She was admitted quickly by—yes, the sexy P.I.

More alert now, he wondered why the late-night visit? Had the local LEOs already somehow connected the P.I. agency to Bree's murder? How much longer before they got around to interviewing him?

His mouth took hers in a punishing kiss.

Tamsyn startled awake and glanced at her watch. Nearly one. She dragged herself off the sofa. She shook her head and tried vainly to erase the sensual dream she'd had about a certain, way too sexy man. Mouth parched, she tried to swallow. She headed to the kitchen for a drink of water when the doorbell rang. Making a 180, she changed course and opened the door.

"Sorry I'm so late," Tess said, heading to the den.

Tamsyn followed Tess. "It's all right. No problem. Scott kept me company."

A smile wreathed Tess's face as she gazed at his sleeping form. "So I see." She rushed over and gave his forehead a quick kiss.

"I couldn't sleep anyway," Tamsyn said.

"Liar," Scott said, stirring in his recliner.

Tess sat on the sofa and leaned forward, her elbows on her knees. "The notification didn't go well—not that any death notification goes well, but this was one of the worst. The mother collapsed. Before I could talk to the father, a doctor had to be called to sedate her. Once she'd been taken care of, the father lost it. Difficult to get him calmed down enough to question. Now, what about her fiancé, the one you had in your sights earlier this evening?"

Tamsyn picked up her iPad and pulled up her notes from the office. "His name's Jason St. John—pronounced *Sinjin*, according to Bree. She met with me earlier in the week and hired me to see if he could be tempted. Nothing unusual. Just one of my typical cases except..." She hesitated, then continued, "I should tell you I knew Bree from school. Green Hills Academy."

"I need all the background you have. Everything she told you about him and their relationship."

Wondering whether she ought to tell about the long-kept secret of Bree's rape, Tamsyn scanned the case notes on her iPad. "They were newly engaged. He's a financial counselor. Moved to Nashville three months ago from a large firm in Atlanta. They met at a charity fundraiser. Basically, he swept her off her feet. She'd begun having second thoughts, starting to think they were rushing things. She wanted to be sure he would be faithful. The thing that bugged her most was he seemed awfully interested in her father's business dealings. That maybe he was using her to get close to her dad. She figured if that was the case, given an opportunity, he'd cheat."

"So what happened?"

Stifling a yawn, Tamsyn set the iPad aside. "I hit Gatsby's at a little before six. He was already there just as she said he'd be. I dropped my purse, one of my usual ploys, and he didn't bite. In fact, he thought I was a hooker, and he pegged Justin for my pimp!" She gave an eye-roll. "*As if...*"

Tess was taking notes while Tamsyn spoke. "Go on. What happened next?"

"I handled it wrong. I should've continued playing him. So what if he thought I was a working girl. Instead, I got all flustered, got indignant, and got the hell out of there. But here's the kicker: he followed me home."

Tess straightened. "Whoa!"

"Yeah, he totally followed me all the way from Green Hills, circled the block, and then slowed down in front of the house just long enough to peg the address before he left. Justin was behind him."

Tess arched a quizzical brow. "Back to why you were so flustered? Was there something about him that made you uneasy?"

"*Uneasy*?" She took a deep breath before continuing. "That's not exactly the right word. I was physically *attracted to him*. That's never happened before. *Never*. When he returned the lipstick, the touch of his hand—" Was she actually about to admit how his touch had made her feel?

Tess's eyes widened. "What? He touched you?"

"Yes, just a brush of his fingers. He didn't grope me or anything. And, honestly, if he'd tried to lead me out of there, I *might've* been tempted to go with him. He was rather compelling. I was definitely attracted. Tall, dark and handsome. I mean, what's not to like?" She lifted her shoulders in a casual shrug. "I'm losing my touch, being attracted to a mark."

"Seriously, sis?" Scott shook his head. "Are you nuts? I'm *right*. We need to shut these cases down."

"Not again. You should've stayed asleep." Tamsyn stood arms across her chest. "I'm sick of hearing about cutting out my caseload. I might've been attracted, but I would *never* get involved with a mark. Trust me."

Scott rose from his chair and pulled her into his arms. "Look, sis, I'm sorry your friend was murdered. But that fact alone connects our agency with a murder investigation. We don't want or need the kind of publicity that comes from such an association."

A ball of anger roiled through Tamsyn, hot enough to explode. She jerked from his supposed-to-be comforting hug. "This is no time to be questioning our business practices when an innocent young woman has been murdered. It's not my fault. It's not our agency's fault."

"What if it is? What if her fiancé realized what you were up to and got pissed. He goes over there to have it out and ends up killing her as a result?"

"That only works if she was killed after I saw him," Tamsyn said with a huff.

Tess interrupted, "Hold on, you two. Let's nail down the timeline before we arrest St. John. Okay?"

Tamsyn took a deep breath and tamped down her temper. "Right," she said, her breathing ragged. "It was a little before six when I entered Gatsby's. He was already there. He glanced at his watch which made me check the time. It was," she paused, her eyes shut, concentrating, "seven minutes until six exactly."

"And what time did you leave?"

"I barely had time to order a drink, spill my purse, and talk to him. Five to six minutes max. I didn't even take a sip of the wine."

"What time did you get home?"

"Six-fifteen or so. And remember he followed me home with Justin on his tail. What was her time of death?"

Tess gave a cagey smile. "Can't comment on an active investigation. Let's say I'm very interested in Jason St. John's whereabouts *before* he turned up at Gatsby's." Tess made an entry in her notebook. "Anything else?"

Tamsyn shook her head. "I can think of a lot of questions, which I'm sure you won't answer, but I don't have anything to add." Well, she could've told Tess about the old rape, but it probably wasn't relevant.

Standing and giving a wide yawn, Tess said, "All right, husband. Let's get home before the sun rises."

After hugs and the good-byes were said, Tamsyn locked the front door. God. What an evening and night. Losing a client to another agency was one thing, but to lose one, who also happened to be an old friend, to murder was entirely another kettle of sharks. Yet she couldn't help but hope Jason St. John had absolutely nothing to do with Brianna Tollison's death.

Before changing into her pajamas, Tamsyn slipped off her shoes and padded over to the bedroom window. Intending to draw the draperies, she paused for a moment and gazed out into the silent dark street. Safe and secure, the Richland Avenue neighborhood. But then Brianna Tollison had probably felt safe in her high-rise condo too. She reached to lower the blinds and glimpsed a large dark SUV pulling into the street. A shiver ran through her. Had someone been watching the house or was it her imagination?

More to the point, was it Jason St. John?

Chapter Four

After catching a few hours of sleep, Jason went to his "office" which consisted of two rooms. The outer office/waiting room of St. John Financial Counseling was manned by Ella Buntin, the temp he'd hired. It was decorated with a sleek desk and two client chairs. A decent grade gray carpet and four framed modern prints made up the bulk of the decor. Ms. Buntin performed receptionist/PA duties. Given he wasn't an actual financial adviser, his clientele was somewhat limited, as were her duties. Usually, the redhead of a certain age occupied her time devouring mystery novels by the stack.

Ella looked up when he entered. "Good morning, Mr. St. John." She offered him a slip of yellow notepaper. "You have one message from a Detective Holt. She'd like you to return her call."

Jason nodded. "Thank you, Ella." He took the message. "I know what this is about."

"I hope you're not in trouble," she said in a tone rife with mischief as she arched her thinly plucked eyebrows.

She probably thought he *should* be investigated. The local FBI office helped legitimize his operation by sending in newbie agents occasionally to act as clients. But he didn't want things to look too legit. After all, Randall Tollison would be more likely to trust him if he didn't appear squeaky clean. In fact, part of his deeper cover as Jonathan Steele was that he'd spent thirteen months in federal prison for securities fraud.

He set his briefcase on the desk and reached for the phone. He could just imagine the questions the detective would ask.

"Detective Holt," she answered, her tone no-nonsense.

"Jason St. John here. I'm returning your call."

"It's about your fiancée."

"I assumed as much. I'm at your disposal, Detective."

They quickly agreed she would come to his office at ten-thirty. He set the phone back on the charger, then scooted back from the desk. He stood and walked over to the window. From his corner office on Union St., he overlooked the Metro City Hall and beyond that the Metro General Sessions courthouse. Not a bad view, all things considered.

The light on his phone blinked. If that was the detective, she was early. He answered, "Yes?"

"Detective Holt is here, sir."

"I'll see her now." He rose as the tall redhead entered, wearing a light green pants suit and looking more like a runway model than a homicide detective.

Noting the wedding band on her third finger, he said, "Have a seat." As striking as the detective was, she just didn't do it for him, not like her sexy sister-in-law.

She gave his office a quick once-over, then her steady gaze settled on him. Oh yeah, she had him pegged as a suspect, all right. "When did you hear about your fiancée's death?"

"Her father came over to my condo last night and broke the news."

"What time was this?"

"Around ten."

"Can you give me a rundown of your activities for

yesterday?"

"Certainly." He hesitated, dreading what came next, then pulled up the appointment schedule on his computer. "I came to the office at six."

"Why so early?" she asked with a frown.

"Foreign markets. Some of my clients are heavily invested there."

She nodded. "Go on."

He leaned back, endeavoring to appear more relaxed than he was. "Ms. Buntin, my assistant, came in at nine. I went out for coffee—Starbucks—then returned to the office in time for my ten o'clock appointment. My assistant will give you the name if you need it. She can confirm I was here until eleven. I gave her the rest of the afternoon off because I had no additional appointments."

"I should think you'd be busier than that."

"I'm new in town." He gave her a tight smile. "It takes time to build a steady client base."

"Your assistant left at eleven. What did you do after that?"

Here was where things got tricky, meaning he had to lie convincingly to an obviously skilled homicide detective who, no doubt, would take in every nuance of his body language. "Did some research. Made some cold calls," he said offhandedly as if he weren't a suspect. "Left the office around five-fifteen. A little before six, I stopped at Gatsby's in Green Hills for a drink and some jazz. Nice place, a rare find in Nashville, though."

"How long did you stay at Gatsby's?"

"Not long." He scratched his head, frowning. "Something unusual happened at Gatsby's. A hooker tried to pick me up. Didn't expect that at a jazz bar in Green Hills."

A muscle in the detective's cheek twitched as if she

were hiding a smile. "Did you go with her?"

"No! I'm engaged—or thought I was at the time. What time was my fiancée killed, Detective?"

"That hasn't been determined yet. Of course, I wouldn't comment about an on-going case, if I did know." She glanced down at her notes. "I need more detail. The way things stand now you don't have anyone to confirm your whereabouts from eleven until you showed up at Gatsby's."

He held up a hand. "Hold on. I went out for lunch. Walked down to Puckett's around 12:30. They were busy, but the waitress might remember me."

Her gaze widened. "What did you have?"

"Barbeque and potato salad. Guess I'm a kid at heart." He gave her a smile he hoped would soften her gaze. "My mom made the best potato salad. Puckett's is even better." Both of those statements were true. The most believable lies always contained a particle of truth.

The detective allowed a smile this time. "What time did you get back to the office?"

"Around 1:30."

"So from that time until Gatsby's you don't have anyone who can verify your activities."

"It would appear so." He shrugged. "My computer's activity log should show I was here and the research sites I accessed. My phone records will also document my whereabouts and phone calls."

"So I have your permission to pull those records?"

He stirred in his seat. "Due to confidentiality concerns, I'd prefer you get warrants, Detective. I have nothing to hide, but as I said..."

Her shoulders sagged, and her expression flattened. "Confidentiality concerns. All right, St. John. I'll obtain the warrants. I'm done...for now." She stood. "Thank you for your cooperation. But I'll need you to come down to the precinct for a formal statement. And more questions," She added with a wry smile as she strode to the door. She stopped, apparently unable to resist the temptation to do a Colombo. "One more thing," she said holding up her smartphone. "If you don't mind..." Without waiting for his assent, she snapped his photo. "Easier to verify your whereabouts." She gave a quick nod.

"Of course." He managed to get that out without clenching his teeth. He held his breath. Was she really leaving or not?

Yes.

He waited until she shut the door behind her before he let out the breath he'd been holding. He reached into his inner pocket and removed the burner he used to contact his Bureau office. No doubt the bureau techs were already busy creating his phone logs and computer activity reports, but it wouldn't hurt to give them a nudge.

After a hurried consultation with his SAC, he sat. Not entirely satisfactory. Not at all. The Bureau would create the needed digital and phone trail but warned if he *were* involved in Brianna Tollison's death, the Bureau would hand him over along with their falsified records.

Why would I kill her? She was my entree into her father's world.

Tamsyn poked her head into Justin's office. "Morning, Justin. I need to know what kind of vehicle this Jason St. John drives."

"Sure," he said with a smirk, making no move toward his keyboard. Instead, he leaned back, his hands linked behind his head. "Any particular reason?"

"I thought I saw someone watching the house last

night when I went to bed."

"Someone outside?" He straightened, shook his head and frowned. "That's not good."

"Not exactly. I went to pull the drapes, and an SUV pulled out."

With a frown, he straightened. "Where was it parked?"

"Across the street in front of the Duncans' house."

"Could've been one of their guests leaving."

She shook her head. "I don't think so. Their house was dark. In fact, the entire street was dark, except for this one SUV." She drummed her fingers on the doorjamb. "Are you going to check one of your handy databases or not?"

"Easy." He grinned as if she were dim. "He was driving a big-ass Ranger Rover. I told you about it last night. Don't you remember?"

"Right." She dope-slapped her forehead. How stupid. She'd let the news of Bree's murder wipe out everything that came before. "Then it had to be him."

"You didn't get a plate number?"

"No." Exasperated, she gave an eye roll. "What about the dark street didn't you get? Besides, it started up *after* I walked to the window and looked out. I don't like this. Not at all."

"Neither do I," Justin said, reaching for his keyboard. "I'd better do some digging on your Mr. St. John."

She flashed him a quick smile of gratitude. "Thanks."

On her way back to her office, she passed Carrie's desk. "You have a call on line two. He sounds *very* sexy, and he asked especially for the short, dark-haired detective," Carrie said, fluttering her lashes.

"I've had enough of sexy for now." Since most of her clients were women, she didn't know what she could do for a male client. Whatever, she wasn't about to turn away business, even if the caller was male.

"Tamsyn Holt," she answered briskly.

"Jason St. John here."

On hearing his name and resonant voice, Tamsyn nearly dropped the phone, but recovered quickly, unless she discounted her racing heart. "What can I do for you, Mr. St. John?"

"I'd like to hire you."

Her chin dropped. "Hire me? For *what*?"

"To find out who killed my fiancée."

"Your fiancée?" she bluffed, pretending she didn't know exactly who he was.

"My fiancée, Brianna Tollison, was murdered sometime yesterday. She was one of *your* clients."

"Was she?" He'd certainly done his research since the previous evening. Who was he really? "See here. I'm sorry for your loss, but our agency doesn't get involved in ongoing police investigations. You need to let Metro handle this."

"But I'd prefer *your* input."

"Why me?" She could think of a dozen reasons—none of them good. Was he stalking her now? For real?

"I *know* you knew her. She was one of your clients."

"If she was... I don't comment on my clients or their cases. But if I were inclined to take on a male client, I wouldn't do anything that might be construed as a conflict of interest."

"That tells me she *was* your client."

His tone was insistent. Clearly, St. John was used to getting his way. "No. I was speaking hypothetically. Besides, I specialize in cases pertaining to women's issues."

Give it a rest, dude.

"Are you a fully qualified detective or not?"

What an ass! "I *am*," she said, her jaw clenching.

"My fiancée has been murdered. She is—or was—a

woman. I'd say that qualifies as a woman's issue."

She sucked in a deep breath. Maybe a different approach and tone would work. "Mr. St. John," she began sweetly, "this office has very close ties to Metro PD. I'm not willing to do anything that might jeopardize their investigation *or* that relationship. My answer remains *no*."

"I never take *no* for an answer."

"You will this time." She punched the off button. Honestly, disconnecting with a button wasn't nearly as satisfying as slamming down a receiver. Dammit. Infuriating and arrogant, as well. Not qualities her friend had ever mentioned. Except for his propensity for secretiveness, Brianna had thought Jason St. John a little too good to be true. Now, his true personality was emerging. And not a very pleasant one, at that.

Carrie appeared in the doorway. "What was that all about? I could hear you out at my desk."

Tamsyn let out an exasperated huff. "That was Brianna Tollison's fiancé on the phone. He wants to hire *me* to find her killer."

Shoving her glasses up on her nose, Carrie shook her head. "Well, *that's* not gonna happen."

"Tell me about it! Honestly, the man simply would *not* listen. So I hung up on him."

"Better let Scott know. Give Tess a head's up, as well."

"Right. The fiancé's bound to be Tess's number one suspect. As if this office would have anything to do with *him*." As if *she* would have anything to do with him. A possible killer. Yet without conscious effort, his heavily-lashed bedroom eyes invaded her mind's eye. And his steel-blue gaze had seemed to know her deepest desires.

No. Enough of that kind of thinking. Thinking about his eyes or his sensual lips or the longish dark hair that made her want to mess it up could only lead to trouble.

"Hey! Mothership, to space cadet…"

Startled, Tamsyn looked up. "What?"

"What on earth were you daydreaming about?"

Tamsyn started to protest, but the heat of a flush burned its way to her scalp. She opened her mouth, then shut it.

A knowing smile spread across Carrie's face. "Right. Don't bother lying. Your neck is splotchy and your cheeks look as if they'd scorch me if I touched them."

"For Pete's sake. I lost my train of thought for a second—that's all." She jumped from her seat and stalked by her sister. "I have to update Scott." She promptly stubbed her toe and had to grab hold onto Carrie.

"I've never known you to be clumsy," Carrie said with a laugh. "I'd love to meet the man who's turned you into such a klutz."

"Get a grip." Tamsyn squared her shoulders and held her head high. "No such thing," she muttered. "It was my shoe."

"Seriously? Please repeat. I don't think I heard you correctly." More of the Carrie eye flutters.

Since history had proved there was no way in hell to win a pissing contest with this particular sister, Tamsyn gave an eye roll and beat it for Scott's office.

Shaking his head, Jason stared at the phone in disbelief. Damn. She'd actually cut him off. Granted, he'd exhibited an uncharacteristic amount of arrogance and determination, but he'd never considered she wouldn't, at least, agree to see him.

And he *really* wanted to see her again.

Chapter Five

From the Market Street parking lot, Jason sat in his car and surveyed the historic building where the Holt Investigations office was located. Should he wait for her to emerge or just invade her territory? This pint-sized seductress had him stumped for the moment. He'd called her earlier just to throw her off her game, but it hadn't had the desired effect. The more insistent he'd been, the more stubborn she'd become.

He glanced at his watch. He planned to meet Bree's father for lunch at one. Presumably, he was occupied making arrangements for his daughter's funeral. Preliminary ones, at any rate, since when the medical examiner would release her body was anyone's guess.

Even though he hadn't been in love, the idea of someone taking Bree's life was appalling. She'd been a bright and amusing young woman, even if a trifle spoiled.

His one experience with close loss was that of his mother. Late one evening, she'd died in a car accident after dropping him at boarding school when he was fifteen. He'd blamed himself ever since, as had his father.

His old man had never come right out and said her death was Jason's fault. No, SSA Marcus Stone was too subtle for that. Afterward, it was the frequent glimmer of hostility in his father's gaze, as well as his voiced disapproval with Jason's choice of school, career, and life, in general.

No matter what honors he'd achieved in school or how

he'd excelled in his training at Quantico, his father's underlying hostility never wavered.

He shook away the painful memories. Better not to dwell on what he couldn't change. Now, the detective was something else, again. Should he wait until she emerged for lunch or invade her turf?

Sit and wait. No way.

Before Tamsyn could update Scott about St. John's phone call, newlywed P.I. Nick Vitelli ambled into the office.

"*Hello*, there," Carrie greeted him from her desk. "Would you just check out the smile on this guy? Have a nice honeymoon, did ya?"

His cheeks darkened a bit. Hooking his thumbs in his jeans pockets, he inclined his head. "Very nice. But I'm ready to get back to work. Allie's cracking the books. And she says I'm a distraction."

Tamsyn smiled, then said with a broad wink. "Guess that means the honeymoon's over."

"Just as well," Carrie said. "There's a new client coming in about thirty minutes. You can have him."

Nick nodded, rubbing his hands together. "Good deal."

"Details are on your dashboard."

"I'll just let Scott know I'm back," he said, nodding at Tamsyn.

Somewhat reluctantly, she went back to her desk and sat. Might as well give Nick and Scott a few minutes to get their brotherly-in-law bonding out of the way. She drummed her fingertips against the desktop, her manicured nails beating a sharp rhythm.

When she heard Nick exit Scott's office, she stood, ready to apprise him of the latest development. She walked down the short hall, tapped on his door, and opened it. "Just me. I want to let you know something odd happened right before Nick came in. Jason St. John called and tried to hire me to investigate Brianna Tollison's murder."

Frowning, he reached for a pen. "I hope you told him a resounding *no*."

"I did, but he was most insistent. I just wanted you to be aware. I'll give Tess a head's up as well. He doesn't strike me as the type to give up easily."

"Are you afraid of him?"

She shook her head. "No, not really. Irritated is more like it." No point in telling her brother how compelling she found Jason St. John. Or about the XXX-rated dream she'd had last night.

"Don't worry about him. Tell Carrie if he calls again to refer him to me."

"Will do." She turned to leave.

Scott's phone buzzed. "Wait a sec," he said to Tamsyn. He answered, then scowled. "He's what?"

Holt Investigations occupied the second floor of a historical Market Street building. Jason entered, nodded at an attractive thirties-something blonde, C. Lackey, the office manager, according to the sign on her desk. It really was a family agency.

"May I help you?" Her tone was polite and businesslike, her accent well-educated southern.

"Jason St. John to see Ms. Holt."

At the mention of his name, the blonde's chin dropped. Her brows drew together in a frown. "Do you *have* an appointment?" Her tone not-so-gracious, this time.

"No. I was hoping she could fit me in. It's rather

urgent."

"Mr. St. John." Ms. Lackey rose, setting her hands on her hips. "I believe Ms. Holt informed you that this agency couldn't help you in what is an on—"

"Yeah, I know. 'An ongoing police matter.' I just want to speak to her."

"She's unavailable at the moment. I'll let her know you came by." She remained standing, glancing at the door as if encouraging him to leave.

No way would that work on him. He wasn't leaving without talking to the sex-bomb detective. "I *really* need to speak to her." He kept his tone friendly, but firm. He finished with a smile, one ensured to guarantee success.

The office manager glared over her wire-rimmed glasses, picked up the phone and punched in what he hoped was the extension of the dark-haired beauty.

But no.

"Scott, come out here." The blonde shot Jason a smug smile. "Jason St. John is here. He insists on seeing Tamsyn."

Through the intercom, Jason heard Holt's response. "He's what?" So big brother was going to deal with the interloper. Not unexpected.

Scott Holt emerged from one of the offices. He was about Jason's own height of six-two. He moved easily, balanced on the balls of his feet. With his fists clenched at his sides, he looked as if he could hold his own in a boxing ring. Not a problem. Jason had no intention of challenging Holt to a fight. All he wanted was to see Holt's sexy sister. How else could he get her out of his mind?

"What's the problem?" Holt asked, his shoulders squared, giving him a belligerent air.

"No problem," he said. "I want to discuss hiring Ms. Holt."

"You want to hire her to investigate your fiancée's murder?" Holt shook his head. "We don't do that kind of work in this agency. We do insurance fraud, corporate security, and a few domestic cases—that sort of thing." Holt paused, his gaze level and uncompromising. "We do *not* investigate murder cases. We leave that to the police department. If you have any further questions, I can give you the name of the detective who's handling the case."

"No need. I've had the pleasure. But if could I speak to Ms. Holt about why she was trying to pick me up, the same day Brianna was murdered. I *would* like to know what was on my fiancée's mind. Why didn't she trust me?" Forcing an emotional tone he didn't feel, he continued, "I *need* to understand."

Holt's shook his head. "Ms. Holt can't betray a client's confidence."

"I *will* talk to him, though."

He'd been so intent on conversing with Holt that he'd missed seeing the small brunette slip from behind Holt.

Holt turned to face her. "You don't have to, Tamsyn."

Jason clenched his jaw. *Dude, stay out of it.*

"I *will* speak to him—in generalities—perhaps, it'll ease his mind."

"If you really want to..."

"I do." For once, her stubbornness worked in Jason's favor.

"Bear in mind, St. John," Scott interrupted. "I'm here, as well as two other investigators. We'll toss your ass out if you give her any trouble."

Tamsyn smiled up at him sweetly, which had the effect of making Jason's heart rate soar. "I'm sure I'll be fine. Mr. St. John will be a perfect gentleman. Won't you?"

That was more like it.

"Of course."

***

Tamsyn hesitated. While her first rash inclination was to grab his silk tie and drag his hot bod into her office, he was a murder suspect. So, not gonna happen.

Instead, she flipped her hair over her shoulder and fluttered her lashes ever so subtly. His emotional plea had gotten to her. She'd tell him what she could in somewhat vague terms and then send him on his way. Her brother's intervention wouldn't be needed. In spite of St. John's former engagement, the man was interested...and in more than what she knew about Bree's state of mind. St. John was attractive all right. And attracted. His insistence on seeing her was as much about the chemistry between them as her friend's death.

She led him into her office and shut the door.

He placed his hand on the knob. "If you'd rather leave it open..." he offered rather smoothly.

She dismissed the idea with a wave. "Not necessary. This will be a private conversation." She gestured for him to be seated. He sat, but only after she did.

Nice manners.

"Speaking in generalities, Mr. St. John...."

"Please call me Jason."

She smiled. "In that case, you should call me Tamsyn."

"Unusual name."

"Yes, here in the States it is."

"British?"

"Yes, it's the feminine form of Thomas. I'm named after my great-grandmother Tamsyn Elizabeth Morton Stanley. But enough about my genealogy."

"When did Bree contact you?"

She gave a quick shake of her head. "That's *too* specific. Let me tell you how I work. A client, almost always a woman, will make an appointment. She'll come in, express her concerns, and reasons behind them. She'll give me locations where I might run into her significant other. I'll surveil him for a couple of evenings to get an idea of where he really goes after work and what he does."

His gaze widened. He shot her a sharp look. "You followed *me*?"

She gave him a non-answer answer. "That's my usual routine. I make the approach, and normally, I don't get taken for a prostitute. My timing must've been off last evening."

"Perhaps I'm wary of strangers." The corner of his mouth lifted in a half-smile.

"Yes, well...." She shrugged.

He leaned forward, his expression earnest. "What *can* you tell me?"

"Quite often, again I must speak hypothetically. The client's concern might be her significant other's secretiveness, or her inability to reach him at times when she thinks he should be reachable. That sort of thing."

"Is that all?"

"Or the client might feel the relationship is moving too fast and just wants to make sure she isn't making a mistake."

His brows twitched. "I see." He glanced down at his watch, a nice Rolex.

"Do you have another appointment, Jason?"

"Yes, I'm meeting Bree's father for lunch to discuss whatever arrangements he's made."

She rose and extended her hand. "I'm very sorry for your loss. Ms. Tollison was a lovely young woman with her whole life ahead of her. And in addition to being my client, she was a personal friend, that is, we were close when we attended a girls' school. We grew apart."

"Any reason for that?"

"She went away to Parsons in New York. I stayed here." Yes, there was more to it than that, but he didn't need to know.

"Thank you." He held her hand just a little longer than necessary. Her heart sped up as his blue gaze locked with hers. Her mouth dried. Reluctantly, she pulled her hand from his, clenching it in her lap so he couldn't see it tremble. She took a breath, then continued, "I'm sorry I couldn't be more specific, but client confidentiality, even in a case like this is..." Her voice trailed off. What else could she say? Nothing that would soften the blow.

"Thank you. At least, I have a general idea of what Bree was thinking." He stood, but his gaze held hers.

No matter how she tried she couldn't avert her eyes from his searching gaze. Her neck and face heated. Damn. Why did this man affect her so?

Her line buzzed—thank you! Finally, she could tear her gaze away from his relentless scrutiny. "I have to take this." She grabbed the phone. "Yes?"

"Are you all right in there?" Carrie asked.

"Yes. I'm fine. Mr. St. John is just leaving." She rose, intending to open the door. Somehow, before she even knew it, he closed the distance between them. Without touching her, he inclined his head as if to kiss her. She raised a hand to ward him off.

He stepped back with a rueful smile. "I don't know what it is about you," he began softly, shaking his head. "I can't get you out of my mind."

"I—uh, think it's time you left." How did she manage to get the words out with him so close he could surely hear the racing of her heart?

"Perhaps, you're right."

She reached for the doorknob, ready to show him out

and regain her composure.

He spoke, so low she could barely make it out. "I hope I'll see you again soon, Tamsyn," he paused, "under more congenial conditions."

"That won't be happening. I've answered your questions. We're done."

"But what about *your* questions, Tamsyn?"

His tone was insinuating something, but what? "I don't have any questions."

"Really?"

"Really," she said with an emphatic nod, then opened the door. "As I said, we're done."

He nodded. "If you say so." This time his tone indicated they clearly weren't *done*.

As soon as he left the office, she leaned against the desk to catch her breath. "Damn!"

Carrie sprang from her chair, took Tamsyn by the hand and led her down the hall to the staff kitchen. "What the hell happened in there? You said you were *all right*."

Tamsyn pried her sister's fingers from her wrist. "I *was* when I said it. He was leaving. I stood to see him out, and the next thing I knew, he was a mere inch away, about to kiss me."

Her sister leaned in, her green gaze widened. "And then?"

"And then...nothing." She shrugged, stunned he'd had her at his mercy, ever so briefly.

"You sound disappointed."

"Don't be absurd." She stood. Placing her hands on the table, she leaned forward. "I'm not continuing this conversation. You're entirely too animated by all this."

"Oh, well..." Carrie averted her gaze and scratched the back of her neck. "Some of us have to live vicariously."

"Only when you choose to."

Carrie leaned back with a wide grin. "Sa-nap. Aren't *you* the smart one today?"

On the way back to the Range Rover, Jason tried to fathom the reason for the chemistry between them. Tamsyn Holt was short, dark-haired, and dark-eyed, not his usual type, if indeed he had a *type*. And she came from a large and protective family.

Make that one damned large and protective family.

But before she'd rejected his advances in the office, she'd exuded a heady sensual scent that sent his head reeling. No, it wasn't perfume. Something more tantalizing, hypnotic even. Pheromones?

Yes. Pheromones, those she had in abundance.

At that moment of dazzling realization, he received a text on his encrypted cell phone: Digital trail good to go.

Whew. Subpoena away, Detective Holt. Subpoena away.

Chapter Six

Using his GPS, Jason located where he was meeting Bree's father. The posh 360 Bistro was located in Belle Meade in a small shopping center on Hwy 100. It had a reputation for serving great food and an extensive wine list.

Randall Tollison rose, as Jason entered. The man was haggard, seemingly having aged and deflated overnight. His skin and gaze were ashen. "Mr. Tollison."

"Jason." Tollison nodded, then sat down wearily. "This is a hell of a thing. Burying one's only child."

"I know, sir." Jason sat, not bothering to look at the menu. "What have you decided?"

Tollison took a long swig of red wine before answering. "Marshall Donnelly Combs will pick up her body once it's released."

"When do you think that'll be?"

"Possibly as soon as tomorrow. I'm afraid I used my influence to get her—" He broke off with a shudder. "—her autopsy prioritized."

So Tollison had influence with someone in authority. Interesting.

"This is a nice red. It's a Pinot Noir, Belle Glos Vineyard, California 2013. Have some." He handed the bottle to Jason. Less than half remained.

Jason poured, set the bottle between them, and then sipped. The complex flavors awakened his palate. "Very smooth. Berries and subtle notes of smoke and other spices."

"Indeed, although I can barely taste anything now. I've had too much." He pushed the bottle away. "What the hell. Nothing matters anymore." Tollison grabbed the bottle of pinot noir and poured himself another glass.

The rest of the day in the office, Tamsyn found concentrating difficult, if not impossible. Once she finished with her two-thirty client, she closed her computer and pulled her hobo bag from the drawer. Extricating her smartphone from the bag, she texted Carrie she was leaving for the day.

Her sister gave an absent-minded wave as Tamsyn slid past Carrie's desk. "Have fun."

Tamsyn stopped short, then faced Carrie. "Have fun? I'm not going anywhere except home, and then I going to have a long soak in the tub and maybe a nap."

"A nap?" Carrie shot a look of disbelief in Tamsyn's direction. "Yeah, right. You haven't taken a nap since you were in diapers."

"That's the plan. Besides, *you* didn't know me when I was in diapers."

Carrie held her hands up in a gesture of surrender. "Whatever..."

Tamsyn gave a huff and made her escape. The damned office was stifling.

Outside was no better. No, it was worse. The humidity hit her like a wet blanket. Unusual for an early October day.

She walked quickly to her sports car, glancing around to make sure she wasn't being followed this time. Good. No sign of St. John's big black Range Rover.

In spite of the sun's warmth, she couldn't repress a shiver, remembering the intensity of sensations she'd experienced for the oh-so-brief instance when St. John had come so close to kissing her.

After a long soak in the tub, Tamsyn dressed quickly and flew downstairs. Her stomach insisted it had to be time for dinner. Ravenous hunger, along with the mesmerizing aroma of burgers on the grill, drew her to the kitchen. "Those burgers really smell great," she said to no one. She opened the fridge and pulled out a can of Diet Coke. She popped the top and took a long swig. Through the French doors, she observed Allie and Nick hovering over Justin while he grilled, and Scott supervising from a deck chair. Caroline and Tess were setting the picnic table for a full family gathering.

Tess opened the French doors and stuck her head inside. "We need condiments."

"Condiments coming up." Tamsyn gave a quick nod. "Looks like we're having a party. What have I missed?"

"The newlyweds have emerged from their cocoon, so we're welcoming them home." Tess gave a wink.

"Good idea. The heat has died down. We won't have many more good grilling days."

Tess flashed a quick smile. "Actually, any excuse will do."

"Sounds good to me." Tamsyn pulled a jar of dill pickles from the fridge and started to carry them outside.

"By the way, Brianna Tollison's funeral is the day after tomorrow with visitation tomorrow evening," Tess said while she rummaged through the pantry.

Tamsyn stopped, setting her drink on the counter. "That soon? I thought they'd keep her body longer for evidence."

"Apparently, her father has friends in high places. The

autopsy was done first thing this morning. They're releasing her body to the funeral home later this evening. The rest of the work is forensics and pathology. Those reports are pending, but it's unusual, to say the least. If someone is arrested and brought to trial, his attorney may ask for an independent autopsy which will mean her body will have to be..."

"Dug up again. Oh, crap." Her poor parents. Poor Brianna. Her horrible death seemed like a nightmare. Who could've killed her? Somehow, it was difficult, not to say impossible, to picture Jason St. John as a killer.

Her arms full of condiments, Tess sighed. "Not exactly a pleasant thought when we're about to have dinner."

"I don't know how you do it."

"I compartmentalize. So no more talk about work."

"Agreed." Tess headed for the French doors. *No more talk about work.* Easy for Tess to say, but Tamsyn wasn't sure she could erase the thoughts her mind's eye brought to bear. This morning's *Tennessean* had been entirely too graphic in the description of the crime scene.

She shook herself. Time to welcome home the lovebirds. A sudden longing hit her. If only she could find someone as steady and sound as Allie's Nick.

Tamsyn tamped down her slight feelings of envy. Instead, she pasted on a smile and stepped outside. Allie was in blushing-bride mode with a dazzling smile that wouldn't quit as she gazed up at her new husband. Her sister deserved every bit of the happiness she'd found with the handsome P.I.

Tamsyn slid an arm around Allie's waist. "Hey, sis. Welcome home. How's married life?"

"Tam!" Allie gave a little squeal. "It's wonderful." She shot a radiant smile toward her new husband. "I highly recommend it. And *you* are next," she said, pointing a well-manicured nail at Tamsyn.

"Hmph. Guess that leaves me out," Carrie said with a wry smile as she surveyed the picnic table.

"Not at all," Tamsyn said. "You'll marry before I do. Marriage is the *last* thing on my mind." Not exactly the truth. But where would she ever find a man she could trust? Certainly not Jason St. John. Even if he wasn't a killer, he was certainly a player.

Jason St. John. Merely thinking the man's name was enough to rev her heart rate. Why on earth did have such an effect on her? He was the antithesis of everything important to her: honesty and family.

"Earth to Tamsyn Starbuck. Come in, Starbuck."

Startled, Tamsyn glanced around. "What?"

Justin set a tray of burgers on the table. "Just looked like you were somewhere *out there*." He did air quotes with the last two words.

Before Tamsyn could respond, Nick scoffed, "Dude, you just depleted your testosterone level by half."

Tamsyn chuckled at Justin's mystified response. "What?"

"Finger quotes. Really?" Nick elbowed Justin, then snorted with laughter.

Assuming a solemn expression, Justin brushed his fingers back through his longish blond hair. "I admit my manhood may very well be in question. Too many females in this household. Not my fault, dude!"

"No more girlie air-quotes. Seriously, I had to call you on it."

"I see. Just doing your brotherly-in-law duty."

"Right on." They fist-bumped.

"Oh-my-God. Now, we have too many male hormones surging," Carrie said. "Let's eat."

Grateful that no one had questioned where her mind

was now that Justin had sidetracked everyone, Tamsyn took a seat. "Yes, let's eat."

After dinner, Tamsyn waylaid Justin, pulling him aside. "Spill. What have you found out about Jason St. John?"

Justin's expression grew cagey. "Let's take a walk down the alley."

Interest spiking, Tamsyn nodded and followed him down from the deck to the alley that ran behind the Mission Style house. Leaves on the trees were already starting to turn. Another month and they'd be gone.

He brushed a stray strand of hair behind his ear as they walked along. "He's kind of interesting. On the surface, he appears completely clean as you would expect for a financial counselor. Then I dug into some better-off-not-mentioned sources and discovered St. John isn't his real name."

"What?"An alias was never a good sign. Who was this guy who was tormenting her sleep?

Justin strode along. "He bears a striking resemblance to a certain Jonathan Steele, who served time in a federal pen for securities fraud."

Tamsyn almost had to run to keep even with his long strides. "So he's a fraud all the way around! But is he a killer?"

"I don't know about the killer part, but there's definitely something hinky about him...*and* his background."

She stopped. "Hinky how?"

Slowing, then stopping, he turned to face her. He responded with a shrug. "It's just a hunch."

"*Tell* me." *Yes, by all means, tell me before I find*

myself in bed with this guy.

"Whoever covered up his jail time knew what he was doing. I found a couple of news articles on the web about Steele, but nothing from any major news sources." He lowered his voice, mumbling, "St. John might be a Fed."

"What?"

"Told you it was a hunch." He started walking again.

"Wait! I can't keep up." She grabbed at his shirttail. "What makes you think he's a Fed?"

"Because if I was creating a false background on someone that was supposed to be clean on the surface, but he had some skeletons in his closet, that's what it would look like."

"How can we know for sure?"

"That's just it. We can't. Any inquiries are bound to trigger alerts at the Bureau. I'm already on their radar. They don't mess around. Believe me. I've experienced the honor of their interest before. I'm not anxious for a re-run."

"I just wish I knew what he's up to."

"What difference does it make if he's a crook or a Fed?"

"None. Absolutely none." She turned and stomped back toward the house. Oh, no. No difference unless she really wanted to hit the sheets with St. John, or whoever the hell he was. Damn it anyway. If he was a Fed, even better.

Chapter Seven

Early Thursday morning, Tess stood in front of the murder board. "We now have served warrants for Brianna Tollison's phone records and her computers, as well as those of her fiancé, including his office and personal computers. IT will go over those. We'll see if St. John's timeline matches his statement." Tess adjusted the victim's photo on the board until it was straight.

She continued, "We still haven't located her cellphone. Maybe the killer took it as a trophy, or perhaps there's something on it that he didn't want to be seen. As for Mr. St. John, he wasn't particularly helpful, so we'll take a hard look at him. He could've had time to kill Miss Tollison and make it to the jazz bar. Malik, what about your interview with the bartender?"

Sampson nodded, pulling his notebook from his pocket. "I spoke with the bartender on duty, Hank Stevens. He remembers Mr. St. John coming in around 5:30. However, he never noticed anything amiss about his clothing—no obvious signs of blood."

Sampson was thorough and an excellent addition to her team. Tess hid a smile, then nodded. "Good point. That was a hell of a bloody scene. Go on."

"Says St. John's a regular. Comes in a couple of times a week. Weekdays, but Stevens doesn't work weekends. He has a music gig."

Everyone wants to be a star. "Do we have a formal statement from him yet?"

"Yes, ma'am. He came in after his shift last night."

"I want St. John down here for a formal interview. Seth, you handle that."

"Right." Foyle reached for his cell phone.

Tess held up her hand in a delaying gesture. "Wait. Let's hold off on interviewing St. John until we see what we come up with on his phone and computers."

Foyle frowned. "And if something does?"

"Then," Tess said, smiling, "we'll have cause to obtain a search warrant on his home." She rubbed her hands together. "And that's what I really want."

Later in the morning, Tess scanned the list of calls dumped from Brianna Tollison's cell phone. Damn. She must've spent her entire day on the phone. "Irby, coordinate with her partner, Sophie Nunley. See how many of these calls were to clients. We'll need to check all of them, anyway. Did she have a separate phone for business use? Check on that too." No, it couldn't be that simple. Nothing was ever simple in a murder case.

"Will do."

"These numbers without names—burners?"

"I'll follow up on those too."

"Good." She nodded. Learning to delegate hadn't been a natural gift when taking on her own team of detectives. But she'd chosen well, and she trusted them.

She stood and strode over to the murder board. There were still gaps in Tollison's timeline. In the design studio from 9:30. Lunch at her desk at one. Left the design studio at 1:45 for a two o'clock appointment at Charmaine's Bridal to look at wedding dresses. According to Susan Dyer, Brianna's best friend and maid of honor, she was supposed to meet Bree and three of her bridesmaids, but Bree was a no show. They waited a full forty-five minutes, trying her phone multiple times before giving up. According to neighbors who heard a disturbance, Tollison died around five, at her condo.

So, where the hell was she from 1:45 until she entered her building at 4:45? Three missing hours. Long enough to meet her killer. Was it by chance? Or by design?

"Ron, let me see that list of calls." Tess scanned the list down to the last call before the victim left her office. 1:40 call lasted two minutes." She highlighted the number. "I want to know who this is." She reached for her phone and tapped in the number. Crap. "Out of range or not turned on. Let's get IT to keep pinging this sucker and see if it gets turned on. We need a location. One more thing, I want to get her last boyfriend before St. John in here for an interview. Seth, will you see to that."

"On it, boss."

Tess looked over Seth's report on Eric Chapman, Tollison's relationship prior to St. John. "What do you think, Seth? Is this our guy?"

Seth shook his head. "From what we have here, I'd say no. He's clean on paper, but that doesn't always tell the whole story. He's a successful entrepreneur specializing in technology, communications & media services."

"According to her friend, Susan Dyer, he was abusive that one time and Brianna dumped him. One strike and he was out."

"He could definitely have a bone to pick, but smash her face beyond all recognition? Why wait this long?" Tess walked over to the whiteboard and placed Chapman's photo in the possible column. "First, there's the funeral to get through. We'll see who shows up. After that, let's get

Eric Chapman in here for an interview."

Tamsyn stared at the computer display and yawned. Another sleepless night, well almost—not counting the sex dream she'd had. What a quandary. If Jason St. John was a federal agent as Justin suspected, then he was one of the good guys. Acting on her impulses could be a good thing. And fun. That way she could get him out of her system, and more importantly, out of her dreams. But if he wasn't a Fed, then he most likely was a white-collar criminal, at the very least, and definitely not someone with whom she should even contemplate a booty call, much less act on it.

And tomorrow was Bree's funeral. Losing a friend was a new and unsettling experience, especially one who'd been murdered. Even though she hadn't seen Bree since she'd left for school until she'd called for the appointment, they'd been close, once.

Very close. Through their teenage years, they'd shared tons of laughs... Tamsyn was the only one who knew Bree had been raped after a high school dance. And some secrets were meant to remain secret.

Now, what to wear? She hadn't been to a funeral since her father and stepmother died. She'd filled out a bit since then. She picked up the phone and called Hattie, her personal shopper at Dale's, an upscale boutique in Green Hills. "A simple black suit suitable for a funeral," she told her.

Fortunately, they had something in her size. "I'll come by and pick it up at noon."

"Any accessories?" Hattie suggested.

"No. I'm good."

Okay, that was done. She mentally ticked off the list of things she needed to do. After she picked up the suit, she had a one-thirty appointment.

She glanced up at the sound of a tap on her door.

Carrie stuck her head inside. "Coffee?"

Tamsyn nodded.

"You look down."

Tamsyn sighed. "I just ordered a black suit for Bree's funeral. I'll pick it up on my lunch hour."

"You *could* borrow mine."

"The skirt would come down to my ankles." Tamsyn gave an eye roll.

"Might that have something to do with my being nine inches taller? And we both know where you have more inches than I do. You'd never be able to button the jacket."

Tamsyn shook her head. "Y'know we're sick. Actually, my heart is aching, and we're here discussing clothes and the size of my boobs.

"Sometimes, that's all life boils down to. Clothes. Boobs. Yada-yada-yada."

"The sad truth is Bree is beyond caring what anyone wears to her funeral, but it's a matter of respect. Maybe I just don't want to face what really happened to her. Someone bludgeoned her to death. Someone hated her that much. Can you imagine?" She shuddered.

Carrie shook her head. "I'm sorry you lost your friend. She seemed like such a nice person the day she came for her appointment."

Tamsyn nodded. "More confident and self-assured, but still the same old Bree. I was so glad to see her. The years seemed to just fade away. Just like old times."

"I'm going to get you that coffee now." Carrie turned, leaving Tamsyn alone.

Yes, alone with her thoughts. Carrie was still the caring one of the family and had been ever since their parents died.

Bree's poor mother. She must be devastated.

Flowers.

Tamsyn picked up the phone and ordered flowers for the funeral and a Peace Lily to be delivered to the Tollisons' home. That way, something would go on living in Bree's memory.

Chapter Eight

On Friday, the funeral home was crowded ass-to-elbow. Bree would've been pleased to see so many of her old friends and acquaintances queued up to offer their condolences. Plus, it was common knowledge a murder always brought out the looky-loos and the downright nosy.

Off to the side, Tamsyn spied Tess, respectfully dressed in a black pants suit, her gaze moving casually, but systematically, over the crowd. Tamsyn wove her way through the throng to stand beside her sister-in-law. Tess's fiery red hair hung in smooth waves to her shoulders. Her sedate black pants suit fit her body perfectly. She didn't look like any homicide detective Tamsyn had ever seen, other than those seen gracing the television screen.

"Do you usually attend the funeral of a murder victim?" Tamsyn asked under her breath.

"Always," Tess said with a slight smile. She nudged Tamsyn with her elbow. "Know any of those guys?" she asked, nodding toward a group of young men.

"Yeah. The tall blond is one of the Chapman boys, either Chris or Eric. They're so much alike I could never tell them apart."

"How do you know the Chapman *boys*?"

"I guess it sounds stupid to call them boys, but when we were in school there were three of them. Chris and Eric are fraternal twins, but they look enough alike to be identical. The third Chapman brother is Bruce. He's darker. Not as tall as the twins. Why?"

"We'll be interviewing Eric Chapman, for sure. He was the guy she dated and dumped before becoming engaged to Jason St. John."

"That could be a motive."

"Haven't ruled him out, either. What about the others? Know 'em?"

"Can't say as I do." The idea that Brianna's killer could be in this very room sent a chill up Tamsyn's spine. "I could chat 'em up for you. Make a little light conversation."

Slowly, Tess shook her head. "Really don't want to involve you any more than you already are."

"Safe enough with all these people around."

Tess took a deep breath as if considering her response. "Okay. Conversation only. Don't ask any pertinent questions like: where were you when?"

Tamsyn rolled her eyes. "Don't worry. I know I'm not a LEO," she said, using cop lingo for law enforcement officer. "I'll be circumspect. Very casual."

"Okay, then." Tess nodded. "I'll be watching."

Tamsyn flashed a quick smile. "Counting on it."

She made her way over to a young slender man who wore a hangdog expression. His dark hair was overlong and kept falling into his eyes. She held out her hand. "I'm Tamsyn. I went to school with Brianna. Isn't this just awful?"

The young man swept his hair from his eyes and took her hand awkwardly. "J-Jerry. Jerry Ames. We w-worked together...I mean, I worked *for* her."

"At the design firm," she finished for him. "So you got to know her really well. I haven't seen her since we went away to college. Well, *she* went away, and I stayed here for school. It's so sad."

"Y-yes. She was n-nice. N-nice to everyone." He ran a finger around his collar as if it were too tight.

"So nice to meet you," she said, then nodded and excused herself to make her way over to the Chapman boy. "Chris or Eric? I could never tell you two apart. I'm Tamsyn Holt. You probably don't remember but we were at school together."

"Uh-uh," he stammered, giving her the old up-and-down once-over. "I'm Chris. I remember you. How are you?"

"I'm fine, but I'm so sad about Brianna."

His jaw tightened. His lips thinned. "Yes, well, it was bound to happen sooner or later."

"What?" What an inappropriate remark to make about a murder victim. Geez.

Flicking a loose thread from his navy wool suit, he gave an arrogant sniff. "She wasn't very particular about her choice of companions."

Chapman glared at the attentive, almost-son-in-law, Jason St. John, who was positioned at Mr. Tollison's elbow. Bree's father was bearing up, but her mother appeared pale and fragile. A gentle breeze could knock her over.

"Excuse me," he said, brushing Tamsyn aside. "I see someone I must speak to."

Rude. Brusque. Arrogant. Not a favorable impression. After all, he wasn't the one Brianna dumped for St. John. Or was he? But why would Eric attend the funeral and pretend to be Chris?

Intending to head over to the Tollison's to express her condolences, she stopped short at the sight of a tall and hefty, broad-shouldered man joining the mourners.

Was it? Could it be? How dare he show his face here and now, after all these years?

Yes. Brad Oliver.

What the heck? She watched him make his way to the

Tollison's, only to be greeted with obviously warm affection. Her parents couldn't possibly know. No one knew. Only Brad and Brianna knew. Now, other than Brad, only Tamsyn knew. And she'd sworn never to tell. Could she? Should she tell Tess?

But she'd promised Brianna. Why bring all that up now? It was so long ago. And what good could it possibly do?

"Well?" Tess said from behind Tamsyn.

Swallowing the knot in her throat, she turned. "The geeky guy with dark hair is Jerry Ames. He worked at the design firm with Bree," she said in a rush. "That was Eric Chapman's brother Chris—at least he said he was Chris."

Tess leveled her gaze. "You think he might really be Eric?"

"Just a feeling. Chris was never arrogant and rude back in the day. Eric was the jerk. Otherwise, you have to wonder why Eric hasn't bothered to show." She took a breath, willing her nausea to subside. "I need to go home. I can't deal with any more of this." Without waiting for Tess's response, Tamsyn beat it for the door.

As she placed her hand on the knob, someone tapped her shoulder. Unable to contain her surprise, she gasped and turned. "Mr. St. John, you startled me."

"And here I thought we were on a first-name basis." Leaning closer, he said, "You haven't offered your condolences to Bree's parents. Don't you think you should?"

"I just needed some air. It's very close in here." And getting closer. Her breathing grew rapid. Her cheeks heated, hot enough to scorch. Damn the man.

"Looked as if you were running away. And I have to ask myself why." He kept dogging her steps, nudging her through the crowd, moving her toward the Tollisons...and

Brad Oliver.

She hung her head. "It's just so awful. I couldn't take it any longer."

"I doubt there's much that fazes you. But you're obviously upset. What or *who* was it?"

"Were you spying on me?" What nerve. But he had nerve in abundance, as she well knew.

"Merely curious to see what you were up to. You seemed to be on a mission until something upset you. Are you going to tell me, or must I figure it out for myself?"

If they'd been any place but where they were, she would've smacked his insolent face and flat-out bolted. As it was, she clenched her jaw. "None of your damn business." She glanced around to see if anyone heard her.

He leaned in close, his words just above a whisper. "Behave yourself or people will start to wonder." He took her gently by the hand, his strong fingers interlaced with hers.

They reached Brianna's parents and Brad Oliver who loomed at their side. Her heart sped up, her insides quivering like Jello. "Mr. and Mrs. Tollison, I'm so sorry for your loss. Brianna and I were at school together."

"In New York?"

"No, here before college." She kept her gaze averted from Brad Oliver's. No way could she face him. Not like this. "I'm Tamsyn Holt. We were at GHA together. Again, I'm so sorry. If there's anything I can do, please let me know."

"Thank you, dear," Mrs. Tollison managed weakly.

Poor woman.

Tamsyn moved on, making way for those behind her. Thankfully, Jason had released her hand. "Satisfied?" she hissed. "Heaven only knows what they thought about you dragging me over like that."

"Relax. I didn't drag you over. Besides, you hadn't expressed your condolences." He shot her an arch smile. "I could've told them about the honey trap Bree paid you to set for me, but I didn't think the time appropriate."

"Hah." She gave a snort. "Do you somehow think her death is *my* fault? If anything..." She paused, unwilling to accuse him outright.

"What?"

"Never mind." Now that her nerves had settled, all she wanted was to get away from the noisy drone of the crowd and away from Jason St. John. The man was entirely too distracting. And it had been too long since— Never mind. She pulled herself together. "You had no business manhandling me. If you know what's good for you, you won't try it again." That should settle him.

"I merely took you by the hand. If you want to call that manhandling, so be it. I must confess I quite enjoyed *manhandling* you." Again, a smile flitted about his sensual mouth.

"You would." She let out a small exasperated sigh. "Your behavior is *so* inappropriate. We're at the visitation and funeral of a young woman who was murdered. And I might add, a young woman to whom you were *engaged*. Yet here you are, already flirting with me, I suppose, in some lame attempt to fill your bed."

He stiffened, then added, his tone scathing, "Aren't you the presumptuous one? What makes you think—?"

"Oh, I *know* when someone's coming on to me. *And* I know when to leave." She spun toward the door. No way could she tolerate his odious presence another second longer. She made a bee-line for Tess's position on the far side of the room. That was one spot where St. John wouldn't follow... especially if he had anything to do with Brianna's death.

"So what's going on with you and St. John?" Tess murmured, her intense gaze continuing to survey the room and belying her soft tone.

Tamsyn folded her arms across her chest. "Nothing. Nothing at all."

"Didn't look like nothing to me."

"I've had enough of this. I'm leaving."

"Wait. One more thing. Who is the tall guy standing next to the Tollison's?"

"He's—" Tamsyn broke off. "I'm not sure. Brianna knew a lot of people. I can't be expected to know them all." Okay, that was a little snappy, but she'd had enough.

Air. She needed air.

Once outside, she stopped to take a deep breath. Her hands shook as she tried to unlock her car door. Why had she lied about not knowing Brad Oliver? To Tess of all people.

Could the rape ten years ago conceivably have something to do with Brianna's murder? Not likely. Bringing all that up would only serve to heap additional pain onto her parents' already heavy load. Nothing could be done now.

Jason shook his head, watching the tempting P.I. make her escape from the funeral home. What or who had set her on edge—other than him, of course? For some inexplicable reason, he couldn't seem to keep his mind off her.

Thinking back, he'd observed her stiffen when Brad Oliver entered the funeral home. In fact, she hadn't acknowledged his presence when she offered her condolences to Bree's family. What was that about? Couldn't say he blamed her, though. He'd met the man at one of the exploratory meetings he'd had with Bree's father. As Tollison's attorney, Oliver was a favored member of Tollison's inner circle and would certainly bear watching. The lawyer had all the charm of a barracuda with eyes as flat and expressionless as a serial killer's. Tollison, however, seemed to rely on Oliver's brand of ruthlessness.

"Need to speak to a prospect," Jason said, excusing himself from the Tollisons. He shouldered his way through the crowd and outside. Standing on the covered porch, away from the cloying scent of lilies, he sucked in a lung of fresh air. He caught the tantalizing aroma of grilled steak from the Texas de Brazil Steakhouse just up 25th.

Somewhat amused, he watched Tamsyn pull her Porsche Boxter onto 25th and zip right toward West End, never giving a glance in his direction.

It's all right, hon. I know where you live.

Driving down West End, Tamsyn's shoulders twitched, as if Jason St. John's relentless gaze continued to bore through her. When she'd pulled from the parking lot, she'd caught a glimpse of his unmistakable tall, toned form on the funeral home's porch.

Just a glimpse.

But enough.

Telling her, she could run, but she couldn't hide.

She adjusted her shoulders. Anything to get rid of the sensation he was still with her, hovering over her shoulder.

Watching.

Enough! She pounded the steering wheel in frustration. A run—that was what she needed. Say goodbye to all her frustrations and and get rid of all that nervous energy.

All she had to do was nip home, change...and run.

***

Fifteen minutes later, with her hair pulled back with a terry cloth headband, Tamsyn had changed into grey running shorts and a bright yellow tank top. She emerged from the house and started jogging gently down the sidewalk to loosen her muscles. In spite of the summer-like heat, Richland Avenue was thankfully shady and lined with convenient sidewalks. Normally, she'd run on the street, preferring that surface over concrete, but afternoon traffic was already picking up in the neighborhood.

As her muscles warmed, she increased her speed, but try as she could, images of Jason St. John kept intruding. Damn the man. He was a distraction, pure and simple.

Not so pure...or simple.

Damn the man.

So she picked up her pace.

Before she knew it, she'd reached West End Place and turned left, heading for the cul-de-sac at the end. Up and to her right, traffic was heavy on the I-440 Loop. Maybe running at a time when exhaust fumes were at their height wasn't the best idea.

Never mind. Anything to get Jason St. John out of her head.

She circled the cul-de-sac and headed back home. Sweat gathered between her shoulders and breasts. She wiped the perspiration from her forehead with the back of her wrist. Slowing her pace a bit, she took a long swig from her water bottle, then pulled off the headband and poured the rest of the water over her head. Walking along, she replaced the headband.

Wonderful.

All she needed was a hot shower and a wine cooler.

As she neared home, she spied a black Range Rover

parked in front of the house.

Oh, no. Better not be.

The driver side door opened and a long leg emerged.

It was.

She picked up her pace to an all-out run. She slammed into his chest, knocking him back against his Rover. "What the *hell* are you doing here, *Saint* John?"

Chapter Nine

Startled by the force of her abrupt attack, Jason held up his hands in surrender. "You must be one hell of a football player, Ms. Holt."

She stepped back, giving him some breathing space. "Are you stalking me now?" Red-faced, she glared up at him, feet planted apart and her hands on her slender hips. "You're supposed to be at your fiancée's funeral. Some fiancé *you* are."

He gave a casual glance at his watch. "I have time. Besides, I thought she was your friend. *Some* friend you are."

Damn, she's hot when she's feisty.

"Why have you followed me home...again?"

"Excellent question." He studied her with care. Her lush breasts rose and fell with each breath. "Why *are* we here? Why are any of us here? It's man's existential question—"

"You *know* what I mean. And in case you don't understand words of more than one syllable, I mean what are you doing at my house?"

"I believe 'doing' has two syllables." That response received an eye roll.

"Yes or no—are you stalking me?"

"I can see how you might think I am." He favored her with a smile. "Technically, my answer is no."

"Yet you *are* here."

Abrasive or not, she made a tantalizing picture. "You

rushed from the funeral home so precipitously I was concerned you might not make it home safely."

"I see. In other words, you followed me." Her tone was flat, her expression no-nonsense.

"Technically, yes. But if I were stalking you, I wouldn't have waited here so patiently while you were on your run. Feel better now?"

"Yes." She pulled the headband from her head and shook the dark damp waves loose. "Now if you don't mind, I'm hitting the shower."

"I don't suppose—"

"*No.*" She straightened her back and added in a scathing tone. "I don't need *anyone* to wash my back."

Great. He was really getting under her skin. "What a suggestion, Ms. Holt. That was the furthest thing from my mind." *Liar. Liar.* "Unfortunately, my attendance is expected at the funeral, otherwise I'd be delighted to oblige you...with your shower." He kept his expression neutral, repressing the smile which would only serve to piss her off even more. Sparring with this hot dark beauty had just made his day—maybe his month. Maybe even his year.

"Enough!" Her delicately flushed cheeks grew redder by the second She clenched her fists. "If you don't leave immediately, I'm calling the police."

He took a step back. "The charge?"

"Harassment. Stalking. Whatever!"

"And I'll be forced to have you charged with assault."

She let out a groan. "I'm out of here. I advise you to do the same." She whirled, ran up the sidewalk to her house, leaving him alone. And amused.

Damn. He shook his head. Tamsyn Holt was a helluva woman.

For a moment, he considered following her but decided against it. He'd jerked her chain enough for now.

And he really needed to get back to the funeral home.

Finally, the funeral service ended. Tess took a position on the front porch, carefully watching the mourners. Such a tragedy and so poignant when a young woman like Brianna Tollison died. But this young woman hadn't merely died. She'd been murdered. There were so many unanswered questions. Who did it? Why? And the family would ask what they could've done to prevent it. If only...

Unlike the grief-stricken families, Tess never bargained. The who and the why were all she needed to know. *Why* would likely tell her *who*. Like many homicide cases before, she wouldn't give up until she had those answers. And the perp.

Tomorrow, she'd send her new partner, Seth Foyle, to the interior design firm where Brianna Tollison had been co-owner for initial interviews. But for the moment, Jerry Ames was flashing on her radar. She'd observed him throughout the proceedings. He was a jittery, nervy mess, and indicators like those always set off alarms in the pit of her stomach.

But she'd also kept a close eye on Jason St. John. He'd returned from wherever he'd gone barely making it back in time for the service. Logically, he held the *numero uno* spot on her suspect list. Husbands and significant others always held that spot. Refusing his permission for her having his phone records pulled without a warrant pissed her off. She shook her head. Not a smooth move, dude. Any detective worth her gold badge would have to wonder what he had to hide.

And she certainly did.

Back to Jerry Ames who was about to emerge from the funeral. Might as well give his cage a rattle.

"Jerry," she said. "Ames, is it?"

Startled, he stopped, his body trembling. "Y-yes. What?"

"I'm Detective Tess Holt." She gave him a quick look at her badge. "I'm investigating the circumstance surrounding Ms. Tollison's murder. I understand you worked with her."

Ames's eyes widened. He glanced around the muscles in his neck twitching. "Uh—yeah."

"I have a few questions." She indicated they should step aside, away from the other mourners.

"*I* don't know who killed her." He pulled at his collar as if it were too tight.

"We'll be interviewing everyone at the firm tomorrow, but since we're both here, I wondered if you knew anyone who might've wanted to hurt her?"

"No. No."

"You know what I mean," she said soothingly. "Clients who might've been unhappy with her work. Anyone who came to the office and gave her trouble."

"No." He shook his head. "Brianna was a superb interior designer and a genuinely nice person. Everyone loved her."

"Did *you*?"

"Kill her? No!" His eyes widened with alarm.

Tess smiled. "No. I mean did *you* love her?"

"Me?" His voice rose to a squeak. "I'm just a design assistant. I worked for her and Sophie. Bree was always nice and polite to me."

"How long have you worked there?"

"I did a six-month internship while I was in my last year of design school. They hired me after I graduated, and I've worked for Bree and Sophie going on eight months." He loosened his tie, swallowing so that his prominent

Adam's apple jerked, visible even in his thickset neck.

Tess gave a quick nod. "I'll see you tomorrow."

"Yeah. Sure. Okay. See ya." He scuttled off as if he couldn't stand another moment in her presence.

Definitely something off about him. Or maybe he was just a nervous wreck all the time. Now, where was her *numero uno*? She surveyed the thinning crowd and spied him still dancing attendance on the Tollisons. No matter. She'd question him again, once she had his phone and computer records.

She motioned to her partner across the room. Seth was a head taller than most of the other mourners. Giving a quick nod, he made his way to her side. "I think one of us should go to the internment," she said. "Check out any onlookers who seem out of place."

"*One of us* would be me," he said with a wry smile.

"Correct." Her phone dinged, indicating a text. Glancing down she saw it was from Tamsyn. ST. JOHN FOLLOWED ME HOME. SO PISSED OFF!

Tess texted back to make sure Tamsyn was okay. She was.

ON MY WAY

So that was where St. John had gone.

Interesting.

And worrisome. No wonder Tamsyn was pissed off.

Jason kept his tone soft and solicitous with the Tollisons while he kept one eye on the red-headed detective. He had to be her prime suspect. Even so, she was working the crowd. He'd seen her pull aside a geeky-looking guy for questioning who'd high-tailed it ASAP. Then he'd seen her glance at her phone and frown. Had Tamsyn texted her sister-in-law about their run-in? Wouldn't put it past her.

The detective shot him a "look." He could spend all afternoon trying to decipher what that look meant. But for now, she was heading out. And she wasn't smiling.

He would've given anything to follow her, but he needed to continue playing the attentive fiancé a while longer. There was still the internment and, at the Tollisons' mansion in Belle Meade, something called a "bereavement dinner."

Basically, for the remainder of the afternoon and evening, he was screwed.

How much had Detective Holt confided in Tamsyn? Maybe he could find out more about how the investigation was proceeding from her instead.

Now, *that* was something to look forward to.

Chapter Ten

When Tess entered the house, Tamsyn breathed a sigh of relief. St. John's little habit of showing up unexpectedly was a bit of an irritation. On one hand, she was undeniably attracted to him, but on the other, his behavior bordered on stalking. Sighing, she pulled a wine cooler from the fridge. "Want something?"

Tess looped her shoulder bag over the high-backed stool. "I'll take a Diet Coke. Still on duty." She accepted the soda and sat on the stool. "So St. John left the funeral home, and he *followed* you home."

"That's right." Tamsyn took a long swallow of her wine cooler. "I couldn't stand much more at the funeral home. My nerves were on edge. Know what I mean? So I went for a run. Figured I could drain some of that nervous energy. I ran the first leg of my usual route, and when I circled back, there he was, big as life and twice as ugly." Definitely not ugly.

Tess frowned. "What did he want? Was he trying to pump you about the case?"

"No." Tamsyn set the wine cooler on the counter. "More than anything, it seemed as if he just wanted to bug me. Everything he said was total BS. Said he thought something might be wrong since I ran out so quickly."

"So he was harassing you?"

"Basically, that was it." Tamsyn shrugged. "I told him to move on because I was ready for a shower. The nerve of that guy. He said he was sorry but he didn't have time to wash my back. As if..."

Tess gave an eye roll. "He said that? Really?"

"Yes! It ranks right up there as one of the stupidest conversations I've ever had with anyone. It was a *non-conversation*."

Tess gave a sideways glance. "Sounds as if there's some kind of chemistry thing going on between you."

"Not on *my* account." Okay, so that was an out-and-out lie. "Besides, I had Justin dig into his background." She leaned forward. "Get this. He thinks St. John might be a Fed."

"Whoa!" Tess straightened. Definitely a new wrinkle in the fabric of her case. "If Justin's right, it means there's a government operation going on we aren't privy to."

"How did Justin put it?" She traced circles in the moisture ring left by the wine cooler. "He said it was the kind of background he'd create to get someone dirty to trust him. Does that make any sense?"

Tess rubbed her forehead. "In a way. For instance, if you want to place someone undercover, he'd need to have something in his background that would make the target of the investigation believe they could trust him."

"And he has another name—oh, what was it? A Jonathan Steele served time for securities fraud. Justin says the resemblance is uncanny."

"Hm." Tess's eyes sparked with interest. "So whirlwind engagement to Tollison's daughter. Maybe Papa Tollison is shady, and the Bureau, or whoever, is investigating *him*. I'll have to dig a little deeper."

"Do you think St. John might really be a Fed?" If he was one of the good guys, then she didn't have to fight all those feelings and urges that popped up whenever she was within twenty feet of him.

"We don't know any such thing." Tess shook her head.

"Be careful. Fed or not, he still could've killed your friend. As yet, he doesn't have an alibi. Normally I wouldn't reveal that, but he seems focused on you. So keep your eyes open and *keep* your distance."

"I promise." Easier said than done, given St. John's propensity for turning up wherever she happened to be.

Tess drained the Diet Coke and tossed the can into the recycle bin, her steely gaze focused on Tamsyn. "Now, back to the funeral home, why *did* you leave so abruptly?"

Under Tess's eagle-eyed scrutiny, Tamsyn's cheeks heated. Her mouth dried. "Uh." Grabbing her wine cooler, she took a couple of long swallows. Was it time to come clean about Bree's rape. It was so long ago. She'd made a promise to her friend. But maybe she shouldn't have, after all.

"Well?" Tess's nails drummed on the granite countertop.

"Funerals affect me that way. Don't they bother you?" She shrugged. "No, I guess not. You must attend quite a few considering your line of work." Yes, she was babbling. Anything to get Tess to exit detective-mode. "I mean Bree was so young. You never think about someone you know, or knew, becoming a murder victim. Something like that makes you think about it could be you. And you feel grateful to be alive. And guilty because you are." She stopped to take a breath. All through this gobbledygook that was coming out of her mouth, Tess's eyes had glazed over. Maybe now she would leave.

"You know. One of the first things you learn as a cop—no, as a cadet—everyone lies to the police. Everyone. Even when they don't have to." Tess sighed. "But it *really* pains me to have to listen while someone in my family lies."

"But—"

Tess held up her hand, stopping Tamsyn. "I know

you're hiding something. You might as well tell me. Keeping a secret never turns out well. And the wrong secret can turn around and bite you in the ass. Even worse, a secret can get you killed."

Damn. Talk about a mind reader. "Your psychic abilities must come in handy. No wonder you're so successful." Tamsyn averted her gaze. "I've kept this secret for a long time—twelve years. Besides, it might not have anything to do with Bree's murder."

Tess leveled her gaze, her toe tapping. "I won't know unless you tell me."

"Not my secret. It was Bree's." She swallowed hard, then plunged ahead. "When we were at Green Hills Academy, Bree was raped by a Nashville Military Academy student. It happened after a school dance. She came to me afterward and swore me to secrecy. I tried to get her to go to the hospital or to the police, but she wouldn't. Said she knew she'd be the one blamed. He came into the funeral home this afternoon. He's the reason I left so abruptly."

Tess rummaged around in her shoulder bag. Pulling out her digital notepad, she opened it. "Name?"

"Brad Oliver. I don't know anything about his life now, but he certainly seemed to know her parents well enough."

Tess entered the name, then waited. "Description?"

"Tall, beefy. At the funeral, he was wearing a gray silk pinstripe suit. Maroon tie. Very tan."

"I remember him." Tess nodded, then slipped the device back into her bag. "I'll definitely dig into him. Something's bound to pop. A rapist seldom stops with one."

"He was with Bree's parents when St. John nudged me over to offer my condolences. Seeing him again pretty much freaked me out. Big time."

"You did a good thing—*finally* telling me."

"He got away with it. He was never punished. Now... It's too late, isn't it?"

"There used to be a fifteen-year statute of limitations on Class A sexual assault cases. But in 2014, the Tennessee legislature removed the statute of limitations on Class A sexual assaults when a rape case is filed within three years of the crime."

"We were sixteen. I'm twenty-eight now. So..." Tamsyn shrugged, denying the heaviness burdening her heart. In protecting Bree's secret, she'd not done her friend any favors. "We were kids. You don't make the best decisions at that age. I wish I'd told someone. Anyone."

"I remember how it was. I'm not *that* old," Tess said, offering Tamsyn an understanding smile. "It's too late for Bree's rape case. On the other hand, Oliver makes a helluva person of interest in her murder." Tess got to her feet. "Gotta go." Retrieving her bag, she slung it over her shoulder.

Tamsyn followed her sister-in-law to the door and locked it behind her. Alone in the house. No point in taking any chances. A shiver slid up her spine. Goosebumps prickled her upper arms. No. Not gonna be threatened by the unknown. Squaring her shoulders, she rubbed the goosebumps away.

In the midst of the most uncomfortable gathering, Jason's FBI phone had beeped, signaling a text. More than ready to make his escape, he excused himself from the Tollison's. Bereavement dinner or no, he couldn't take any more sympathetic looks and pawing hands of well-meaning, well-liquored, and well-heeled septuagenarians, both men and women. He strode outside to the Tollisons' patio. The expanse of lawn was still lush green, in spite of it being October. That had to cost a pretty penny.

He retrieved his cell phone, glancing at the screen: FYI, search warrants granted.

"Jason?" Bree's father had followed him onto the patio.

Acknowledging his almost-father-in-law with a nod, Jason casually slipped the phone back inside his jacket. "Randall. This has to be the worst day of your life."

Tollison nodded. His cheeks quivered. His hang-dog expression was now a permanent feature. "Just wanted to say how much we appreciate your support." He offered his hand to Jason.

Jason took his hand. "If there's anything I can do, you only have to ask."

"Matter of fact there is. We'll discuss it tomorrow." He glanced back over his shoulder toward his guests. "I need to get back in there. Marge...you know?"

"Right. Tomorrow." Just what he'd waited for. Had to be about *business*.

"I'll call."

Jason nodded. Tollison moved wearily back inside the house. Time to make his escape for real. Now that the warrants for his phone records and computer activity had been issued, the detective would be in touch sooner rather than later.

Instead of heading toward Green Hills, Jason left the Tollison's semi-palatial home in the exclusive city of Belle Meade, turning onto Harding Road which became West End Avenue closer into town. A single street in Nashville could have as many as three or four names, depending on whichever section of the city it ran through. The desire to see Tamsyn Holt again was beginning to unnerve him. He turned off West End into the Richland Place neighborhood.

The closer he came to her house, the stronger the pull. What was it about her? Sexy as hell—yes. Beautiful—yes, check that box too. But it was the snap of intelligence in her deep brown eyes that... Pulled him in like a freaking Neodymium magnet.

Get out of my brain.

Bedding her once should do it. Sure it would. Twice, at most.

He'd always been a love 'em and leave 'em kind of guy. The closest he'd come to a long term relationship was with one of his fellow NATS at Quantico. Completing the course had put an end to that. Assignments took them in opposite directions.

About time too.

Unable to stop himself, he parked in front of the house. The house was substantial and probably historic. A real family home. During his delving into the Holt-Lackey's background, he'd discovered the house actually belonged to the Lackey side of the blended family, inherited from their mother.

He emerged from the Range Rover and strode up the sidewalk to the porch. He'd had a hell of a day. She would likely slam the door in his face. Maybe not.

No. She wouldn't. This sizzle of attraction between wasn't all one-sided. She felt it. He'd bet on that too.

He rang the doorbell. Waited.

Finally, she opened the door but stood blocking his entrance and gazing up with a speculative glint. "What the hell do you want?" Her voice was low and seductive, belying the inherent discourtesy of her words. She wore a white top with thin straps that tied on the shoulder. Resisting the temptation to reach and loosen one of the straps, he forced his fingers into his palms.

Finally, he had the presence of mind to make his

mouth form a coherent sentence. "Long day. You could take pity on me. Offer me a drink...or something."

A faint eye roll. "Are you for real?"

Playing with her, he took inventory of his arms and legs. "I'm real. And *you* didn't stay for the funeral."

"I told you it was too emotional. I couldn't take it." She opened the door a bit wider, not an invitation to enter...yet. "I had to get out of there."

"Gonna invite me in or not?"

"I'm—"

Whatever she'd started to stay, apparently she'd thought better of it and stopped.

"—home alone? Are you afraid of me, Ms. Private Eye?"

"Not at all. My sister's upstairs." Her chin lifted in a defiant jut. "And my brothers will be here in a few minutes. Just so you know."

"They keep late hours." Hell, anything to keep her talking. Anything to keep her from slamming the door in his face. In spite of his stalkerish behavior, she didn't appear afraid. Maybe intrigued.

"Sometimes. They've gone out for Chinese. Just down West End," she said with a shrug. "They *won't* be long." Her tone held a warning. Was she bluffing?

"Your brothers and sister all live here together?"

"And it's your business why?"

"Just curious."

She wrinkled her brow. "You've heard the old saying about the cat?"

"I might've heard it, once or twice." He shifted his stance. "You could let me come in, and we could talk. I'd like to know more about you and your friendship with Bree. I still don't understand what I did to make her think I would be unfaithful."

"Why would I allow a man, who just happens to be the person of interest in my friend's murder into my house?"

"I won't be a person of interest much longer. I have an alibi."

"You do?" Her brothers would be home soon. She wasn't lying about that. Surely, she could trust him, especially since he might be a Fed.

"I do." He leaned against the doorjamb. "In fact, Detective Holt has my phone and computer records for the time period during..." He shook his head, remembering.

"Sorry. I didn't mean to remind you." She let out a sigh. "You might as well come in." She stood back and let him enter. "Come on," she said, then walked through the foyer toward the back of the house.

"Big house." He followed gladly. Her shining ebony hair swung free to her shoulders. Her tight ass in a pair of faded jeans—inspiring.

She padded along barefoot, surely aware of the havoc she created within any red-blooded male. Had to be. "As for who lives here, there used to be six of us." Walking along, she pulled a ruffled band from her wrist and used it to secure her long hair on top of her head. "My eldest brother, Scott, lives with his wife. Tess—you remember her, the homicide detective. My sister Caroline—you met her at the agency—lives here. Our other sister Allison's newly married, and only recently moved out."

"So who ends up with the house? The last one to marry?"

She lifted her shoulders in a casual shrug, the thin strap of her top slipped, revealing the smooth skin of her tanned shoulder.

"Never really thought too much about it." She led him into a kitchen furnished with the requisite granite countertops and a professional range. "I guess either Justin or Carrie will own it. It belonged to their mother before she and my father married."

"That's only five. Who's your sixth?"

Her expression grew grave. "Kim, our youngest—she ran away over ten years ago. We've never been able to find her. Great bunch of detectives, aren't we?" Her tone, laced with a wry bittersweet sadness, touched him.

"A runaway? Ten *years*. How do you deal with not knowing?" How did anyone?

She stopped in front of a humongous fridge. "Beer?"

He nodded.

"How do we deal with not knowing?" She lifted her tanned shoulders in a casual shrug. "We've found traces of her whereabouts from time to time—always out west. But she has always moved on by the time we get there." She pulled two bottles from the fridge. Beer for him, and another wine cooler for her.

She nodded toward the French doors. "Let's sit on the deck. There won't be too many more evenings like this."

He stepped out onto the large deck. The fall colors of the red and gold maple trees lining the perimeter of the property were at their height. They'd fall soon, but not yet. She crossed the deck to a large picnic table and sat. Claiming a place opposite her, he took a seat, then took a long pull on his beer.

Damn. He'd had every intention of jumping Tamsyn's bones, anything to get her out of his system. No way could he concentrate on the Tollison operation until he did. But learning about her runaway sister, hearing the sadness in her voice—hell, seeing Tamsyn Holt as a fully dimensional woman with troubles of her own, not just as a seductive annoyance. That played hell with his plan.

"It must be difficult. It's small consolation, but at least, you know she's alive," he said, bringing the conversation back to the runaway sister. He'd been an only child. A large blended family like this was beyond his realm of experience. "Why did she run away? Was it drugs?"

"That's just it. No drugs. She and Caroline had a spat. She grounded Kim for something—I don't even remember why. Next thing we knew, Kim was gone. The police declared her a runaway. And even though our late father had been on the job, they refused to investigate. No Amber Alert. Nothing. Carrie blamed herself. Truth be told, she still does." She took a long sip of the wine cooler.

"Are you sure she ran away?" Puzzled, Jason had to know more. "What about the authorities? Could she have been abducted?"

Tamsyn shrugged. "We didn't think so at the time. You see, Kim *had* been acting out when she and Caroline argued. Kim sneaked out of the house that night. She took some clothes and some money. There was never any indication that she'd been taken."

"She must've had help." Jason frowned. "A teenage girl doesn't just disappear into thin air without help...or encouragement."

"You think someone might've groomed her to run away, for..." She worried her bottom lip. "That's too horrible to think about. What we know, for sure, is she took a bus to Memphis, but we lost her trail there."

"But you said you've had leads since then?"

"We're pretty sure she made it out West. New Mexico and Nevada. We've had tips and sightings, but she'd always moved on by the time Scott or Justin could get there."

"And she's not contacted you, not once?"

"No."

He leaned forward. "When was the last lead?"

Setting the wine cooler aside, Tamsyn let out a sigh. "Four years now. We don't even know if she's alive or healthy or what she's had to do to survive."

Tamsyn's eyes glistened with unshed tears, then she leaned forward. Instinctively his gaze flicked to her cleavage. His mouth dried, but he forced his gaze to meet hers.

"The weird thing is," she said, "all this time, I've had a lurking fear that someone took her. But I guess with the various sightings, that's not a viable theory. She's certainly old enough to come home now if she wanted to."

"A sighting doesn't necessarily mean she was there. The authorities always have numerous sightings whenever there's a kidnapping or a disappearance."

Tamsyn took a sip of her wine cooler. She nodded thoughtfully. "True."

"So your father was a police officer?" Even though he knew the bare bones of her father and stepmother's history, he wanted to keep her talking so he could enjoy her presence a little longer. And yes, get to know her better.

"Yes, he was a homicide detective. He retired and started Holt Investigations. A couple of years after that, he and my stepmother were killed in a car accident. All of us were still in school. Scott was the oldest, so he dropped out of law school and took over the agency. Carrie managed to finish her degree, but took over here at home, then later in the office. Justin, same thing. He manages our IT. Allison went on to nursing school—she just recently married one of the agency investigators. Last year, Scott married a Metro PD detective, Tess, but I told you that already. Sorry to be so repetitive."

"I've had the pleasure of meeting Detective Holt." An absolute exaggeration. "What about you?"

Tamsyn shot him a rather smug smile. "I majored in criminal justice for a couple of years at MTSU. Enough for an AD, but not a bachelor's. Still, the A.D. mollified Scott enough I could work for the family agency. As you've already guessed I'm the honey trap specialist, but the agency has several large corporate clients, as well as individual ones. We're growing all the time."

He nodded his approval. "I saw signs of new construction, so the agency is expanding. Interesting range of clientele."

Chapter Eleven

"A diversified clientele is necessary." Tamsyn nodded. Hearing the irony in his tone, she slanted a smile in his direction. "I bring in a lot of the rapid turnover business. My cases close quickly. I like it that way."

"I hope you're more successful with your other clients than you were with Bree."

She stiffened her spine. "I *never* said Bree was one of my clients."

"You didn't have to. I'm a keen observer."

"I imagine you're a lot of things." Like a Fed.

Before he could respond, Justin pulled into the backyard with his bile green Nash Metropolitan. He and Scott emerged from the vehicle with the latter's usual complaint. "Dude, you need a new car. I feel like a pretzel riding in this thing."

Then Scott stopped, stared at Jason. "What's going on?" His body language took on a confrontational air. He set the bags of takeout on the picnic table. Squared shoulders. Jutting chin. The dreaded stink-eye.

Tamsyn waved away her brother's concern. "It's all right, Scott. Mr. St. John and I are having a nice getting-to-know-you chat. Aren't we?" She reached over and patted the top of his hand as if reassuring a child.

A cheeky gesture to be sure. But he jumped as if she'd run her hand along his thigh and grabbed his dick.

He swallowed, his Adam's apple bobbing.

Justin cleared his throat. "Where's Caroline? She left

the office before we did."

"Don't worry." She gave a chuckle. Now, St. John would know she'd lied about not being alone. "Carrie texted. She's at Target. Something about a baby shower gift."

St. John raised an eyebrow. Busted.

Justin visibly relaxed, his shoulders slumping. Giving a nod, he set down his share of the takeout on the table.

Scott, not so much. "How can we help you, St. John?"

St. John stood. He and Scott were eye-to-eye now. "As your sister said, we were just getting acquainted."

"If you're trying to pump Tamsyn for information about your fiancée's murder, you've come to the wrong place. She doesn't know squat. We don't interfere in ongoing police investigations."

"I heard something along those lines from Detective Holt." He winked at Tamsyn. "And from Tamsyn as well."

"You're wasting your time." Scott picked up his bags of food, still eyeballing St. John.

His gaze narrowed. "It's mine to waste. Besides, I wanted to know more about Bree's state of mind. Why she thought I would cheat?"

Had she imagined it or had St. John issued a challenge?

"Stay away from my sister." Jeez, had Scott really played the sister card?

"Or what?"

"Hold on." Tamsyn set her cooler down with a thump. "I'm an adult. That means I get to choose my friends."

"So now he's a friend?" Scott's brows rose almost to his hairline. "He's a suspect in his fiancée's murder. That's what he is."

"Yes, and now I'm inviting him for dinner." Why was she acting like a teenager? Maybe because Scott was treating her like one. She offered St. John a smile guaranteed to get what she wanted. It always had. "Jason, will you stay for dinner?"

A flash of uncertainty flickered across his handsome face. "If you're sure?"

After Scott stomped into the house, Tamsyn gave a dismissive wave. "Don't worry about him. His bark is worse than his bite."

"Hope so." He sat and took another long pull on his beer. "He's your brother. He's protective. Must go with the territory."

"I'm used to it. But I have to put my foot down once in a while so he doesn't forget I'm the boss of me."

He let out a quiet chuckle, his blue eyes shining with amusement. "So will the detective be coming by?"

Stalling for time, Tamsyn swished the remaining liquid in her bottle, then took another swallow. "Probably. Scott still eats here most nights since Tess is usually involved in a case. She comes by whenever she's through, grabs a bite of leftovers, and then they go home." What was Jason's real reason for coming by unannounced?

"I'd like to talk to her."

"So you really came by to talk to Tess?" She nodded. "I should've known it wasn't my charming company you were after."

"Want the truth?" he asked.

"If it's not too inconvenient." Cocking her head to one side, she waited for his answer.

The hint of a smile curved his mouth. "I came by to—uh, hookup."

"You did?" She straightened. *Good answer.* "Was I going to have any say in the matter?"

"Definitely. But I had second thoughts."

"Please, flatter me some more."

"Oh, I'm still interested," he said, lowering his tone to a seductive range than resonated deep within her. "But I decided I ought to get to know you better."

"Let me see if I'm translating this correctly. You wanted some slam-bam-thank-you-ma'am sex. But you had second thoughts."

"You're driving me crazy. I need to get you out of my head."

"So you thought a one-off would do the trick."

"I hoped it would." He shook his head. "I have a feeling it won't."

"Still not terribly flattered over here." She drummed her nails against the tabletop. "Nope. Not remotely interested. And here's why. I think you're a jerk. You should be in mourning for Bree, but instead, you're putting the moves on me. Did you *ever* care about her? Were you in love with her? No wonder she hired me." Her hand went to her mouth. "Oops."

He squirmed under her steady gaze. Good. He deserved to feel uncomfortable. "Well?"

"It's complicated. Bree was fun. We had a good time. But the whole thing happened pretty fast. I *was* having second thoughts. I assume my uncertainty was what Bree picked up on. It's not because I was screwing around or picking up sexy private investigators in jazz bars."

So, he thought she was sexy. His throwaway comment shouldn't have cheered her so much.

But it did. In her line of work, she'd run across his type too often. Handsome. Imbued with an inborn certainty of his never-ending appeal. And with an answer for everything. Why was he the one who made her want to throw caution to the wind? How was he so different? Sooner or later, she'd figure him out. She would. "I can certainly vouch for the latter."

"Don't you have a *date* tonight?" He lifted a single eyebrow lifted with his rude question.

She lifted her chin a defiant notch. "As you might imagine, my line of work plays hell with my attitude toward men."

"Damn shame." He gave her a wry smile.

Yeah, go ahead smile. "If you're not careful I'm going to rescind my dinner invitation." She kept her tone modulated as if she could care less.

"What have I done?"

"You *buried* your fiancée this afternoon. Shouldn't you be with her parents, instead of here toying with the idea of our hooking up?"

"I *was* there. I spent two interminable hours with her parents. Then I had to get out. I believe you're familiar with the feeling."

Before Tamsyn could make up her mind whether or not to kick him to the curb, Caroline pulled in and parked beside Justin. She emerged carrying a big bag from Target and wearing a WTF expression. "Tam?" She walked up onto the deck.

"One more for dinner," Tamsyn replied through clenched teeth.

"Right." Caroline turned her attention to Jason. "Mr. St. John, I hope you like take out—" She turned to Tamsyn. "What *are* we having tonight?"

"Chinese."

He stood smiling at her sister. "Jason, please. Mr. St. John's too formal...especially to eat Chinese." He opened the door for her. "Allow me."

Smooth. Oh, so smooth.

Caroline's gaze widened. She awarded him with a bemused smile, then handed over the bag. "Thank you...Jason."

Jason might win over her sister with his perfect manners, but her brothers wouldn't fall for his perfect manners or a perfect line. Neither would Tamsyn.

The last visible rays of the sun had disappeared behind the neighboring house. The fall evening air, cool on her skin, she shivered. "Might as well go inside."

Chapter Twelve

Eager to observe the family interactions between Tamsyn and her siblings, Jason strode into the house. A plethora of food containers were spread over the kitchen island with a stack of paper plates and chopsticks occupying the far end. The spicy aroma of Chinese fast food heavy in the air, his mouth watered. His stomach growled.

"Help yourselves, everyone." Tamsyn gestured toward the food, then focused her dark gaze in his direction. "Tonight's my night to cook. And since I'd rather have a root canal than cook, Friday night is now Chinese food night."

Enough food to feed a small army. "At least your family won't starve."

"No danger whatsoever." Mischief sparkled in her dark chocolate eyes.

Nudging his elbow, Caroline reached for the Target bag. "Thank you. I can manage it now."

"My pleasure." Somewhat distracted, he handed it over, but his gaze was inevitably drawn back to Tamsyn's very fine figure as she shrugged into a light sweater. Bummer. No more temptation to untie her straps.

Back to reality.

Like bookends, at the far end of the kitchen, Tamsyn's brothers stood watching him, their arms folded across their chests. Opposing—make that imposing—bookends. Scott the dark. Justin the light. No mistaking their protective glares. Or stances geared for battle.

He raised his hands in surrender. "Okay, guys. I get it. Your sister's off-limits."

"Why are you *here*?" Scott asked, taking a step forward.

"Tamsyn invited me to dinner."

"Before she invited you, *what* were you doing here?" Scott took another step toward Jason.

He paused before speaking. The truth might've amused Tamsyn. The brothers, not so much. "It's complicated. Let's say I needed a break from the funeral festivities."

One more step. "What I don't appreciate—"

Caroline stepped between them. "Hold on. Dial down the testosterone. Jason, for the time being, is a guest in our home. I say he's welcome until he makes an ass of himself like *you two* are in imminent danger of doing."

Scott took a step back. "Fine. But I have my eye on you."

So Caroline was the peacemaker/diplomat of the family. Interesting. Scott—he wouldn't want to meet in a dark alley. Long-haired Justin was more of a nerd, but his manner aside, he obviously was no stranger to the gym.

Tamsyn let out a piercing whistle. "People! There's food on the counter, and I'm starved."

Now, *she* was the riot police. And a major distraction. A lovely one, though.

Jason watched while the brothers filled their plates with a variety of dishes, then tromped their way to what they called the man cave. Let 'em. Hanging out with the sisters was more to his liking. Especially the one sister.

He filled his plate slowly, not as agile with chopsticks as they were. Tall and slender, Caroline chose vegetable-prevalent dishes. On the other hand, Tamsyn dipped into the meatier ones with gusto. "I'm staying in the kitchen. Closer to the food that way," Tamsyn said, slurping up an errant lo mein noodle. With a wide smile, she wiped brown sauce from her chin. "Did I mention I *love* Chinese?"

Basically, she ate with abandon. Did she engage in other earthy pleasures with the same degree of passion? *Sure hope so.*

"I'll have to hit the gym tomorrow morning for at least two hours to burn off all these calories. But it's *so* worth it." She took a bite of General Tso's chicken, moaning with pleasure.

So she favored the hot and spicy dishes. No surprise there.

"Aren't you hungry?"

He gave her a sheepish smile. "You caught me. I couldn't help but watch you eat."

With a smile curving her sensual mouth, she admitted, "I'm an enthusiastic eater. Food should be enjoyed. Eat up." Her dark eyes caught his gaze and held it.

He cleared his throat. "I confess I had something at the Tollison's. Nothing this good, though." Abandoning the chopsticks, he forked a bite of pepper steak.

"Leave anything for me?" a female voice called from the hall. All too well, he recognized the owner. Detective Holt had arrived.

"There's plenty." Tamsyn almost sang her reply.

The detective sauntered into the kitchen. "Well, I see y'all have company."

"Detective Holt. Nice to see you again."

She shot him a skeptical stare. "Likewise I'm sure. Also very convenient. Maybe we can talk after dinner?"

"Of course. I'm happy to assist the city's finest."

"Right." She filled her plate. "You'll find me in the man cave. Strange as it may seem, I need to see my husband once in a while."

Tamsyn leaned closer, lowering her voice in a conspiratorial manner. "Are you still a suspect?"

He nodded. "Until she tells me otherwise. What about you? Am I still a suspect in your book?"

"That's where things are a little tricky. We don't have anything resembling an interrogation room." Her tone was playful. Playful was good.

"I doubt our conversation will be anything formal."

She cocked her head to the side. "You have an attorney?"

"No. I don't need one. I *didn't* kill Bree."

"Very good to know."

Her response was casual, but did she believe him? "You should probably be careful about whom you invite into your home."

"I am, usually." A playful grin.

Time to change the topic. "So where do you work out?"

"Green Hills Y or if I'm going from the office, the Downtown Y."

"Maybe I'll see you." Hell, yes, he'd see her.

"Maybe."

He turned to Caroline in order to include her in the conversation. "The family agency seems to be doing well, and you seem to get along without too much drama."

"We do. Scott's the lead. Justin is our IT. You're already familiar with Tam's part of the business. More and more, though, we're venturing toward corporate security and personal protection, but we still do some domestic cases, other than Tam's. I'm not involved with fieldwork. I run the office. We're already expanding the office space, and now we own the entire floor. As soon as the remodel is finished, we'll have more room to expand. We're already interviewing and hiring more staff." Caroline nibbled a minuscule bite of her broccoli and chicken. "We have another P.I., but since he married and our younger sister, Allison, he's family too. I can only suppose they're still enjoying married life too much to bother with us. They'll be here Sunday, though. That's my day to cook."

This was a family. A *real* family. Bonded by time and circumstance. Clearly, they cared about one another. Worked together and, in spite of a couple of marriages, basically lived together.

What would it be like to be part of such a tribe? Intrusive at times...probably. And finding alone time...non-existent.

But the warmth of this group surrounded him, her brothers notwithstanding. Jumping ahead, could he get used to it? Wouldn't mind finding out. At any rate, it was nothing like his tension-filled family had been. Doting mother. Jealous and dismissive father.

He'd barely finished his pepper steak when the detective emerged from the man cave. "Let's talk."

Her jaw clenched, Tess led Special Agent St. John into the rarely used formal living room, pulling the pocket doors closed behind them. She gestured for him to have a seat while she took the Stickley chair opposite. "I see you've been making yourself at home." She leaned forward. "What're you doing here, St. John?"

"Your sister—she's fascinating." His face warmed. No way. He couldn't be blushing.

"Really? That disturbs me on several levels." She eyeballed him. "You just *buried* your fiancée today."

"That fact is ever-present." He nodded gravely. "Plus, people keep reminding me."

"So one down, time to move onto the next?"

"I'm not that shallow, Detective."

Really? "If you're not filling a space in your empty bed, then you're digging for information on how the murder investigation is going. I'll tell you now that you're wasting your time. Even though our family is close, there's a definite line between what *I* know and what you *think* Tamsyn might know."

"My interest in your sister-in-law is more..." He shrugged. "...complicated."

"Your *complicated interest* is what concerns me. I'm advising you to stay away from her."
Wait for it.

Shoulders squared, his chin rose a determined notch. "Isn't that up to her?"

So the Fed wouldn't back down.

"As long as you remain a person of interest in my investigation, it's up to me. I'm warning you: make yourself scarce. If—and that's a big 'if'—the investigation clears you of Brianna Tollison's murder, you may pursue Tamsyn to your heart's content."

He let out a bark of laughter. "I expected this conversation from one of her brothers. Nice to know who wears the balls."

She smiled. "We took a vote. I won."

"Just curious. Is 'person of interest' police-speak for a prime suspect?"

"You know damn well it is."

He shifted in his chair. "*How* would I know?"

"How indeed?" She let out a huff of exasperation. "I received an interesting phone call earlier this evening. It came from the Nashville FBI Field Office Special Agent in Charge, Michael Chase. I was informed to keep you as a person of interest if I must, but that you were involved in a sensitive undercover operation and to keep hands-off."

"So now you know I'm one of the good guys. Why the strong-arm tactics?"

"Pure and simple. I don't like you."

"But now that you know I'm an FBI agent, you must realize I have no intention of harming a hair on Tamsyn's head."

"I don't know any such thing. You were prepared to marry my murder victim just to keep your cover going. And now you're pursuing my sister-in-law. I find that distasteful. Make that very distasteful."

"And there you have it. I didn't murder Bree. Far from it. Her untimely death makes my operation that much more difficult."

"You're going after her father?"

"*My* turn to draw the line, Detective."

She smiled. "I'll take that as a yes."

He stood. "I take it I'm free to go?"

"For now." St. John might be one of the good guys, but trust him? No way. "One more thing. Ms. Tollison's killer is still at large. If he has anything to do with her father or your mission, there's a chance you could draw that danger to Tamsyn. If you're really interested in more than a one-night stand, hold off until we find the killer."

His eyes appeared to glaze over. "My dinner's getting cold."

Glancing around for something to throw, she gritted the word, "Fine."

Calm down. Tamsyn will see through him soon enough.

Chapter Thirteen

Curiosity getting the better of her, Tamsyn had her ear plastered to the living room door. Damn oak doors. Too freaking thick. Couldn't hear a blinking word.

Without warning, the door opened. She stumbled into Jason's arms.

"Careful."

His strong arms surrounded her, holding her a moment or two longer than necessary for regaining her stability. Her breath caught in her throat. "Thanks," she murmured when she could catch her breath.

"*My* pleasure."

"So are you under arrest?"

"No." He smiled down at her, his gaze warming her in places already blazing hotter than normal. "Still a free man."

"That's good to know. I—uh, just came to warn you the food's getting cold."

He leaned against the wall, the corner of his mouth twitching with amusement. "Of course, you did."

What did he have to smirk about anyway? "I'm just being a good hostess."

With a blank expression, Tess glided by them giving Tamsyn the briefest eye roll before model-walking to the kitchen.

Tamsyn tapped the toe of her shoe against the oak floor. "Anytime you're ready..."

He seemed to catch his breath. "Ready for what?"

"...to finish your dinner. I certainly didn't mean *anything* else." She uttered that statement with a bit of heat.

"A man can hope." Jason leaned his head closer and murmured, "Just so you know, a man *always* hopes."

His breath warm against her neck sent chills of excitement up her spine. "I see." Okay, losing control of the conversation. She turned to head to the kitchen and bumped into the wall.

"Kitchen's this way." He jerked his head toward the back of the house.

"There's something about you," she muttered, elbowing his ribs ever so slightly. "I turn into an absolute klutz when you're around."

He slipped his arm around her waist. "Let's see if I can accept your statement as the truth. I've observed you drop all the contents of your purse, but that might've been on purpose. You stumbled around in your office. You just fell into my arms when eavesdropping, and now you've walked into a wall. Consider this: maybe you really *are* a klutz."

Facing him, she set her hands on her hips. "But I'm not. I took ballet and dance until my teens. Under ordinary circumstances—"

"That's just it. We're not in ordinary circumstances territory. And neither of us is ordinary." With that arrogant statement, he took her hand, pulled her into a dance position, and then twirled her around the foyer. Only with extreme focus and concentration did she avoid tripping over her own feet. "See there?" She looked up, challenging him.

"You're extraordinary, or I wouldn't be here." While she considered the meaning of his words, he led her, still waltzing, down the hallway into the kitchen.

"You've had a lesson or two yourself." She extricated

herself from his embrace, not that she really wanted to, but Caroline and Tess's wide-eyed expressions were too much to contend with. Who needed that?

"You're quite graceful when you quit trying to lead." He reached over and ruffled her hair.

"Enough with the patronizing sexism," She knocked his hand away and made an attempt to smooth her hair.

"It's getting late. I'm afraid I must go. Thank you for dinner." He nodded. "Caroline. Detective."

"I'll walk you out." Tamsyn took his hand and dragged him to the front door. "I trust you can find your way to the car without me."

"I can."

She opened the door, but just as quickly he closed it. He backed her against the foyer wall and kissed her. His mouth was soft against hers at first, then demanding. Heat pooled between her thighs. She couldn't get enough of him. This was what she wanted. Needed. Only she wanted more than his lips on hers. The hard length of his erection pressed against her hip bone. Her knees weakened. He could have had her against the foyer wall with her brothers in the den and her sisters in the kitchen. Let the world watch. She didn't care. She would have given him anything. Done anything, just to have him inside her.

But he pulled away. "To be continued."

Grabbing his shirt in her fists, she gasped for air. "Soon."

Dipping his head once more, he kissed her forehead. "Very soon." He opened the door and slipped away into the night.

Still breathless, she leaned against the wall until a modicum of sanity returned. Instead of returning to the kitchen, she slipped into the first-floor bathroom where she turned on the water faucet. Cupping her hands she splashed the cold water over her burning cheeks. Now if she could just regain her composure, she would attempt to face Caroline and Tess. She peered into the mirror over the sink. No amount of cold water was going to take away the shine of excitement in her eyes.

Nothing could.

Elated by Tamsyn's response to his kiss, Jason whistled all the way to the Rover. She was every bit as passionate as he'd suspected. Hoped. He'd felt her mind and body's surrender to his touch. Her body was lush and giving, and he could imagine no greater happiness than to sink into her hot, wet depths. Still, he wanted more than a one-night stand. She was as eager as he, but losing control and indulging his fantasy could mean the end of his assignment.

If discovered, Tollison would never understand Jason's having a relationship with another woman this soon after Bree's death.

Success would mean admission into Tollison's inner circle. Bringing Tollison down would mean a promotion.

And maybe his father's acceptance.

Nah.

Pulled back from the abyss of insanity. Tamsyn sucked in a deep breath. Yes, that was exactly how it felt when he'd broken their kiss. Time to face Caroline and Tess. She emerged from the bathroom.

Oh crap!

Not only were her sister and sister-in-law in the hall waiting for her but so were Scott and Justin. Like a lineup, they were aligned against the wall, arms folded over their chests. "What?"

"That's what we want to know," Scott said. Naturally, he was the first to speak. "What the hell's going on with you and that guy?"

"Nothing that's any of your business." She gave a huff. "I'm going to bed." Darting toward the stairs, she wasn't quite fast enough.

"Hold it!" Scott grabbed her wrist. "That guy's no good."

"Hell of a kisser though." She tried not to smile.

"Have you lost all common sense?" Scott again, definitely in over-protective mode. "He's a person of interest in his fiancée's homicide. You *know* what that means. Just stay away from him."

"Or," Justin interjected, "he's a Fed and mixed up in something you don't need to get involved with."

Caroline sighed. "I think he's nice. He's clearly interested in Tamsyn. And she's interested in him. I don't see why y'all can't just leave her alone."

"Scott's right." Tess's turn, again—groan. "You need to steer clear of him."

"It's been a year since I've had a real date. I've heard enough." Tamsyn pried Scott's hand from her wrist and then ran upstairs. "More than enough."

Taking a calming breath, she resisted the intense impulse to slam her bedroom door. They might treat her like a child half of the time, but she didn't have to act like one.

Chapter Fourteen

Saturday morning, Tess sat at her desk, double-checking the forensic IT report. St. John's alibi was solid. One of the waitresses at Puckett's had remembered serving his lunch on the day in question. His phone and computer records showed activity during the window of opportunity for the murder.

Should she tell Tamsyn he was cleared? Technically, he was undercover, so Tamsyn had no need to know. Neither did Scott, and he was definitely in big brother protective mode.

St. John was a Fed, but she was the only one of the family who knew that particular piece of information, for sure. If she let matters between the two to continue, Tamsyn would only get her heart broken when he moved on to his next assignment.

Still, this was Tamsyn they were dealing with. It was her life. Her heart. Knowing Tamsyn's stubborn streak, she'd do whatever the hell she wanted.

Tess pulled the phone from her belt. Might as well get it over with. She tapped in St. John's number. Maybe St. John, or whatever the hell his name was, would be reasonable.

"St. John," he answered, still sounding half asleep.

"Detective Holt here. Just wanted to let you know per your computer and phone records, you've been cleared as a person of interest in Miss Tollison's murder."

"And the fact that I'm a federal agent doesn't enter

into it?"

"I don't care if you're J. Edgar reincarnated. I follow the evidence." Steeling for an argument, she said, "As for my sister-in-law, I hope you'll give her a wide berth."

"I've taken time to consider, Detective. I will do as you ask."

Too easy. But no point in looking a gift horse in the mouth. "That's a relief, but I have to wonder why?"

"As you surmised, I'm involved in an undercover operation targeting Randall Tollison. Getting romantically involved this soon after his daughter's death would blow my cover."

"Understood. Agent—I don't suppose St. John is your real name."

"No. My surname is Stone—but you can forget that for now."

"All right, then. We're done." Tamsyn wouldn't thank her. That much was obvious.

"Will you contact me when the case is closed? I'd like to know who killed Bree. She certainly didn't deserve what happened."

"No one does. And yes, I'll let you know when someone is charged."

"And keep watch on Tamsyn. She's special."

"We'll keep her close, never fear."

"Thank you, Detective Holt... for everything."

Tess terminated the call.

Would keeping Tamsyn safe be that simple? If it meant keeping her away from St. John. Tess sighed. Probably not.

Rolling over, Jason set his phone on the bedside table. One obstacle overcome, at least. Two if he could keep his word. But keep it he would. If today's meeting with Tollison went well, then his operation was about to get complicated.

He reached for the phone, this time calling SAC Chase. "We're proceeding as planned. I'm meeting with Tollison later this morning. I should have a better idea of what he's up to by this afternoon. Either that or you'll be a long time searching for my body."

Tollison's butler showed Jason into Tollison's study. From the man's overt physique and the way he moved, he was more bodyguard than butler. The furnishings were a testament to Tollison's privilege and power. Centuries-old mahogany paneling and what appeared to be an antique French desk—one of the Louie's. Marble floors and lustrous leather. Very Old World.

"Sweep him for bugs, Hughes." Tollison shrugged. "Sorry. Necessary precaution."

Jason nodded. So planting a surveillance device wasn't an option.

Tollison indicated with a nod that Jason should sit on the settee. Tollison was already downing very old and very expensive Scotch. "Glenfiddich, bottled in 1937." He picked up another glass. "Can't go wrong with this."

Jason shook his head. "No thanks. Too early for me. I like to keep my head about me when I discuss business."

"Good man." Tollison nodded his approval and set the bottle on the table. He sat, leaning back. "I have a new revenue stream I need to—shall we say—launder."

"How can I help?"

"You have contacts in the Cayman's, of course?"

"Of course."

"I will be taking delivery of a large shipment of

something the government would rather not see in this country. Consequently, I'll be selling it at a premium. I'd rather not have to explain to the authorities where all that lovely cash came from."

Jason nodded. "The money can be laundered through various shell companies. Laying the groundwork is simple. I just need your approval to go ahead." Drugs or arms? What was Tollison into?

Tollison shot him a smug smile. "I've had you thoroughly checked out. You're not as squeaky clean as you appear on the surface."

"I counted on that. Why else would we be having this conversation if you hadn't uncovered my alias and the history of my unfortunate incarceration?"

"You did an excellent job, though."

"Reinvention came at a price. I have losses to recoup." Jason arched a brow. "What's my commission?"

"I'm willing to cut you in for five percent. That will be a considerable amount. A fortune, in fact."

"Five? Is that the best you can do?" Jason shrugged. "Twenty-five would make me *considerably* happier."

"A quarter? You expect me to fork over a quarter. Hells bells!" Tollison huffed. "I have other partners to take into account. Seven."

"Twenty," Jason countered. Walking out of this negotiation, as if he were dickering over the price of a car, wasn't a viable tactic. Unless he fancied disappearing forever. He held his breath.

Tollison's eyes shuttered; a muscle in his neck twitched. Jason's gut quivered. Had he been too bold? Was he about to meet Tollison's inner thug?

"Ten. Final offer." Tollison's gaze became focused and deadly. He pointed directly at Jason, emphasizing his growled words. "But know this: you'll earn every blasted cent."

Jason swallowed, then nodded. "Ten it is."

"Good. You know your worth." Tollison smiled, once again his affable self.

Jason exhaled. He held out his hand to shake on the deal.

"You'll work with my attorney, Brad Oliver."

"Oliver? Do you really deem it wise to bring your legal adviser into this? Until FinCEN's recommendations take effect, I'm not bound by the AMLs. And then, I'm still not bound unless I oversee over 100 million dollars in assets."

"Brad's a major player *whatever* I do."

"I see." Right. Oliver was definitely bent. "Now that I'm on board, I need more details."

"You know enough," Tollison grunted, attempting to rise. "All you need to know, for now."

Damn.

Jason sprang forward to assist Tollison, offering him a hand. "You still have reservations?"

Tollison waved him away. "I haven't come this far without extreme diligence. You do your part. You'll be paid. That's all *you* need to know." He poured himself another shot of scotch and downed it. "Just be ready. If all goes well, this should go down in a couple of days."

Making it Monday. "I *will* need to be present to make the initial transfer to the Cayman account."

"You will be."

"I'll be available whenever you call." Ready to leave, he stopped, turned to Tollison. "How is Bree's mother doing? Should I say goodbye?"

"That's kind of you." Tollison shook his head. "But she's in no condition to see anyone." He let out a bark of rueful laughter. "For me, it's still business as usual."

"I'm so very sorry for your loss. I thought our future

was set. Now, she's gone."

"Of course. You're grieving too." Tollison poured and downed another shot.

"Yes." He schooled his features to approximate a semblance of his grief. While he truly grieved Brianna's death, it wasn't the gut-wrenching anguish of one who'd lost his future life partner.

"Hughes will show you out."

The butler/bodyguard appeared quickly. Too quickly. Had he been listening at the door?

"This way, Mr. St. John."

"Thank you, Hughes." Yeah. Dude was a bodyguard all right. And in spite of Jason's training, not someone he'd relish meeting in a dark alley.

Jason let out a sigh of relief as soon as he passed the city limits of Belle Meade and turned onto Harding Road. Time to show up at his office and go through the motions of being a financial adviser. Might as well give his SAC a head's up about the upcoming money exchange. Using the Range Rover's onboard Wi-Fi, he called Agent Chase. "Something's going down—best guess Monday. Tollison's being very close-mouthed about what. It involves the delivery and resale of something the government won't want in this country. Arms or drugs are the most common, but what if it's a bioweapon? It could even be a weapon of mass destruction? Tollison says the money involved is substantial. My cut is purported to be a considerable fortune."

"Details ASAP."

"Will do. According to Tollison, his attorney, Brad Oliver, is a player in all of his business deals. Wouldn't hurt to have a two-man team surveilling each."

"Agreed."

"Tollison had his bodyguard sweep me for bugs. So no wires. I have to go in cold."

"That's not what we planned."

"Can't be helped. I'll transfer the money he pays from his Cayman account. Then when he sells it on, I'll transfer that money into the cloned Cayman account. He'll never know the difference."

"We'll institute long-distance listening devices."

"I'll have little notice. He won't call until it's ready to go down."

"We'll be ready."

Sure as hell hope so. Otherwise, he'd prove his father's estimation of his abilities right. In other words, a loser.

If Jason St. John could waltz into her office and rattle her cage, Tamsyn decided two could play that game. When she entered his office, St. John's PA, Ms. Ella Buntin according to her nameplate, didn't look too pleased to be working on a Saturday.

"The office closes at noon...sharp," Ms. Buntin said, glancing at her watch.

"Keeps his own hours, doesn't he?"

"He's the boss."

"Do you have any idea why he's so late today?"

"He had an appointment at a client's home at ten. Perhaps *you* should've made an appointment." She picked up what appeared to be a mystery novel.

"Does he have any others? Appointments, I mean."

Ms. Buntin's gaze narrowed. "Not this morning."

"I'll wait." Tamsyn picked up a copy of the *Wall Street Journal*. Scanned the headlines. Boring.

"Mr. St. John has it delivered daily." Ms. Buntin

smiled, then went back to her novel.

Smart guy. Good cover.

At a quarter till twelve, Jason strolled into the office. He nodded at the P.A., then noticed Tamsyn. What the hell was she up to now? He clenched his jaw. "Ms. Buntin, you might as well call it a day."

She huffed and started gathering her things.

"This way, Ms. Holt."

Tamsyn flashed his PA a wide smile, but then followed him into the inner office.

In a flash, he slammed the door behind her. "What the hell are you doing here? I promised —"

"Excuse the hell out of me. I was under the impression we'd made plans." She jutted her chin up a notch. "You promised *who* what?" Glancing around the room, she shrugged away from him. "Boring furnishings, by the way."

He stiffened, walked around his desk, and sat. Needed some space. Otherwise, she'd probably smack him if he touched her again. Not that he'd blame her.

"Sorry, I wasn't aware you had a background in design. Should I have hired you?"

She wrinkled her nose and swung a lock of midnight black hair over her shoulders. "Don't change the subject."

"You're the one—" He spread his hands, signaling he was done. Fed up. Whatever. "Fuck it. What *do* you want?"

"It's very simple." She pulled at her short skirt, drawing his gaze to her legs. "I'd like to open an investment account."

"Like hell, you would."

Smiling, she crossed her legs, tugged at her skirt again. "Aren't you an investment adviser?"

"Of course." He smiled a patently false smile, one for

show. "How much do you have to invest?" Seduction 101. *Deliver me.*

"Is there a minimum?" She leaned forward, her elbows on his desk.

His gaze darted to her full breasts. His mouth grew dry and his dick hardened. Damn the woman and the effect she had on him. He forced his gaze back to her face. Beautiful oval face. Dark arched brows. Warm brown eyes. Lush perfect mouth.

He drew in a shaky breath. "The more money you have to invest, the greater your return." He clenched his jaw. His muscles tremored.

"Is that guaranteed?" She shoved his desk calendar to the floor and climbed onto his desk.

Trying to swallow the lump in his throat, he loosened his collar. "There are no guarantees." He managed this with a decided croak.

Reclining on her side as if she were a courtesan in a renaissance painting, she murmured, "Not sure I like the sound of that."

He stood, forcing his expression into a stern mask. "Stop this. Stop it right now."

She got to her knees and snaked her arms around his neck. "Are you sure you want me to stop? I'm certain you really don't." She ran her forefinger down the zipper of his jeans, finding his erection.

"Dammit, I promised." He grasped her wrists, forcibly removing her hands from his body. He stepped away from the desk, his heart beating like a snare drum.

"Promised who?"

"Tess—Detective Holt." He took another ragged breath.

Tamsyn calmly slid off the desk, exposing an inordinate amount of tanned thigh, and rearranged her clothing. "*When* did you talk to her?"

"Earlier this morning. She called to tell me I was cleared, but I promised her I would avoid you." He stepped back.

Away. Get away from her or you're lost.

"But why?"

"That's *all* you need to know. I mean to keep my promise."

"Justin was right. You *are* an agent of some kind."

"You don't know any such thing. Just know it's not safe. *I'm* not safe. Go home, Tamsyn. Have a picnic lunch with your family. Forget you ever met me. You don't know me."

"That's just it." She took a step forward. "I want to."

"You *want* to get to know me? That's what this display was about?"

She smiled. "Almost worked."

"Not even halfway." He shrugged. All right. He'd lied. Another five seconds of her antics and all his good intentions would've hit the fan.

She walked around the desk. He sucked in a breath. *Dear God, no. Go away.*

"I thought we'd have some fun." Playfully, she ran her finger across the desktop. "Desk is kind of hard. Oh, well."

"You need to leave... Now."

"And if I don't?"

Heart pounding, he leaned in. "You're in grave danger of finding out how hard that desk is."

"Really?"

"Really."

"Prove it." She closed the distance between them. Her arms went around his neck.

"Just once." Cornered.

"What if *once* isn't enough?" She nipped his ear.

Her breath was warm on his neck, but chills raced up his spine. Lost. "It'll have to be. This mission is too important."

He bent his head and kissed her. She opened to him meeting his tongue with hers. He hiked her skirt. No panties. Not even a thong. She'd come prepared. But he hadn't. "I don't have protection."

"I do." She slipped a condom packet from her black lace bra.

He grabbed her ass and set her on the desk. She unsnapped the fastener on his jeans and unzipped them. She tore the packet with her teeth, sheathed his cock, then lay back with her body open to him.

"Slow down." He slipped the knit top over her head, then unfastened her bra. Her breasts were lush. Her nipples perfect pearls of pale milk chocolate. He cupped her breasts, groaning at their softness. He took a nipple in his mouth and sucked.

She moaned under him, her hips writhing. He licked down her belly to the thicket of black curls where her toned thighs met. Unable to resist, he tasted her, flicking her clit, inhaling her musk. She begged him to hurry. "I'm dying. Please."

He slid a finger inside her. Hot. Wet. Wild. He nudged her slit with his cock. She arched her hips, rising to meet him and take him inside.

Before he could thrust, his cellphone trilled. The one he used with Tollison. Groaning with frustration, he straightened, struggled for sanity, and willed his cock to behave. He reached for his phone.

She levered onto her elbows, then grabbed his wrist. "No, don't!"

"I can't afford to miss this call." He glanced at the Caller ID: Brad Oliver, not Tollison. He stifled a groan.

What did *he* want? "St. John here. What's up, Oliver?"

"Thought we should talk this through before it happens."

"Anytime."

"How about now? I'm just outside your building."

"Now's fine. I'm in six-oh-two." He terminated the call. "You have to get out of here. Like now. I have someone on his way up."

"Now? You're going to leave me high and dry?"

"Correction: you're not dry. And if you value your life, get the hell out of here now." He pulled her off the desk and yanked her skirt to cover her thighs.

She snatched up her bra and top from the floor. "Great. Just freaking great." She pulled the top over her head, then stuffed her bra into her purse. "Next time..."

"Next time, make an appointment. Better yet—*no* next time."

She finger-combed her hair and shot daggers over her shoulder. But thank God, she left his office, muttering curses on his head, no doubt.

He groaned a sigh of relief. Damn the woman. Bewitched—that was it. And powerless to resist her wiles. He'd barely picked up the desk calendar from the floor when Oliver strode into the office.

"Who was the broad?"

"What broad?" Damn. Oliver had seen Tamsyn.

"Dark hair. Dark eyes. She just left your office. I've seen her before...at Brianna's funeral."

"Not *my* office." He managed a casual shrug. Oliver had not only noticed, but he'd also remembered her from the funeral. "Six other office suites on this floor." Never blinking, he shoved his chair under the desk. "I was about to go for lunch. Hungry?"

"I could eat."

"What do you recommend?"

"The Southern on Third Avenue South. Know it?"

Jason nodded. "Good choice. I'll meet you there." Tollison's attorney was a former jock who'd softened around his middle. Still, he moved with an easy grace belying his bulk. With shark-dead eyes and the seeming ability to read others' minds while shuttering his own thoughts...definitely not someone to mess with.

Tamsyn managed to stay upright and ran to her car in the parking garage, her heels echoing sharply across the concrete. Her hands trembled so hard, she could barely unlock the door. Once inside, she locked her door and sucked in a deep breath. Calm down. Meeting Brad Oliver at the elevator ranked at the top of the chart as her second least favorite moment of all time. Was he somehow involved with Jason's mission?

Brad's speculative gaze traveled up and down her body before the elevator doors closed—unnerving, to say the least. Had he recognized her from the funeral...or from twelve years earlier?

Should she call Tess? Then she'd have to explain why she'd been at Jason's office in the first place. Knowing Tess, she'd dig out all the details if Tamsyn wasn't careful. She reached for her phone to call Tess's private cell.

"Detective Holt."

"I don't suppose you can meet me for lunch. I don't care where. I just need to see you."

"I can't. Got a briefing in ten minutes. It'll go on for a while. Can it wait 'til this evening?"

"Sure." It's not as if her life were in danger. Nevertheless, Brad Oliver was one scary dude.

"You don't sound all that sure."

"I'm okay—really. Later is fine. Have a good briefing." She ended the call, forcibly shaking off the uneasiness gathering in the pit of her stomach ever since she'd run into Bree's rapist.

Focus on something else.

Coitus interruptus. Dear heaven. Had she lost her mind? Talk about being saved by the bell.

No. Focus on something else. Something else entirely.

The sun was shining. The fall colors were at their height. What could go wrong on such a beautiful day?

Chapter Fifteen

Still puzzled by Tamsyn's call, Tess entered the briefing room. What had upset Tamsyn so much that she'd called to have lunch? Talk about an unexpected occurrence. Fitting into her husband's family of blended siblings had been a breeze. But Tamsyn was the edgiest of the sisters and the least inclined to spend time chatting over a salad.

All right, focus. Take care of Tamsyn's problem later.

Right now, catching Brianna Tollison's killer was number one.

Detective Seth Foyle, her partner of three weeks, was already seated. He nodded. He'd transferred from another precinct, as had she, to the new Midtown Hills Precinct. He'd been a defensive tackle at Vandy, graduating with a degree in criminal justice. Dark hair and green eyes made him pleasant to look at, and his dogged reputation made him someone she could trust to have her back.

The younger detectives on her team stumbled in right behind her. Ron Irby, an almost brand-spanking-new transfer from the south precinct. Dark blond hair, blue eyes, an all-American, boy-next-door with a temper—he'd bear watching. Malik Sampson, all smooth southern charm when it suited him and a bit of an attitude when it didn't. His wiry build and not quite six-foot height made him less physically imposing, but she'd watched him since he was in uniform. Not a pushover.

All in all, a good team with an assortment of strengths

and weaknesses. Balanced.

"Good morning. Let's go over what we know, then concentrate on what we still need to know. "Ron?"

"I've re-interviewed the neighbors on her floor, as well as the floor above and below. Background checks on all. Nothing pops. Negative on the victim's cellphone. Last use was an hour before her murder."

"Malik?"

"I've re-interviewed the office, cleaning, and maintenance staff. Landscaping is contracted out, and I've done backgrounds on all of 'em. Nothing popping there, either. I've gone over the CCTV footage three times, including the time-window and two hours either way along with the concierge. No one shows up who shouldn't be there, but there's a fifteen-minute window where the footage is nothing but static. I'd say our perp used a jamming device."

"You're probably right, Malik. Ron, I want you to contact the Tollison's and ask them nicely for the memorial book where the people who attended the funeral signed. Interview all the men and run their backgrounds. We can agree our killer is a man. Since the funeral was well attended, that's going to be a long list. Ron, you and Malik can split the list."

Seth spoke next. "I've interviewed everyone at Ms. Tollison's workplace. I'd like to bring Jerry Ames in for another go. He was just squirrelly enough to set off alarms."

Tess nodded. "I spoke to him for a few minutes at the funeral. I agree. I'd give anything to get a warrant to search his place. So far, we don't have enough grounds. Definitely, bring him in for a sit-down."

"Will do." Seth cracked a smile. "You know he lives with his mother."

She snapped her fingers. "That does it. He's our killer."
Tess nodded but gave her partner an eye roll. "Moving on.
Phone and computer records have cleared her fiancé,
Jason St. John. All we need from him is his signature on
his statement. But I'll take a run at a couple of other men in
her life. Eric Chapman was involved with Brianna before
her current fiancé. And Brad Oliver." Especially these two
because they played very significant parts in her life at one
time or another. "Oliver was at the funeral, but Eric wasn't.
I'll do their interviews, but, Ron and Malik, you should go
on with the background checks. Do both of the Chapman
brothers and Oliver first. I need those backgrounds done
before I interview them. And since someone jammed the
condo's CCTV during the time in question, dig into their
capabilities in that area. That's it for now."

Her team rose to get started on their assignments.
"Seth, a moment."

He stopped at the door. "Sure."

She hesitated, allowing Ron and Malik time to clear
the room. "Close the door."

Seth complied. "What's up?"

"St. John's a Fed and undercover. As far as I can
determine, it's something to do with her father's business
dealings. Steer clear. Let him do whatever the hell he's
supposed to be doing."

"I wondered why you gave him an easy pass."

"I already had my suspicions. The local SAC gave me a
head's up last night."

"And if our murder and his operation intersect?"

"Let's hope they don't." Tess shrugged. "We'll deal
with it, then. Carefully, dig around in Randall Tollison's
background. Nothing to set off the Feds' alarms. I'd just
like to know more about him. And before I forget, I want
Brianna's previous ex in here, Eric Chapman, ASAP."

"Will do." Seth nodded. "I'll rattle his cage now."

Frustrated and still shaken, Tamsyn changed into her running clothes. Her feet hit the pavement. Yes, exercise was exactly what she needed.

She'd been running about fifteen minutes when she heard a vehicle coming up behind her, speeding a bit from the sound. She moved over to give the driver plenty of passing room and took a quick peek over her shoulder.

Dammit. He was headed straight for her. Another second and...

She sprinted onto the sidewalk and into the front yard of an Italianate house and kept running. The SUV's brakes screeched. He'd stopped.

Heart pounding, she tried to catch her breath. What if she'd waited for another second to glance over her shoulder? He would've hit her. She'd be bloodied and sprawled on the street.

She ran. *Think.* What kind of vehicle? SUV—was there anything else? Color? Dark green. Or blue. What was the emblem? Tried to remember. Couldn't.

What had she done? Who was pissed off enough to try running her down? One of her client's significant others?

Or just some general perv and anyone handy would do.

All-out she ran until she couldn't hear his vehicle. She dashed for the alley that ran behind the houses. *Get out of sight. Now.*

Two more blocks and she'd be home. If she could just keep the driver from seeing where she lived. Sweat trickled down her face and chest. She slowed her pace just enough to wipe her face with the hem of her T-shirt.

An engine gunning. Again. *Damn. Give it up, dude.*

Where was he now?

Before crossing the next street, she checked both directions.

She tore across the street. Brakes squealed. A door slammed.

She kept running. Behind her, the heavy footfalls of someone giving chase.

One more block.

He grabbed her wrist, yanking her off balance. "No!"

Damn. Big mother—

She struggled, trying to wrestle free from his grasp. She kicked backward. Anything to throw him off balance.

He yelped, spewing a stream of obscenities.

She let out a 100-decibel screech. No. Not going easily or quietly. Reaching over her shoulder, she clawed at his face. DNA. *Yeah, cocksucker.*

A man rushed from his house with a shotgun. "What the hell's going on out here?"

"Help me!"

As quickly as he'd grabbed her, the attacker dropped her. Off-balance, she whirled to catch a glimpse of him. Tall. Big. Fleshy. White dude in a black hoodie.

Very fast on his feet. Dammit.

She chased after him.

"Let him go!" the neighbor called behind her. She heard him huffing behind her.

Not that she expected—or wanted—to catch the SOB. Get his damn plate number.

He gunned it, then sped away, but not before she made out his vehicle and the three letters on his Williamson County plates. Justin—George—Victor. Not enough, but a start.

"JGV" she repeated. Can't forget them.

Still puffing, the neighbor and his shotgun caught up.

"You crazy? Chasing him like that."

"I wanted to get his tag number."

"Thought I was going to have to shoot him."

"Did you see his face? He grabbed me from behind so I couldn't see anything."

Her guardian angel shook his head. "Hoodie covered his face." He continued gasping for breath. "Out of shape. Twenty years ago, I could've caught him."

Tamsyn smiled. "Out of shape or not, you helped me out of a jam. Thank you. I don't know what would've happened if you hadn't come along when you did."

He aimed the 12 gauge at the ground. "Glad I could help. Don't know what this town's coming to. Never used to have incidents like this—not in *this* neighborhood anyway. If you like, I can walk you the rest of the way home."

"It's all right. I just live in the next block. Again, thank you!" She dug in the pocket of her running shorts and pulled out her house key. "See you around."

Home. Safety. Family.

No way was she telling her family about this incident. Correction—she'd give Tess a head's up. No point in pushing her brothers into an over-protective mode.

Lunch at the Southern. First, Oliver kept Jason cooling his heels in the bar for a good forty-five minutes. Confusing—not the food. It was great. Once Oliver arrived, appearing out-of-breath and harried, the attorney seemed more interested in Jason's past relationship with Bree than business. Why was that?

"You know I used to date Bree. Long time ago. I took her to a high school dance. Guess that's only one date. Nice gal. Too bad how she bought it though." He gulped his second bourbon.

"Bought it?" Jason clenched his fists to keep from pasting Oliver across his fat kisser. "They couldn't open the casket. I'd say *bought it* is pretty dismissive when you consider how she was murdered. It was a vicious—no, a horrific attack."

"A tragedy, of course." Oliver shrugged. "But dead is dead."

"Yes." Jason clamped his jaw. What a jerk. A real piece of work.

"Kind of sudden, wasn't it? The engagement, I mean. Randall thought she was rushing things."

"Doesn't matter now, does it?" Jason still nursed his first bourbon. So Tollison had discussed their relationship with his attorney.

The waiter arrived with another round of drinks. Oliver ordered the Southern Burger while Jason went for the fish tacos. Oliver downed his third bourbon less than fifteen minutes. Not exactly a reliable attorney.

"Go on. Have another. Randall won't ever know."

Jason shook his head. "I prefer to keep my head clear when discussing business."

"Just like he won't know you're already getting your knob polished. Yeah, I saw that fox coming from your office."

"Told you she wasn't in my office."

"Sure she was. I saw her come out. No doubt about it."

"Fine. None of your business. Nothing to do with you. Working girl."

"I knew you were all right." Oliver guffawed, reached over, and slapped Jason's shoulder. "Yeah, you're all right."

"About this upcoming transaction?"

Oliver's gaze grew steely. "You'll be called. It's taking place at an empty warehouse, up for lease on Centennial. No harm in you knowing that." He wiped his mouth.

"Randall's way too paranoid about shit."

Oliver talked too much when he was drinking. But that could come in handy.

As soon as Tamsyn reached the house, she locked the doors, even going so far as to set the security system. As soon as the system was alarmed, she leaned back against the door and let out a loud sigh of relief.

Call Tess or not? What a stupid question. Of course, she could call Tess.

Her mouth dry as the Mojave, she tried to swallow. Water. She kicked off her running shoes and padded into the kitchen. She opened the fridge and retrieved a bottle from the bottom shelf. After opening the bottle, she downed at least half the contents without stopping.

Wiping the sweat from her forehead with the back of one hand, she reached for her phone with the other.

Tess answered, quickly and brusquely. "Tamsyn. What's up?"

"We still need to talk, even more now. I was out for my daily run. Someone tried to attack me."

"Are you all right? Tell me more."

Tamsyn gave her sister-in-law the quick and dirty version, then added, "It was a dark green Grand Cherokee. I got part of the tag number: J-G-V as in Victor. Might've been a one after that, but he was gone too quick."

"Where are you now?"

"Home. Security alarm on."

"Good. I'm in the middle of something, but I'm going to send one of my team, Seth Foyle, over there to take an official report. Okay? See you tonight. I promise."

"Sure. I'll be here."

Tess ended the call.

Tamsyn would stay put all right. She peered out through the blinds to check the street, just in case. No way was she leaving the house. That creep could be anywhere circling the neighborhood. Ready to pounce again.

She sniffed her underarm. Jeez. Better get a quick shower before Tess's partner arrived on the scene.

After a speedy shower, Tamsyn pulled on a pair of navy capris. The doorbell rang just as she was pulling a white short-sleeved French T-shirt over her head. Damn, that was quick.

She sped downstairs and rushed to the front door. "Who is it?"

"Detective Foyle, ma'am. Detective Holt sent me over."

The name matched, but it always paid to be careful. "Come over to the window, and show me your badge and ID."

"Happy to, ma'am."

Through a space between the wood blinds, she eyeballed his bona fide MNPD badge and ID.

One button at a time, she punched in the security code, deactivating the security system. Letting out a sigh of relief, she unlocked the door and opened it with a smile. "Come in, Detective Foyle."

She craned her neck to see all of him. The hunky detective was at least six-four and built like a defensive tackle. His wavy dark hair and dreamy jade green eyes would've made her swoon if she were accustomed to such silliness, and *if* her attentions weren't already taken up by the ever-so-mysterious Jason St. John.

Wishing she'd had time to apply a little makeup, she led the detective into the kitchen, stopping in front of the fridge. "Would you like a cold drink or bottled water?"

"No thank you, ma'am. I'm good." He perched on one of the stools at the kitchen island, then pulled out his notebook. "Detective Holt said you were out for a run and someone tried to attack you."

Tamsyn chose the stool opposite the detective and sat. "That's right." She took another long drink of water.

"Would you start from the beginning? What time was it?"

"About one. Maybe a little later. I didn't check the time. I'd been running for about fifteen minutes, just getting loosened up and really into the zone, you know?"

Foyle nodded. "Go on."

"I heard an engine revving behind me. I moved over to the side of the road to give him space. Luckily, I glanced over my shoulder and realized he was headed straight for me. I darted onto the sidewalk and into the front yard of one of the houses. I think I ran back toward home, but then I heard a car door slam and heard him running after me. He caught me from behind, and—man, he was a big guy. I never saw his face. I screamed and one of the neighbors came out with a shotgun."

"The neighbor's name and address?"

She shrugged. "Sorry. I was so flustered I didn't get either, but he lives two blocks down, middle of the block, the American Four Square of tan brick with pale blue trim."

Foyle smiled. "He might have more information. Then what?"

"The creep let me go, but I chased after him."

"You did?" Foyle's eyes widened. "What?"

"Yeah, I wanted to get his license plate number and a better look at his vehicle."

A frown clouded the detective's face. "You took a big risk."

"I know, but I got part of his plate: J-G-V with a one, I think. He got away before I could make out the rest. He drove a Jeep Grand Cherokee, dark green."

"What was he wearing?"

"Dark sweats and a hoodie. No logo or anything helpful."

"You said he was 'big.' How big?"

"As tall as you, almost. He was heavier though."

Foyle closed his notebook and slipped it into his jacket pocket. He pulled out a business card. "If you think of anything else, you can reach me at this number."

Nodding, Tamsyn took the card. "Thanks."

The detective ambled to the front door. "You *will* lock up after I leave?"

"Damn straight, I will. Besides, my brothers will be coming in soon after the Vandy game. My sister will be home soon too."

Foyle nodded. "Good deal."

She locked the door and engaged the security system. Tamsyn gave a sigh of relief that, for now, the ordeal was over.

Two hours later, Tamsyn was in the kitchen. Saturday was always a cookout night. Only a tornado or an ice storm would keep her brothers from firing up the grill. Chicken breasts and ribeye steaks were thawing in cold water, while she sliced and diced peppers, onions, and mushrooms for kabobs.

The doorbell rang. What now? Had the hunky detective forgotten something? She ran to the door. Still cautious, she paused and asked, "Who is it?"

"Jason."

"What's on *your* mind?" she asked as if she didn't

know. Crap. Why hadn't she taken time to do something with her hair and makeup after the detective left? She finger-combed her hair and gave her head a shake. That'd have to do. St. John could just take her as she was. Or lump it. Still, better to have any company than be alone. The memory of her close call sent a chill up her spine.

"Open the door and I'll tell you."

"Not sure I like the sound of that." She reached up, unlocked the deadbolt, and opened the door. Clad in tight-fitting jeans and a casual pale blue, short-sleeved knit shirt, he presented a tasty treat for the eyes. Her eyes. Especially her eyes.

"Are you going to invite me in, or are you just going to stare?"

Busted.

"Of course." Her cheeks already heating up, she stepped back and stumbled over the hall rug.

He scooped his arm around her waist, keeping her from falling.

"Uh, thanks." Now, her flushed cheeks had escalated from mere warm to an all-out volcano-hot burn. Damn it. Under normal circumstances, she had no difficulty walking and chewing gum at the same time. Why did coming into proximity with this one man turn her into a klutz with two left feet?

"My pleasure." His mouth kicked up at the corner.

So, her clumsiness amused him. Great. Just freaking great.

"Whatever you want, you caught me in the middle of preparing dinner." Okay, maybe that was a bit of an exaggeration. "I need to get back to the kitchen."

"Should be interesting. Watching you actually *working.*"

She huffed and shot him a brief glare over her

shoulder. "I heard that."

He followed her down the hallway. "Nice house. *Great* kitchen," he said on entering the heart of the house.

She glanced around the familiar surroundings. "It really is." Avoiding his intense gaze, she picked up the butcher knife and sliced into a red bell pepper.

"And you all lived here together after your parents died. It's remarkable."

Concentrating on her task, she nodded and ripped the inner core and seeds from the pepper, discarding them in the disposal. "What else could we do? The six of us stuck together. That was when Scott left law school and took over dad's agency, otherwise, we wouldn't have survived." She rinsed the pepper, then started cutting the vegetable into chunks.

Anxious to lift the mood, she asked, "What about you? The *real* you. I'm not interested in whatever cover story the FBI gave you. Brothers or sisters?"

"You're assuming a lot." She watched his expression changed from one of concern to an out-and-out scowl. "Come straight to the point, don't you."

She flipped her hair over her shoulder, then leaned her elbows on the granite counter. "You could say that. What's it going to be? The cover story or the truth?"

"I don't know you well enough for the truth."

"Fine. I already spilled my guts the last time you were here." She gave a casual shrug, then walked over to the fridge, opened it, and pulled out a head of romaine. She ran cold water over the leafy greens, then gave them a shake. She broke off the stalks, then set them aside to drain. Still determined to ignore her unforthcoming guest until he spilled the beans, she pulled out a container of mushrooms.

"All right. You win. I'm an only child."

She couldn't resist shooting him a smug smile. "Figures."

He cocked an eyebrow. "How so?"

"Oh, you can always tell." She shot him a teasing grin.

"Really? Elaborate please."

"For one thing, you exude a sense of entitlement."

"Entitlement?"

"You expect women to fall at your feet just because you're well-educated and passably handsome."

"Just passably?"

She smiled inwardly. Oh, so he didn't like her remark. "I don't intend to feed your ego."

"But you *will* feed me vegetables?"

"Indeed." She favored him with a quick smile. "Vegetables and all the protein your heart *desires*." She purposely lowered her voice with the last word, giving it a sensual emphasis.

He walked, no prowled, around the island. "And, if what my heart desires is *you*?"

"You'll have to wait on fulfilling that particular desire because one of my brothers just drove in from the alley." She nodded toward the French doors where Justin's Nash Metropolitan could clearly be seen.

"Damn. And I was so looking forward to—"

Justin opened the French door and stepped into the room. He took in Jason's presence with a suspicious glance. "What the hell—"

Chapter Sixteen

Jason tamped down an inward groan. Another interruption by one of Tamsyn's brothers. Talk about bad timing. Just when the atmosphere was starting to sizzle. "I'll go." Might as well.

"No!" Tamsyn gave her silky dark hair a furious shake. "Justin, be nice. Jason's staying for dinner."

Justin planted his feet wide apart and set his hands on his hips. "I thought Scott and Tess were clear. You're to stay away from this guy. Agent or not—I don't trust him."

Tamsyn gave her brother an eye roll. "It's a meal, you bonehead. Nothing more."

"Now, Tamsyn—" was all Jason had a chance to say before she shot him a look that clearly said *mind-your-own-business*.

"Normally, you're the most laid-back member of the family, but I've had enough of the big brother attitude from you and Scott to last a lifetime."

Ignoring her brother and Jason, as well as muttering to herself, she went back to arranging the freshly-cut vegetables on a platter.

Jason shrugged, glancing over to Tamsyn's brother. "Sorry, dude. Maybe I *should* go."

"It's okay. I'm used to her beating up on me." Then he winked. "She's the temperamental one. Reckon we should be warning you about *her* instead of the other way around."

She abandoned her food preparations long enough to hug her brother. "All right. I'm sorry." She wagged her finger in his face. "And that gives you the right to call *me* bonehead or any other epithet you happen to choose *once*—and only once—in the next calendar year."

"Hah! Only once? No fair—not with *you*."

Jason leaned forward, his elbows on the granite countertop. This was something he'd missed as an only child, the teasing interplay, the fights, the fun, and the camaraderie that came with a large family. *This* was a family, albeit a blended one, who'd overcome obstacles and still cared about each other. They would always have each other's backs.

He'd always felt like an outsider in his own family when his father was around. Jason had adored his mother, but his father was the man who must be obeyed. There'd been good times when his father was away on assignment. Jason had enjoyed those times with his mother. She'd done everything she could to make up for his father's shortcomings.

Tragically, she'd died after dropping him off at boarding school. His father had never forgiven him. And never would.

Before he could descend into his own version of a pity party, more of the family arrived. Tamsyn's brother Scott breezed into the kitchen, followed by the other detective he'd met in the office—must be the brother-in-law, and a bouncy strawberry blond, the rebel who'd gone into nursing instead of the family business. Scott said nothing. A single elevated brow was his only reaction.

"Who've you entranced this time, Tam?" This from the newlywed—what was her name—Allison?

"This is Jason St. John—at least that's the name we know him by. He's undercover for the FBI or some other federal agency."

Jason let out a groan. "You don't know any such thing.

Some discretion, please."

"What one member of this family knows, we all know." Allison smiled up at him, her blue eyes shining with good humor. "Get used to it."

Get used to it? Did she honestly think he was, in any form or fashion, going to be part of this always-in-your-business family of hers?

Scott said, "Tess'll be late, as usual. But she says we're to go ahead and eat." He helped himself to a beer from the fridge, then clapped his brother on the shoulder. "Let's crank up that grill, dude. I'm starving."

"Yeah." The blond brother stared at Jason but followed Scott outside.

Jason's gaze darted around the kitchen. Allison was whispering into Tamsyn's ear. What was that about? The two women giggled, broke apart, and then cast a furtive glance in his direction. Great. *He* was the subject of their laughter. Freaking great.

Always the outsider. Damn, that's what he felt like here too.

Just then, the newlywed detective came over. "Tamsyn, why so rude? Your fella's looking dehydrated. How about a beer?" A genuine smile lit his face as he held out a hand in greeting. "I'm Nick."

"Beer'd be great. Thanks." Acceptance, at least from one of the family.

"Don't mind this bunch. Just go with the flow. You'll get used to it."

Assume much?

Nick pulled two beers from the fridge. Jason accepted one gratefully—anything to fade into the background.

Tamsyn glanced up from slicing the mushrooms. "Sorry. I don't know what happened to my manners."

"Sure you are. I know you were hoping I'd take the

hint I wasn't welcome and leave."

The slightest of smiles touched her lips as she cut a sly gaze toward him. "Uh, I must've had dinner prep on my mind."

Her evasive response brought a giddy warmth to his mid-section, as did the memory of events right before the family invaded. Truthfully, *he* was the invader, but if her brother had held off coming home another fifteen minutes...

Just as well. Not looking for a hookup. But he couldn't seem to wrap his mind around anything else whenever he came within ten feet of Tamsyn Holt.

Cool it. He took a long pull on his beer, resisting the very real temptation to pour it over his head.

"Outside, lover." The strawberry blonde grabbed Nick's wrist and pulled him along.

With half the family treating him like he was already a member and the other half giving him the evil eye, Jason was torn between diving into the comfortable family gathering and making a quick retreat.

While there was little chance that Randall Tollison would hear about Jason's attending a Holt-Lackey family dinner, he couldn't afford to take the risk.

"Tamsyn, I really need to go. Family dinner with the detective who's investigating my fiancée's murder doesn't jive with my cover. I appreciate your hospitality, but I can't afford to screw up this operation. I really need to get the hell out of here." He set the half-empty beer on the counter.

"I understand." She nodded, but she seemed to have a wistful expression. "I suppose when this operation is over..." She paused to swallow. "You'll be going back to DC?"

"If I'm still alive."

She set aside the mushrooms, then met his gaze, finally. "I've enjoyed getting to know you—sort of."

"Same here." No matter how much he wanted to get to know Tamsyn, and no matter how much he wanted to... it wasn't gonna happen. Better to make his getaway now before temptation got the better of him.

"I'll see you out," she said, wiping her hands on her dark blue Capris. "I guess this is good-bye."

"Yeah." He managed to choke the word out. Damn. When had a simple 'good-bye' ever sounded so final?

They stopped at the front door. He swallowed the lump in his throat. "Take care of yourself."

"I-I'm glad you came by." She gazed up at him, her full lips parted.

What else could he do? He inclined his head and tenderly kissed her forehead. No, not her full ready-to-be-kissed mouth. Danger. "Bye."

He slipped out the front door without looking back. Damn, leaving her was damned hard. But too much was at stake.

Halfway to his SUV, Jason met Detective Holt coming up the brick walkway. She stopped with hands on hips and scowled. "What the *hell* are you doing here?"

"Just stopped by to see Tamsyn. My mistake. And thanks for blowing my cover. From now on, I'm steering clear of you folks."

"I didn't. But flighty as Tamsyn is, she isn't stupid. "She gave him a quizzical smile. "Do I detect a note of regret in your voice?"

"Maybe." He shoved his hands into his pockets.

"Then I'd appreciate if you *would* steer clear. Did Tamysn tell you she was attacked this afternoon? I'd bet my gold shield it had something to do with your operation."

"Attacked? No! When?" Why hadn't she told him about the attack? They'd talked about a little of everything, but not one word about her being attacked.

"Earlier this afternoon."

"Hm. Around lunchtime?"

The detective skewered him with a sharp glance. "What do you know?"

Not wanting to explain why Tamsyn had been in his office on a Saturday morning, he shook his head. "Nothing. What about a description of her attacker?"

"Very big. If a neighbor hadn't intervened, he could've done anything he wanted. Anything." Tess poked his chest with her forefinger. "Listen here, Mr. FBI. You'd better not be keeping anything from *me*. I don't know if this attack had anything to do with your fiancée's murder or with whatever else you're doing in town. You *said* you'd stay away from Tamsyn."

He clenched his jaw. "Noted." Whoa. "Exactly time was she attacked?"

"Noonish."

"Where?"

"She went for a run in the neighborhood. He tried to run her down. When he wasn't successful, he stopped, gave chase, and grabbed her."

Tess's terse recitation of the event stunned him. He grabbed his head. "How did she get away?" Dammit. Why hadn't she mentioned it? He'd had no idea he'd come so close to losing her.

"A neighbor intervened with a shotgun, and her attacker ran away."

Hold on. Oliver had made such a big fucking deal about seeing Tamsyn leave the office. Had he somehow managed to follow her home? Was that why he'd been late for lunch?

"You promised to stay away from her." Tess's blue eyes blazed. "I *mean* it."

"Again, noted, Detective." He reined an angry response. "I don't want to put her in danger any more than you do."

"Good." She gave a sharp nod, then stomped up the sidewalk to the house.

Once inside the SUV, Jason's hand shook as he inserted the key. Brianna murdered, and now Tamsyn had been attacked. Had he already compromised his mission? Was Oliver onto him?

Jeez, if he'd blown this assignment already... Career flat-lined, he could look forward to low-end assignments somewhere like Nebraska or North Dakota. And his father would be justified in his low opinion of his son and heir.

Time to report.

Leaning against the wall, Tamsyn sighed. What the hell? An avuncular peck on the forehead. Better known as the kiss of death. And about as sexy as a wet diaper. She gave a little groan.

Behind her, the door opened. She straightened, feeling her cheeks burn. "Tess. You're early."

Tess yanked off her leather shoulder bag and set it on the hall table with a considerable thump. "Yeah, whatever. What was Jason St. John doing here?"

Tamsyn shrugged. "I think he wanted to see me, but I could be wrong."

"You need to stay away from him—for your sake and his."

"Don't worry. We've said our good-byes. He won't be

around anymore."

"Good." Tess kicked off her shoes. "One thing, though. You didn't tell him about the attack."

"So?"

"Why not? Why was he here? What did he want?"

"I told you he came to see *me*. Is that so strange? Enough of the third degree." Tamsyn huffed, turned on her heel, and headed back to the kitchen. "Besides, we had other things to talk about. Nothing about the case. Just stuff."

Tess followed. "Not *strange*. I just want to know what the hell he was doing here."

All righty, time to change the subject. "You're in a terrible mood. What's wrong?"

"I don't like it when work life and home life intersect."

"Not *my* fault." Back in the kitchen, Tamsyn sniffed. "I think the grill's ready, don't you?" She pulled a large platter from an upper cupboard.

"You called me earlier before the attack. What was that about?"

"Oh, nothing much, really." Determined now to conceal the shenanigans in Jason's office, she concentrated on arranging the thawed meat and chicken on the platter until it was worthy of a full-page spread in *Bon Appétit*.

"Really? Sure sounded like something at the time. What are you hiding?"

"Do we have to do this now?" She picked up the platter ready to carry it outside.

Arms crossed over her chest, Tess stepped into Tamsyn's path, blocking her exit. "If not now, when?"

"Later." Tamsyn shrugged. "After dinner, maybe."

"Okay, I'll let you put me off until then. No 'maybe' about it." She uncrossed her arms and waggled a finger in Tamsyn's face. "But you still need to understand that being around him is dangerous. As of yet, I have no idea whether the attack on you was an opportunistic assault, related to my murder investigation, or to St. John's operation."

"It could even be unrelated. One of my client's significant others?"

"Yes, it could. And *now*, we have to look into your cases."

"I see what you mean. Work life and home life. Getting complicated." She maneuvered around Tess and aimed toward the French doors. "Don't want to keep the cooks waiting."

"Right," Tess scoffed.

Jason sat in the SUV, staring at his iPhone, his thumb hovering over the call icon. How in the hell could he explain why he just might've been compromised without going into all the gory details about Tamsyn Holt's impromptu booty call at his office? He could just hear Agent Chase's questions: Why was Detective Holt's sister-in-law visiting your office? What the hell are you thinking?

"Fuck it." He hit the call icon and waited, his gut starting to twist like it did the first time he came under fire. Real fire. Not a simulation.

"Chase here. What do you have for me?"

"I had lunch today with Brad Oliver. He talks too much when he power-drinks bourbon. Meeting's definitely going down soon."

"Where?"

"According to Oliver, the deal will go down at an empty warehouse—one that's up for lease. Somewhere on Centennial Boulevard."

"Can you narrow the location any better than that?"

"Not without making Tollison suspicious. I suggest we

look into his commercial holdings. I'll email you a list of all his shell companies—the ones I know about. I'm betting he owns that building, otherwise why take the risk?"

"This doesn't give us a lot of time to research and set up surveillance. But it'll be done. We'll take him down with his crew."

"Gladly." Not ideal, but better if he intended to survive.

"You'll be arrested along with Tollison's crew."

"Right. Keep my cover intact as long as possible." He hesitated, still dreading what he had to say next. "As for my cover, there might be a problem."

"What!"

"Oliver. In spite of his loose lips over lunch, he's no dummy. He's suspicious."

"What makes you think that?"

"He saw someone leave my office this morning— Tamsyn Holt. He made a big issue of having seen her leave. I lied, told him he was mistaken. But I admitted she was a working girl. Not sure he believed me. He was almost an hour late for our lunch meeting. And in that interval, I learned from Detective Holt that Ms. Holt was assaulted near her home by someone who fits Oliver's description. I think he either followed her or had someone follow her."

"Okay, back up. What was she doing in your office? We *are* talking about someone in Detective Holt's family?"

Jason paused, then admitted, "Yes. Her sister-in-law." Okay, how to put this? "There's an attraction there, but I've ended it."

"Ended it? Were you *involved*? Are you nuts?" Disbelief was rife in Chase's tone. "You'll blow this op sky high if Tollison finds out you're screwing around with someone, much less a relative of the detective who's investigating his daughter's death."

"No chance of that now. Whoever attacked her, she doesn't think he saw where she lived. According to Detective Holt, the assailant ran off when a neighbor intervened."

"There are some, higher up in the food chain, who have misgivings about your being assigned this operation. I'd hate to see them proved correct. Dammit, Stone. Your future in the Bureau is at stake."

And he didn't have to ask who the 'higher up' with misgivings was. *Thanks, Dad.* "Don't you think I know it? I can still pull this off. A week from now, it'll all be over. I'm sure of it."

"Can you keep it in your pants that long?"

"Definitely."

"There." Tamsyn shut the door to the dishwasher, then hit the wash button. "That's the last of the dishes." She turned to face Tess. No point in putting off the *dreaded* talk.

"Fine." Tess grabbed a bottle of white zinfandel and two wine glasses from the counter. "Now, we're going to sit down and have a little convo about *why* you called me earlier." She nodded her head toward the French doors. "Outside."

"All right!" Tamsyn wiped her hands on a paper towel, then tossed it in the trash. "Jeez. You're awfully pushy tonight." Okay, Tess was right to be pushy. Tamsyn had kept Bree's secret for over ten years. Now, that she was dead, any bit of background information might assist Tess and her team in finding out who killed her. Tess would understand. Surely.

Still, a thought nagged. Was there even the slightest possibility that Oliver killed Bree? If Tamsyn hadn't kept

Bree's secret, would she still be alive?

She stepped out into the deck. The evening's temperature had dropped along with the humidity. The coals on the grill were still warm with the remaining fragrant aromas of grilled beef and chicken.

Tess sat and poured two glasses of the blush wine, then handed Tamsyn one. "Okay, you've been holding something back. I want to know what it is, and does it have anything to do with your phone call this afternoon?"

"Yes, on both accounts." She gulped half a glass of the semi-sweet wine, then let out a sigh.

Tamsyn nodded. "I think Brad Oliver might be the one who attacked me this afternoon. I-I think he followed me from Jason's office downtown."

Tess's eyebrows arched. "*What* were you doing at St. John's office?"

"I figured if he could show up at the agency and get me all flustered, I might as well return the favor. So I paid him a little visit." Just the memory of that visit caused her neck to flush.

"You're making sense whatsoever. Why would you even bother? You've been warned to stay away from him." Tess leaned in. "And why is your neck getting all splotchy?"

Under her sister-in-law's focused gaze, Tamsyn's cheeks burned as if someone had turned on a space heater. "I'm attracted to him, okay."

"No! *Not* okay."

"Anyway, we were getting close when the phone rang—"

"Getting close?" Tess waved her hands in the air. "Omigod, I don't even want to know what *that* means."

"Good thing, since my sex life is none of your business." Tamsyn gulped a large swallow of her wine. "Anyway, the phone—it was Brad Oliver. He called to say he was on his way up to see Jason, so I pulled myself together as quickly as I could and ducked out of there. But as luck would have it, when the elevator doors opened, there he was. I tried to avoid his gaze, but he did a double-take. Oh yes, he did. I ran to the garage and flew home. I didn't see anyone follow me, but he must've. I decided to go for a run. Anyway, a few minutes into my run—that's when I heard this vehicle revving behind me. You know the rest."

"He recognized you from school?"

"Possibly. But it's been at least ten-twelve years. We didn't attend the same schools, but there were plenty of times when the two schools had joint activities. Anyway, he definitely knew Bree, and back then, we were always together. Besides, he was at her funeral. He might've recognized me there."

Tess grabbed her phone.

"Hold on now. *Who* are you calling?"

"Seth. He needs to double-check Oliver's background. Rape isn't a one-off deal. Rapists don't quit. Not for long."

"Do you think that's what he intended when he—uh, came after me?"

Tess's brow furrowed, her gaze narrowing. "At the very least."

And if he killed Bree, why stop at rape? A hard shudder ran through Tamsyn's body. "Do you *really* think he's the one who killed Bree? *Why* after all this time?"

"She could've threatened to tell his wife. His employer. Could be any number of reasons. In my book, he's as good a suspect as anyone. At least, until he's ruled out."

Tamsyn's mouth grew dry. She tried to swallow. "Guess I'll have to start running at the Y again, instead of in the neighborhood."

Tess cocked her head. "Ya think?" She stood and

walked to the far corner of the deck.

Tamsyn couldn't hear what she was saying, but if body language was an indicator, then Detective Seth was getting an earful. Another chill slid up her spine. The hair rose on the nape of her neck. Was he out there now? Watching? Waiting for another chance?

She wrapped her arms around, hugging herself. "I'm chilly," she said, even though Tess was too involved to hear. "Going inside."

She opened the French doors. Allie sat at the island, munching on cashews. She glanced up and smiled. Tamsyn strode over and gave Allison a big hug. "It's easy to see how happy you are. How are your classes going?"

"Considering I just started class this week, I'm still at the very-excited stage. I'm sure the grind will hit me eventually."

"I wish I had something, a goal if you will."

"You're not enjoying the work?" Her gaze widened. "You always did before."

"Bree's death has cast a pall over everything. She didn't deserve to die like that." She shuddered. "Tell me more about what you'll be doing."

"I get to use my medical background and knowledge in cases of negligence and malpractice, insurance fraud, and even criminal cases."

"It sounds fascinating. Lucky you. But I don't have your background, and I really don't think I could cut going to nursing school. Blood and guts—not for me."

Allie laughed. "I can't see you going to nursing school, either. You're more of a rebel than I am." She wiped the salt from her hands, her newlywed-happy expression turning serious. "So what was so grim with you and Tess?"

Not about to risk another lecture, Tamsyn ignored the question. She rubbed her upper arms, then shrugged.

"Geez. Felt like someone just walked over my grave. Know what I mean."

"Exactly."

She shrugged. "I'm just being silly." And being silly wasn't who she was. Not really.

"No." Allie's gaze grew inward. "Pay attention to those feelings. They mean something. Believe me, I know what I'm talkin' about."

Tamsyn nodded. Indeed, her sister did, having been kidnapped by a doctor's psycho wife not so long ago. "Yeah. This family seems to be a lightning rod for nut jobs."

"Yeah, we've had more than our share."

Nick came up behind his bride and wrapped his arms around her. "More than your share of what?"

"Psychos," Tamsyn said. "As in totally freaked-out weirdos who want to ruin our lives."

"Know the name of that tune." Nick nodded sharply. "You're not talking about Jason, are you? I kind of liked him. You could do worse."

Could do worse. What was with all of a sudden receiving so much relationship advice? Tamsyn shook her head. "No, this was someone else."

"Then, I'm taking this bride of mine away from the psycho-danger zone." He backed away, taking Allie with him. "Ready?"

Allie nodded. "I need to hit the books." But there was a gleam in her blue eyes that had nothing to do with avoiding danger or hitting the books. More likely a real need to attack her handsome husband and carry him off to the nearest bed.

A pang of emptiness, maybe even envy, knifed through Tamsyn, staggering her. What the hell was the matter anyway? No way was she jealous of her sister's happiness. Quite the opposite, Tamsyn was thrilled her sister had found true love.

Still... If Tamsyn weren't careful, she'd end up alone.

She'd had relationships before. Men. They came. They went. No big deal. The absence or presence of a man in her life seldom troubled her. Damn Jason St. John. Somehow, he was different. And he'd made *her* feel different. Now, her life seemed superficial.

Empty.

Chapter Seventeen

Justin groaned gave a yawn. The football game cut to a commercial, and his phone pinged. "What now?" He glanced at his phone. "Holy crap! There's been a hit on Kim at a casino in Oklahoma."

Scott straightened and leaned forward. "What?"

"Last month, I updated a software program I wrote for the National Indian Gaming Commission. Just for the hell of it, I inserted a line of code, an alert command that would notify me." Actually, he did the same for all software programs he wrote for outside companies. Illegal or not, it was a shot in the dark.

"Notify you of what?"

"Her last known car tag number, any info that might correspond with whatever Kim's doing today. I even did an age progression photo. The casinos' biometric facial recognition software might pick her up. Look I know it's pissing in the wind, but..."

"It's a longshot all right."

"Her body has never been found. She has to be out there somewhere. She has to have a job. Casinos are big employers."

"She's not a Native American."

"No, but this hit is on her last known car registration."

Scott shook his head. "We've been chasing false leads for ten years. Probably not even her car anymore." He leaned back.

"I have to check it out. This could be the lead that

brings her home."

"If she wanted to come home, she'd be here."

"Oklahoma is closer than Reno. Maybe she's trying to make her way back home."

"Pursue it, of course. But we've been down this road before—just sayin'."

"Just between us. No point in getting Carrie's hopes up." Justin stood. "I gotta get online. Gotta see if it's just the license plate that hit. Maybe there's some security footage of the vehicle and driver."

"You can access that?"

Nodding, Justin grinned. "Better believe it."

Justin shook his head. Damn. No CC footage on the driver. No one resembling Kim showed up in the casino's facial recognition program. Still, the WinStar World Casino showed a photo of her last known license plate and vehicle. That had to be something. If the vehicle wasn't in her possession anymore, the owner might be able to tell him something about the previous owner.

He booked the next flight to Dallas. Maybe this would be the lead that would bring their baby sister home.

He flew downstairs. Scott and Tess were just getting ready to leave.

"What did you find?" Scott asked.

"It's definitely the old junker she was driving when she was spotted in Reno. I'm flying to Dallas in the morning, then I'll rent a car and drive to the casino in Oklahoma. It's close to the Texas border. I know it's a long shot but you never know." He glanced at his watch. "Flight leaves at 11:15. Probably be back sometime Monday if it's another dead end."

Scott nodded. "Keep me posted."

"Good luck," Tess murmured.

Justin grinned. "This could be it. Gotta pack."

Sunday morning Jason awoke to a rainy gray day. He sat up and swung his feet to the cool hardwoods. He yawned. Somehow he had to get Tamsyn Holt out of his brain. Dreams of her lush body had plagued his sleep most of the night. Her full breasts. Firm thighs. Her soft lips.

He shook his head.

Focus.

Losing sight of his assignment and what he needed to accomplish was the quickest way to end up with cement boots in the Cumberland River—or however arms dealers solved their problems these days. Most likely it would be a bullet in the head. Or torture first and then a bullet.

He headed for the shower, turned it on cold and stepped into the icy spray. Flinching when the cold needles of spray hit him, he shook his head. Just what he needed.

Focus.

Tollison's big deal was going down soon. Was it a large shipment of arms designated to arm a private army of goons? A massive supply of drugs? Or a bioweapon of some sort? Would Tollison really be so rash as to buy and sell a weapon of mass destruction? One that could easily be turned around and used on the seller's home country.

Tollison had an end game. No doubt about it. Before her death, Bree had hinted that her father had political aspirations of the highest order. But the man had no history of running for office, public or otherwise. What could he hope to accomplish politically? In the grand scheme of things, he was ostensibly an extremely successful businessman. Never served in the military, using multiple college deferments during Viet Nam, graduating a year after it ended.

Well, he wouldn't be the first who sought the highest office in the land with a similar background. Maybe Tollison's deal was part of building a war chest he could use to launch a political campaign. Other more unsettling speculations came to mind.

Somehow he needed to get into Tollison's head. Whatever the man's end game, he wasn't about to share it with his dead daughter's fiancé. That degree of trust wasn't there. Not yet.

But time was short. Who *did* Tollison trust that much?

Brad Oliver.

Right. Oliver was a junior partner in his father's prestigious law firm. Would he keep anything incriminating in his office? Doubtful.

His home? More likely. Was he as paranoid as Tollison with security measures up the yin-yang?

No. Too arrogant. Too convinced of his superiority. Complacent.

Tonight. That's where he'd start.

But first, surveillance was in order. And while he was at it, maybe he ought to swing by Tamsyn's house, just to make sure everything was in order. He wouldn't stop. What could it hurt, as long as he wasn't seen?

Tamsyn groaned at the sound of rain hitting the slate tiles on the roof. As in *pouring* rain. She wanted nothing more than to pull the covers over her head and go back to sleep.

No. Sleep meant more dreams of a certain FBI agent.

Hell, he even plagued her nights.

She sprang from the bed and ran to the window, sighing. The glorious Indian summer had given way to gray skies. Last night's storm had blown most of the leaves from the trees, their bare branches naked spikes in a dreary sky.

Yuck. No grilling out today. Today called for something like a big pot of vegetable soup or chili. Now, chili she could do. The hotter and thicker, the better.

She drew on a robe and padded downstairs to the utility room. From the deep freeze, she pulled out two pounds of ground round and set it on the counter. After that, she filled the farm sink with cold water and set the packages of beef into the sink to thaw.

Might as well put the coffee on. Yawning, she filled the coffee maker, measuring out the fragrant arabica brew the family favored. She wrote on the blackboard, 'Gone for bagels.' After hitting the brew button, she headed back upstairs to shower.

After showering and changing into jeggings and a warm wool red sweater, Tamsyn pulled on a rain poncho ready to drive to nearby Star Bagel.

At least that *had* been her primary destination. When she was ready to turn onto Richland, a black Range Rover cruised by. Damn! That was Jason. What was he doing lurking around, again? Maybe she should just follow *him* for a change. Serve him right.

She followed him downtown to a condo in the Gulch. So that was where he lived. Good to know. Just in case she ever wanted to place a tracking device on his Rover. She circled the block, trying to decide what to do next. He didn't remain inside long. His Rover emerged from the parking garage, and this time, she followed him all the way to a pricey Brentwood subdivision where he parked on the street. But he just sat there. What was he up to now?

Slowly, she passed the Rover, then pulled into the

space in front of the SUV. She'd just ask him.

Jason groaned. Tamsyn had followed him, very amateurishly for someone who was supposed to be a professional P.I. Fortunately, he'd spotted her before leaving her neighborhood, so he'd driven into his condo's parking garage, figuring she would give up.

Now, she was about to wreck his surveillance on Oliver. He hit his forehead with the palm of his hand. No! She couldn't be that rash.

Apparently, she could. She whipped opened the passenger door and hopped inside. Her impish grin—so infuriating. Damn. "What the hell do you think you're doing, following me?"

"You were stalking me, again. I decided to give you a taste of your own medicine." She pulled off her wet poncho, folded it and tossed it into the backseat. She settled back against the seat as if she had every intention of staying there for the duration. "So what are we doing?"

Do not gaze into her eyes. Focus. On anything but her.

"Get out now," he growled. "I'm doing surveillance."

"Really?" She craned her neck. "And *who* are we surveilling?"

"It's whom. And *we're* not surveilling anyone. I am. Now...get out." He rubbed his forehead. Damn pesky woman. "Go on. *Out.* You're compromising my investigation."

"Not until you tell me what's going on."

From the corner of his eye, he saw Oliver's Lincoln emerge from the back of the house. Off to church, maybe? Oliver never struck Jason as the church-going type.

Damn. Oliver was turning this way. He would drive right by them. As far as he knew, Oliver had never seen Jason's SUV. Even so, he grabbed Tamsyn and pulled her into his arms. "Just go with it," he muttered, smothering her with a kiss, making sure neither of their faces was visible to passersby.

She didn't struggle. And she definitely went along with it. His head spun from the surge of lust that rocked his body and threatened to rip his jeans.

Her lips were soft, pliant under his. Her mouth opened to his, her tongue probing, battling. She wove her fingers through his hair and cemented his hold on her.

Her hand grazed his cock. He sucked in a quick breath. She fumbled with his belt, attempting to reach his zipper.

He slid a hand under her sweater. Oh, god. No bra. He kneaded her firm breast and groaned.

"Fuck me." Her voice was raspy, determined.

"You're not exactly dressed for it," he said with a grumble as he pulled her sweater up, revealing her breasts. He latched onto one tight nipple and sucked.

She whimpered with need. "Fuck me, dammit."

Hitting the seat control to recline with one hand, he slid his other hand inside her tight pants and found her damp core. She clutched his finger with her inner walls as if it were his dick. A spear of lust shot through him as she squirmed. With one hand she managed to get her skin-tight pants down to her knees, then amazingly freed one leg.

Limber and inventive. Deliver me.

"Fuck me!"

He struggled with his zipper.

"Finally." She eased his dick free.

He sucked in a breath and willed himself not to come. She straddled him and then lowered onto his swollen cock.

He grasped her ass and arched upward, pulling her closer, tighter.

Hot. Wet. Heaven.

He bucked and she rode him like a bronco. Hotter Wetter. Her mouth devouring his. Her inner muscles gripping him with each stroke.

Too fast. Too much. Too soon.

His control shattered, they flew over the edge together, his entire body shuddering with the intense release.

What was it about this woman that made him lose himself in her?

He swore. No condom. What the hell was he thinking? Dammit—he wasn't thinking. At least, not with his brain.

Tamsyn collapsed against his chest with a moan. Never had she experienced anything like being with this one man. She straightened. "OMG! We didn't use a condom."

"Right," he said wryly.

When had she ever been this horny in all her life? Was she ovulating? Mother Nature's nasty little trick for perpetuating the species. No. She couldn't be. Not if the implant in her upper arm was still working. She even carried a package of condoms in her bag.

"Damn you!" She pounded her fist on his chest.

"Me?" Jason straightened. "You were the one begging me to fuck you. What did you think was going to happen? I told you I was working. I told you to get out. But no—you made a grab for my dick. What did you think was going to happen?"

"I can see you're a real stand-up guy. And I *wasn't* begging."

"You were. You definitely were."

Come to think of it, maybe she had begged...a little. But now she had him out of her system. Never again. Never.

"Well, I'm definitely getting out *now*." She moved away, breaking their physical connection. Holding back a moan at the loss of intimate contact, she struggled into her jeggings and pulled them up. Her hands trembled. Her thigh muscles jittered. She swallowed hard, then turned around in the seat to find her poncho. Tears welled in her eyes.

"Don't leave like this."

"Yes, just like this. I'm leaving."

Stupid! Who lost control and had unprotected sex in this day and age? She wasn't some hormonal teenager. No, just a non-ovulating supposedly mature woman. If that wasn't hormonal, what was?

He covered her hand with his. "Tamsyn, we need to talk about what just happened."

Again, the all-too-familiar spark of lust zapped through her. "Some other time, Agent St. John." She jerked her hand from his.

The rain pounded on the roof of the SUV. She pulled the poncho over her head, opened the door, and ran for the Boxter.

"Tamsyn..." he called after her.

Ignore him. He's no good for you. Her hands, still trembling, fumbled with the key. Finally, inside, she sat for a moment, her mouth dry and tears spilling down her cheeks.

What the fuck had she just done?

Chapter Eighteen

Jason pounded the steering wheel. Of all the hair-brained acts to pull, he'd made love to Tamsyn almost in front of Oliver's mini-mansion. Not made love. There wasn't anything resembling love in their coupling.

Just sex. Hot. Dirty. Sex.

Groaning, he waited while her little red sports car pulled away. They'd been damn lucky a neighbor hadn't reported them or the Brentwood Police hadn't caught them at it. And explaining that to his SAC, after being warned... No way.

Coming back tonight would be fraught with a different set of difficulties. The large houses were close together on smallish lots. Waiting until after midnight would be best. More like a couple of hours after.

He started the motor and eased into the street. Might as well return to his apartment and gear up for tonight's mission.

As for any consequences that might result from this moment's madness—he'd deal if indeed there were any.

Tamsyn breezed into the kitchen. She inhaled the aroma of freshly brewed coffee permeating the air. Nothing better than that first cup of the day. Justin and Carrie were seated at the kitchen island. Carrie arched one sculpted brow in her direction. "Did you forget something?"

Still, a bit dazed by the early morning booty call,

Tamsyn glanced around. "Huh?"

"Bagels," Carrie suggested.

"Bagels?" Tamsyn's cheeks heated. "Right. I guess I did forget."

"If you didn't go for bagels, where the hell have you been?" Justin fell over, miming starvation.

"Good question." Where the hell had she been? "What have I been doing?"

Stall. Stall. Think of something. Anything but the truth.

Carrie smirked. "Maybe the real question is *who* have you been doing?"

Her cheeks now heading toward spontaneous combustion territory, she swallowed hard. "It's true. I got a little sidetracked—uh, distracted. It's not too late. I'll run back out and pick them up."

Carrie rose, waving away Tamsyn's suggestion. "Never mind. I think this rainy day calls for something a little more substantial than a bagel. Who's up for scrambled eggs and bacon?"

Tamsyn forced a smile. "Me please."

Justin stood with a wry smile. "No time. My flight for Dallas leaves at eleven."

Carrie stopped in front of the fridge and frowned. "I wish you would tell me *why* you're going to Dallas."

"Told you. No big deal. Just a software issue that needs hands-on." He held up both hands and mimicked keyboarding. "Mine."

"I know that's what you said, but I'm not buying it." Carrie opened the fridge and pulled out a carton of eggs and a package of bacon. She glanced over her shoulder at Justin. "I can feel it." She wagged her index finger at him. "You're up to something."

All righty. A change of topic. Exactly what was needed

to get them off *her* back. "Yeah, he's definitely up to something." Tamsyn leaned her elbows on the island. "Spill it, dude."

"No time. Gotta go." He ducked and ran upstairs.

Carrie let out a huff. "Can you believe that?" She screwed her mouth to the side. "He's had a lead on Kim. I know it!" She set the package of bacon on the counter with a smack.

"He'd tell you if that was the case." *Keep her thinking about Kim.* "Unless he didn't want to get your hopes up."

"That's it. Sneaky so-and-so." Carrie cracked four eggs into a bowl and began whipping them with a wire whisk. "Don't think *you're* getting out of here without an explanation," she said without turning from her task.

Tamsyn sniffed, lifting her shoulders in as casual a shrug as she could manage. "Don't have a clue what you're talking about."

Carrie turned and cast Tamsyn an I-got-your-number expression. "Uh-huh. You go out for bagels and come back hours later looking like the cat who ate the canary. I'm surprised there aren't feathers sticking out somewhere."

"Hardly *hours* later."

"Long enough. So spill." She set the bowl of eggs aside, then leaned her elbows on the island. "It's just the two of us."

What could it hurt to tell Carrie? Better to spill than explode. She cleared her throat and plunged into her tawdry story while her sister's chin dropped on hearing the details. "You did *not*!"

"I did—well, *we* did."

Carrie collapsed on a stool, shaking her head. "How could you be so stupid? You barely know the man, and you were bumping uglies on a residential street...in *Brentwood.*"

"The SUV's windows are tinted. It was raining. Not many people out." She shrugged. How many more lame extenuating factors could she come up with?

"Like any of that would've mattered if you'd been caught."

"Appears I wasn't thinking too clearly at the time." No indeed.

Carrie favored Tamsyn with an over-exaggerated eye roll. "Obviously."

"Won't do it again." Duh! She couldn't help but squirm at the thought of seeing him again. This morning had been hot and way too quick. Next time...

"Yeah right. Until the next time you see him." Carrie stood, shaking her head. "I just don't see how you could abandon all sense of caution." She poured the eggs into a hot skillet. The butter sizzled. Tamsyn's stomach growled.

Carrie's ESP must be working overtime. "I can't explain it either. It's just this urge to rip his clothes off overwhelms me every time I get near him."

"If Scott had any idea." Carrie shook her head. "Omigod."

"No! You can't tell him. Jason isn't a client. Besides, it's not like he's a bad guy. He's a Fed."

Carrie whipped around, brandishing her spatula. "But someone killed this Fed's so-called fiancée. We don't know if her death was related to whatever his assignment is. Just being around St. John puts *you* in danger. You *have* to steer clear. Like take-a-vacation-to-Europe clear." Turning back to her task, Carrie quickly arranged strips of bacon on a tray and slid it into the microwave.

"I know. And I *will*. He's an ass anyway." Like he hadn't wanted her as much as she had him. 'Making a grab for his dick.' Well, she had. So what. Next time...

"Maybe after..." Carrie's tone softened. "If anything's

really there..."

"Then he'll move on to another assignment, most likely." Tamsyn lifted her shoulders in a casual shrug, determined not to let her sister know how his leaving would affect her. "But that'll be good. I'll get over this madness if he's no longer around." And then an idea wormed its way into her thoughts: there was a lot more to the world than good ole Music City. And their slightly dysfunctional, but almost always delightful, family. Ah, the family.

"I sure hope so."

Justin poked his head into the kitchen. "What madness? What did I miss?"

"Nothing," they said in unison.

"Jinx!" again said in unison.

Justin gave an exaggerated eye roll. "Grow up you two. And you didn't answer my question."

"You shouldn't eavesdrop," Tamsyn muttered. "Girl talk. *Monthly* madness." That would shut him up.

Justin set his go-bag on the floor, then held his hands up in surrender. "I'm out of here. Probably be back on Tuesday."

"Stay safe," Tamsyn called to his departing back.

As soon as Justin cleared the premises, Carrie turned, giving Tamsyn the stink eye. "Speaking of *safe*...?"

"Honestly," Tamsyn huffed. "I'm going to get my own apartment. Where's the Sunday paper? There's absolutely no privacy in this family."

"OMG! Tamsyn!"

"For Pete's sake. I have one of those implant things. Not that you actually need to know that."

"But that won't protect you from—"

"I'm pretty sure a Fed isn't going to be HIV positive. Probably against the rules, y'know."

Carrie gave an eye roll. "Do you hear yourself?"

"I know I'm definitely going to find an apartment. I *am* not a pre-teen. I don't need this lecture. I'm a grown woman and perfectly capable of taking care of my body."

"Fine. Move out. Ruin your life. Screw every Federal agent in America. Why should I care?"

Every Federal agent? Tamsyn tamped down the urge to laugh, then moved to hug her sister and reassure her. "I know you care. You've taken care of all of us for the last twelve years. It was a moment of madness." She stroked Carrie's arm. "I wasn't thinking. It won't happen again."

Carrie sniffed. "All right. I just hope you mean it."

"I promise. It won't happen again."

Unless I'm alone with him. Then game over.

Chapter Nineteen

Head home. Forget hooking up with Tamsyn Holt. Easier said than done.

Gear up for tonight's recon. That was the plan. Operative word: *was*.

Randall Tollison's phone call put the kibosh on Jason's plan. "Come have Sunday luncheon with us, Jason."

"I wouldn't want to intrude during your time of grief, sir."

"Nonsense. Do us both good. No point in sitting around and moping. With this deal looming, I don't have time. Besides, my wife's grieving enough for everyone."

Now, how to get out of staying for dinner with Bree's father...gracefully.

"After lunch, we'll firm up procedures for the deal."

"In that case, I would be honored." Yes, details. Just what he needed.

"We'll sit down at one."

Jason glanced at his watch. Time for a shower and shave. He could still smell Tamsyn's perfume all over his body, a heady, rich fragrance like the woman herself. But he'd have to make an exit in time to prepare for his foray into housebreaking.

***

Hughes, Tollison's butler/bodyguard admitted Jason, this time omitting the scan for electronic devices, and showed him immediately into Tollison's study. Why was it men of power found it necessary to surround themselves with priceless antiques from a bygone age? Did Tollison imagine that possessing a Louis-the-whatever's desk meant he had the power of a king?

Beware, Randall. The last Louis lost his head. And I'm more than happy to be your Robespierre.

"Welcome."

"Thank you, sir."

Even though it had only been a couple of days since their last meeting, Tollison's physical appearance had declined further. In spite of his earlier remark about not having time to grieve, it appeared as if he weren't eating or sleeping. His skin tone was dull and gray. His expensive suit hung loosely from his stooped shoulders.

"Drink?" Scotch glass in hand, Tollison gestured toward the bar.

"No thanks." Jason strode to the French windows overlooking the garden. He gazed out at the fading plants. Keeping his tone low key, he turned. "I'm glad you're ready to share more details about our upcoming deal."

Tollison grunted. "You'll be given enough notice. You're not all that busy in your day job, are you? You'll be able to leave when called?"

Jason nodded, giving a wry smile. "True, business is taking off slowly."

Hughes entered the study. "Luncheon is served."

Tollison lumbered to his feet. "Let's eat."

Sunday afternoon
Wiping the sweat from his brow, Justin checked into

the WinStar World casino. Who knew Oklahoma could be so dang hot in October, even with the AC on full blast, all the way from Dallas on I-35? After a quick shower and shave, he called Security and confirmed his appointment with their head honcho, Daniel Whitehorse, then headed for the Security offices.

He identified himself and was buzzed into the inner sanctum, security-wise, of the largest casino in Oklahoma.

The receptionist looked up from her terminal and smiled. "Welcome to the WinStar World Casino, Mr. Lackey. Is this your first visit?"

Justin returned the smile. Hard not to. The young woman was certainly gorgeous. Wide, brown eyes and a bronzed complexion that no tanning bed ever created could perfect. "No. I was here during the initial installation of your software system."

"Mr. Whitehorse will see you now." She rose gracefully. "Right this way."

He followed. Heck, he'd follow this beauty anywhere. Her slim hips swayed slightly as she led him to Whitehorse's office. But he was here on business. Family business.

Daniel Whitehorse rose and offered his hand as Justin entered. The security exec was over six feet and well-built. Dark brown eyes that missed nothing and a slightly aquiline profile. Dressed in a navy silk suit, white shirt, and a navy and white striped tie, his only concession to his Native American heritage was the large turquoise and silver ring he wore on his forefinger.

After shaking hands, Whitehorse gestured with a wave. "Have a seat Justin. How can I help? Your voice mail didn't elaborate. I have to admit I'm concerned. Have you detected a hacking intrusion?"

"No. It's a personal family matter, and I didn't feel

comfortable disclosing any details over the phone. What it boils down to is I would like to review your parking lot surveillance and facial recognition films for last night."

Whitehorse's brow furrowed. "A family matter? How so?"

"I have a younger sister. She's been missing for ten years. We have reason to believe she was here, or at least her last known vehicle was here last night."

Whitehorse's gaze darkened. "And how did you come by this information?"

Unsure of Whitehorse's reaction, Justin he stirred uneasily in his chair. "With any software I write and install, I insert a line of code that will send me an alert when certain parameters are met. And not just gaming software. I routinely insert this line of code in everything."

"I see." Whitehorse frowned as he steepled his fingers, considering Justin's admission. In the world of software programming, inserting a back door or other string of code might be considered illegal, but not an uncommon practice, all the same. "So you received an alert and believe it's possible your sister was here last evening."

"I know her last-known vehicle was in your parking lot. I'd especially like to see any CCTV footage you might have for the time period when I received the alert. Eleven pm CST."

"You realize privacy is a concern for many of our clients."

"Of course. I'm only interested in seeing who got out of that car. If it proves to be my sister, I'd like to know if she's still here. If it's a man, then I'll want to interview him about where, when, and how he obtained her vehicle."

Whitehorse's dark eyes flashed at the word 'interview.' "That won't be possible. I'm willing to allow you to view the footage, but as for violating the car owner's privacy—no."

"You don't understand." Justin leaned forward. He was too close to finding Kim to give up. "My sister was a mere kid, only fifteen when she disappeared. Our family has been searching for years. We *want* to bring her home. We *need* to know what happened."

"But you had her vehicle registration?"

"Over the years, we've found traces of her, but she's always moved on by the time we get there. Her car registration was our latest lead. This is the first time we've been this close."

"All right," Whitehorse said with a sigh. "Let's review the parking lot footage."

"Lot Q."

"That's one of the employee lots."

"You mean she could be an employee?" If she was an employee, that meant she would be hanging around for a while. His heart sped up. His hands started to shake. This could be it. Finally.

"Someone is."

Whitehorse's fingers flew over the keyboard. "The car tag number."

Justin repeated it from memory.

"The vehicle entered the employee lot at 10:50 last night and left the lot at 9:10 this morning."

"Ten-hour shift sounds like to me. What about the CCTV footage?"

"Locating it now."

Holding his breath, Justin waited, his toe tapping. He refrained from leaning over Whitehorse's shoulders.

"Here we go. It's dark."

Justin leaned in. "Can you adjust it?"

Whitehorse lightened the image. "Sorry about the resolution."

His heart sank.

Even with the low resolution, it was plain.

Not Kim. Not even female.

"Sorry."

"It was always a longshot. But this guy—he might know her. He might know where she is." If he had to get down on his knees and beg, he would. "You have to tell me *who* he is."

Whitehorse shook his head. "Employee records are private." He sighed. "Tell you what. He'll be back on duty tonight. Same time. I can issue you a permit for that lot. That's the best I can do." He picked up the phone and gave instructions.

Gratitude swept through Justin. He rose. "Thank you. My entire family thanks you."

Whitehorse nodded. "My assistant will have it ready for you."

"Again thanks."

"If there's anything else I can do..."

...*without violating anyone's privacy. Yada, yada. Right.* Concealing his impatience, Justin nodded. "I'll let you know."

Outside, Whitehorse's efficient assistant had his parking permit ready. She handed it over, along with an upgrade in his accommodations. "Mr. Whitehorse was sorry he couldn't do more. He hopes you'll enjoy the rest of your stay with us."

"Cool."

"Your things are already being transferred to your new corner suite on the twelfth floor." She handed him a new key card.

Taking the card, he smiled. "Wow. Thanks."

Justin opened the door to his corner suite. Instead of

the typical double he'd booked, he now had a large sitting room with a wide-screen 4K TV. A balcony overlooked the strip. The shower was oversized and glass enclosed. Nice.

Justin's wallet contained less than a thousand dollars cash. Not exactly high roller status. More minnow than whale. All things considered, Whitehorse had been more than generous

Not anxious to answer any more questions about her Sunday morning tryst, Tamsyn kept to her room the rest of the afternoon. She pulled up the Sunday *Tennessean* on her iPad, scanning the headlines for anything important.

Nada.

She checked her smartphone. Was the damned thing turned on? Yes. Battery charged? Yes. So... Not a word from Jason. Not a call. Not even a measly text. Wham. Bam. Thank you, ma'am.

Never mind that they'd just had mind-blowing sex. And it had been just as good for him as it had for her. No doubt about that. What was wrong with the man? Even with a booty call, shouldn't there be some kind of etiquette?

Late Sunday evening.

Justin glanced at his watch. No clocks in casinos. After a light dinner, he'd headed to the blackjack table and managed to turn his measly thousand into ten thousand. Time to cash out. No. Time for one more deal. Better to let the house win some back, rather than be accused of counting cards. With little effort, he managed to lose half his winnings.

Time to cash out.

And he did.

He returned to his suite, placed his winnings in the safe, and changed into black jeans and T-shirt. Now to take his place in the employee parking lot and find out who was driving Kim's old banger and if he had any intel about her present location.

The employee parking lot was well-lit and massive. He found an open space close to the entrance. As soon at the CCTV recorded the license plate entering the lot, he'd receive the same alert as before.

Finally, he was getting somewhere. All he had to do was wait.

Justin kept an eye peeled on the lot entrance. Doing surveillance wasn't his forte. He much preferred the office end of the business. Tech was his wheelhouse, not sitting in a vehicle until his ass was numb. More and more now, the family business was trending toward security and commercial clients, with less emphasis on catching husbands who were screwing around, Tamsyn's clients notwithstanding. There was any number of agency men he could've dispatched to pick up Kim's trail. Still, this was strictly a family matter. And Daniel Whitehorse knew him from their prior dealings.

At 10:50 his phone alerted. Got him! Now, to find the driver of Kim's car. Would he talk? He spied the vehicle and started his rental car. He followed Kim's old banger, a silver '92 Olds 88 until the driver pulled into an open spot and stopped. Justin parked directly behind the Olds, blocking his exit.

The man jumped out. He was at least a half a foot over six feet and no stranger to the gym. "What the hell?" His meaty fists were clenched as he lumbered forward.

"Hold on. I just want to talk." Tangling with this big bruiser wasn't what Justin had bargained for. "I'm Justin

Lackey. I'm a P.I. from Nashville."

The bruiser's headlong rush slowed. "P.I.? What do you want with me?"

"I need to know about your car. Where'd you get it?"

"None of your damn business." He turned and started to head toward the casino.

"Wait. Let me explain. What's your name?" He purposely kept his tone level and his body language non-threatening.

"Jake. Jake Aguilar."

"The last I knew my sister Kim was driving that Olds. She was in Nevada. She's been missing for ten years."

"Don't know no Kim. Gal I got this car from said her name was Kay Riggs. I found her broken down on I-40 outside Oklahoma City. Gave her a lift to the nearest truck stop."

"When was this?"

He rubbed his chin with his thumb and forefinger. "Spring. I reckon."

"Did she seem to be in good health?"

"Skinny as a rail. Poor kid. Didn't have enough money for a cup of coffee, so I bought her a burger. And then, I bought that piece of shit she was driving for a hundred bucks. Don't know where she went after that. Then, I had the Olds towed to my brother's garage. Worked on it a bit over the summer. Got her going again. Still looks like shit, but she runs good."

Justin pulled up the age-advanced photo on his phone. "Does this resemble the woman you bought the car from? Even a little?"

Jake glanced at his watch. "Look, dude, I gotta clock in."

"Just take a look, Jake. Please."

Aguilar peered at the photo, then nodded. "Yeah, that

could be her. Hair was blonde though. Cut short, spiky kinda. About five-seven or thereabouts." He demonstrated her height with his hands. "Eyes were green, I think. Maybe blue. I gotta go."

"Here's my card. If you think of anything else?"

"Sure." He took the card, shoved it in his hip pocket, and took off in a heavy-footed trot.

Damn. Another dead end.

Still, it wouldn't hurt to follow him in the morning. See where he lived. Talk to his neighbors.

In the meantime, he'd run a background check on Aguilar as soon as he got back to his laptop. While he believed in the kindness of strangers, there was usually only one reason a mug like Aguilar was kind to a woman broken down on the side of the road. Much less give her a hundred dollars for her rusted out junker.

What had he asked or demanded in return?

Monday 2:00 am

Yawning, Jason eased from the SUV parked two blocks from Oliver's house. Clouds and a threatening storm hid the moon. Grass was wet with dew. He'd hoped for a couple of hours of sleep, but getting away from Tollison had been tricky. The old man had inveigled Jason stay for dinner, followed by several hands of five-card stud, accompanied by brandy and cigars. Normally, he didn't smoke, but he'd gone through the motions to mollify the old man and to keep him from getting suspicious. After hours of losing money he couldn't afford to lose, he still he didn't know any more than he had before lunch.

He strode the around to the rear of the house. Better to effect entry from the rear. No point in taking a chance by making it easy for the local security patrol to spot him.

He quickly located and bypassed Oliver's security system. It was a piece of crap anyway. Then he engaged the cell phone and Wi-Fi jammer.

Walkout basement. Great. More than likely if the occupant forgot to lock a door, it would be that glass slider. Gently, he tried the door.

Damn. Locked.

He reached into his bag and pulled out the glass cutter and suction cup. A perfect circle. He removed the circle of glass and set it aside. It would be a clear giveaway that the house had been entered. Would Oliver even notice? Doubtful it would be enough to call off Tollison's upcoming deal. Or would it?

He reached through the opening and unlatched the slider. It slid open silently. Nice.

Once inside, he pulled the night vision goggles down. Less risky than using a flashlight to maneuver around the room.

Right on. A real man cave. Massive wall-mounted TV with theater-style recliners.

He spotted the stairway to the first level. At the top of the stairs, he tried the latch. Locked. Naturally.

He pulled out a set of lock picks and jimmied the simple locking mechanism.

Easy-peasy.

He opened the door, took one step into the hallway, and an alarm blared.

Crap.

He spun. Half flew, half skidded back down to the basement. He blasted through the slider he'd left open...just in case. How had he missed a back-up alarm? Oliver was better prepared than Jason had given him credit for.

He whipped off the night vision goggles, flew around

the corner of the house, and waited, panting, his heart racing. He could hear Oliver lumbering down into the basement. But no sign of the patrol yet. Average response time was ten minutes. He darted for the street and adjusted his pace as if he were out for a late night run until he reached the Range Rover he'd parked two blocks away. Once inside, he started the motor and drove slowly away.

He didn't meet the patrol until he was pulling out of the subdivision proper. Faster response than he'd expected.

Only when he turned onto Old Hickory Boulevard did he let out a *whoosh* of relief.

Chapter Twenty

Arms crossed in front, Tess took her usual position in front of the murder board studying the timeline. Glancing at her watch, she nodded. "Okay, let's see what we have on these guys."

Seth leaned forward on his elbows. "I have Jerry Ames coming in at nine for a deeper interview. Just my gut, but I think he knows more than he's saying. In fact, he started to tell me something but stopped. Said it'd hold until he came in."

"Seth? What about Tollison himself? Do we know more?"

"He appears clean," Seth said with a shrug. "But he runs an import/export business. There's always room for interpretation and illegal deals."

"What countries does he do business with?"

"Eastern bloc—some antiquities. Middle East—primarily rugs. South America—coffee."

"So we can assume there's an opportunity for dealing drugs and arms. Great."

"Malik?"

"I finished my half of the list. Couple of domestic call-outs to the Olivers' address. The wife refused to press charges both times. Said it was a misunderstanding. I interviewed the neighbors on both sides. Neighbors said it gets pretty hot and heavy with them at times. Business-wise, he's Randall Tollison's attorney of record."

"Seth, have you found any other assault reports on

Oliver?"

"None."

"Interesting." Tess nodded. "Ron?"

Irby consulted his notebook. "Eric Chapman was engaged to Brianna for six months. Spoke with her best friend, Susan Dyer. She says Brianna broke off the engagement a year ago when he slapped her during an argument. He said she asked for it by flirting with every man in sight. The kicker is Brianna ended up in the hospital later that evening with a blackened eye and a dislocated jaw. Reportedly, she fell at home. Of note, in the past, he was a software developer. Currently, he runs a company that specializes in technology, communications & media services."

"Okay, so he slapped her in public, but waited until he got her home to really tune her up." Software developer—right. "And he has the wherewithal to interrupt the CCTV at Brianna's condo. We have two abusive men and one squirrelly employee. What about Eric's twin brother? He was pretty dismissive—rude even—at the funeral."

"Chris Chapman—he's squeaky clean," Irby said. "Not even a parking ticket. Owns a home healthcare agency. No complaints with the BBB."

"Seth, you proceed with Ames's interview. I'll observe."

Foyle glanced at his watch, then nodded. "Should be here soon. He seemed eager to help. Maybe too eager. If he's on time, Eric Chapman agreed to come in a half hour from now."

"Okay, folks, we're on a roll."

Tess looked up when Seth tapped on the door. "Yes?"

"Chapman's here."

"Where?"

"Interview two."

Tess rose. "Okay, let's get this show on the road." She strode down the hall and opened the door. Attired in a three-piece navy suit, pale blue shirt and a red power tie, Chapman was blond and blue-eyed. This abuser hiding in plain sight beneath his CEO persona perched on the edge of his chair, appearing as if any moment he'd take flight.

She nodded. "Mr. Chapman, I'm Detective Holt. Thank you for taking the time to make a formal statement."

He gave her a surreptitious once-over. "Detective Holt, I don't know how I can help. I haven't seen Brianna in several months. And may I add, it's a damn inconvenient time. I'm quite busy."

Smiling, Tess sat across from Chapman. "Thank you for your cooperation, Mr. Chapman. We'll get you through this as quickly as possible. First of all, I noticed you didn't attend her funeral."

"I had a conflict. I sent flowers." He shifted in his seat. "Do I need to have my attorney here?

"You're not under arrest. You're just here to make a formal statement. But if you wish to have an attorney present, you're within your rights."

"Fine. Here's my formal statement. I haven't seen Brianna Tollison since we broke off our engagement. I don't know *who* killed her. She was a lovely person most of the time."

He should've stopped with he didn't know who killed her. One of those so-called micro-expressions—the corner of his mouth twitched. Gotcha. Tess tamped down her inner smile. "Most of the time?"

"I felt she was unreasonable when she broke off our engagement, but I'm over it." He stopped to straighten his tie. "I'm engaged to someone else now. I'm very happy."

"Someone more *reasonable*?"

"Definitely." He straightened his shoulders, assuming a mien of smug satisfaction.

"Why did Brianna break off your engagement?"

"She found someone new." He frowned, apparently warming to the task at hand. "Perhaps you should be interviewing him instead of wasting time with me."

"According to one of her friends, we have a statement that she broke off the engagement because you struck her."

"Hmph," he scoffed. "Over-exaggeration. Really."

"How so?"

"I lost my cool—briefly. You may not know this but Brianna was a terrible flirt. One night at a party, I'd had enough. It wasn't much more than a love tap. It would never have happened again."

According to Susan Dyer, Chapman's *love tap* had blackened her eye and dislocated her jaw. "That's what they all say."

Chapman's gaze widened. "*All*. Who?"

"All the men who smack their women around. Like you did."

He shot his cuffs. "I was very sorry. I apologized. And I sent her flowers the next day."

"Typical." She nodded knowingly. She'd seen and heard it all before. "I suppose you sent those flowers to the hospital since her jaw was dislocated."

His gaze narrowing, Chapman stood. "I've had enough. Since I'm not under arrest, then I assume I may go at any time." He headed toward the door.

"You may. One more thing. Where were you on Tuesday from 1:45 until 4:45?"

His eyes widened in shock. Didn't he expect to be asked for an alibi? Or was he deflecting and playing for time to come up with a good response?

"I was with my fiancée. We were making wedding plans if you must know."

"Oh, I do. And *where* were you making these plans?"

"At—uh, my house."

"Anyone else there? Staff?"

"I don't have live-in help." He readjusted his tie. "I use a local maid service."

"I need your fiancée's name as well as the name of your maid service."

"You're not going to drag my fiancée into this, surely."

"We need to verify your alibi."

"Megan Hastings." He spat each syllable with a vehement emphasis.

"Phone number and address." Tess passed him the notepad and pen. "Please."

Chapman hurriedly complied. "I can go?"

Tess nodded. "Main service?" Not that his cleaning service would likely be of any use, but hassling him was fun.

"Centennial Maid Service. They're on the Internet. I assume you know how to use it. Look them up." He huffed, his tan cheeks darkening with suppressed rage. "Believe you me, my friend the Commissioner will hear about this."

"Indeed." She smiled. "Be sure to get my name and rank right."

Whether or not he was friends with the Commissioner or not mattered little. A high profile investigation was bound to rattle a few cages. And she was just getting started.

Back out in the bullpen, Tess sat. "Seth, let's get his fiancée in here for a sit-down. I don't want him anywhere around when she's interviewed."

***

Ames was a no-show for his interview. And now Tess knew why. She walked carefully around the body just pulled from the Cumberland.

At Tess's elbow, Seth Foyle shook his head. "Damn. Sure wish he'd made it to that interview."

"How long?" she asked the ginger-haired M.E.

Foyle kept a respectful distance, but his expression was as avid as hers had to be.

Jacobs looked up from his crouched position beside Jerry Ames's body. The M.E. frowned, screwing his features into a solemn mask. "He's fresh. Given the current water temp..." He lifted his shoulders in a shrug. "Best guess—and it is just a guess because I know from experience how impatient you are. Sometime in the last twelve hours."

Tess groaned. "Suicide?"

"You'll appreciate this." He flashed an evil grin, his pale eyes glinting in the sunlight. "Blunt force trauma. Could be he hit a bridge pylon, and you know I don't like to speculate at the scene, but I'd say someone caved in the back of his head before he took a final swim."

So Jerry Ames was dead. Maybe blunt force trauma. Definitely a suspicious death.

Foyle shot her a wry smile. Now, you can get that search warrant."

"*You* file the paperwork. I'll go on and talk to his mother. I wager she'll let me see his room without one."

Tamsyn dressed hurriedly for the office. She checked her image in the mirror. Gray suit with a pencil skirt, a black V-neck silk blouse, and a red scarf. She wrinkled her nose at her image and removed the scarf. Too fussy. She added silver oval drop earrings. She held up a turquoise necklace. Nah. Instead, she slipped on a fine silver link chain. Anything else was too heavy.

Carrie looked up as Tamsyn strode into the office. "Good morning, hermit. Did you even eat dinner?"

"Wasn't hungry." She pulled her leather bag from her shoulder and set it on Carrie's desk.

"You're upset."

"*No.*" She picked up her bag. "I'm not." Not ready for round two.

"*Yes.* You *are.* Your jaw's clenched. Your mouth's a thin line. And your eyes are blazing. I know mad when I see it."

"Oh, hush. Not today." Tamsyn whirled in the direction of her office and strode away. Fumbling with her office key, she cursed, then hastily glanced over her shoulder. At least she wasn't cursing in front of potential clients.

Once inside her office, she shut the door. Taking a deep breath, she pulled out her chair and sat. *Calm down.* Hurt feelings were stupid. So they'd had a booty call. There was *no* etiquette for a booty call. That was the whole point of a booty call. Just convenient sex. Like scratching an itch.

So *why* did she care so damn much?

Because she *did* care. Maybe she couldn't explain the attraction. Jason St. John intrigued her. Infuriated her. And sometimes amused her. Chemistry, pure and simple. Only in their situation, neither pure nor simple.

She groaned but stopped when her office line buzzed.

After taking the call, Tamsyn set the receiver back on the set. Great. A new client. Not that there was so much to be excited about. Another honey trap. Considering how her last client ended up murdered, maybe Scott was right. Was this the appropriate time to cut out that part of the client base? The family business was doing well, actually, better than well. True, there was a time when she'd brought in a major portion of the agency's clients, and her contribution to the bottom line was substantial.

Now, not so much. Holt Investigations was evolving, taking on more and more corporate security clients, including personal protection. At least five new investigators had been hired. Justin had even interviewed and hired a guy who was the nearest thing to his clone for the emerging computer security division. With the new office expansion in the works, was she still a valuable member of the firm? Or were she and her honey trap client base an unpleasant reminder of what the firm *had* been as opposed to what they were headed as Scott had said?

He'd be thrilled if the agency stopped taking her clients. But what would she do? It was a family business after all. And dammit, she was family.

After notifying Ames's distraught mother of her son's death and leaving Irby to console her, Tess gave the living room a cursory inspection. Seth had been fast in filing for the warrant. The warrant was specific for Ames's room, which according to his mother, was located in the basement. Even though Mrs. Ames had given her permission for the search, Tess wanted to keep things neat and tidy. Legally, she couldn't search the rest of the house, but she could use her eyes. Spotless and neat. Lots of peach and seafoam green. Lots of lace and chintz. Last decorated in the early 90s. Photos of her pride and joy sat in a straight and dust-free row on the top of the upright piano. Jerry Ames had been a cute kid with wavy dark hair, pinch-worthy round cheeks, and big blue eyes. That promise of cuteness had taken a wrong turn in his teens. Severe acne and a tendency to pudginess. Probably bullied in school.

She turned the knob to the basement door, opened it, and descended into a veritable hoarder's paradise. Whoa. What a contrast between upstairs and down.

Gingerly weaving her way through stacks of newspapers, interior design magazines, and Doctor Who memorabilia, she reached Jerry's living area. She sucked in a breath. Not really surprising.

Wall-mounted TV. And at least a hundred photos of Brianna Tollison covered Ames's walls.

Sampson, who had followed her downstairs, rolled his eyes. "Holy shit—sorry, boss—can we say he was obsessed? And a Doctor Who fanatic to boot."

"Let Crime Scene pack it all up. Especially his computer. His cell phone wasn't on the body. Probably lost in the river. I'll talk to his mom some more while you get busy."

"The Doctor Who stuff, too?"

Tess shook her head. "Leave it. Some of it could be valuable. I'd rather not take responsibility for anything damaged or lost."

"Sure, boss."

Tess picked her way back upstairs. Jerry's mom sat on a chintz sofa, red-faced and weeping. Sitting beside her, Irby was looking acutely uncomfortable with the grieving woman. "Ron, could you make Mrs. Ames a cup of coffee? Would that be all right, ma'am?"

Sniffing, she nodded. "That'd be real nice."

With a grateful expression, Ron rose and headed to the kitchen where she could hear him bumbling around.

Tess sat and began gently, "I know this is a difficult time for you, Mrs. Ames, but if you could help me, I have a few questions."

The distraught woman sniffed and nodded. "Go ahead, Detective. I want to find out who killed my son, even more than you do."

"Of course." Tess always hated intruding on a family member's grief. Just part of the job. She pulled out her digital notepad. "Jerry was your only child?"

"Yes. His father left when he was five, so Jerry's been my whole life."

"Did he have a cell phone?" Hell, everyone had one. Still, she had to ask.

"Yes." She sniffed and blew her nose into a tissue. "He was really into that tech stuff."

"We didn't find one with him. Could he have left it here? Maybe in the kitchen when he ate breakfast or something?"

"Oh, no. He wasn't careless. He always had it, in case I needed him. My heart, you see." She patted her chest. "I have palpitations."

Tess nodded. "Do you have someone to call? Someone who can stay with you?"

She nodded. "My neighbor. Do you want me to call her now?"

"Just a few more questions first. Was Jerry acting normally? Did he seem worried or upset?"

"As a matter of fact, he'd been a little edgy ever since his boss, such a nice young woman, was killed. He took it hard. I always thought he was sweet on her. But I'm pretty sure he didn't have a chance. Jerry's shy—I mean, he *was* shy—around women."

"What about his other friends?"

"He didn't go out much. Just to work and back home. I called the police this morning when he didn't come home, but they said he was a grown man and would have to be missing twenty-four hours before I could file a report."

"You called the department this morning?" She'd have to check that out. She stood. "Here's my card. If you think of anything else, be sure to give me a call. It doesn't matter what time."

"Thank you." Mrs. Ames took the card, setting it aside on the end table. "I think I'll call my neighbor, now."

Tess nodded. "Again, I'm very sorry for your loss. I'll do my best to find out who killed your son."

She stuck her head into the kitchen. "Ron, I'm heading back to the house. Check in with me when they're through bagging and tagging. Talk to her neighbors. See if they've noticed anything or anyone unusual in the neighborhood."

Irby nodded as he poured a cup of coffee. "Will do, boss."

She turned back to Mrs. Ames. "Please understand that while we're in the throes of this investigation, you'll only hear from us when we have something definite, not before."

"I understand."

Poor woman. Little did she know it often took months, if not years, to solve a murder, if at all. More to the point, was Ames's death connected to Brianna Tollison's? Ames certainly appeared obsessed with Brianna Tollison. But did an obsession with his boss mean he'd killed her? That line of thought—too obvious. Besides, who killed Ames? Why kill him? And why now?

What did he know? More to the point, had Jerry been stalking Brianna and seen something—like her killer?

Chapter Twenty-one

After a restless night, Justin picked up Aguilar's trail when he left the casino. Aguilar lived in a tract house on the outskirts of Thackerville. No kids' toys in the yard. He drove past Aguilar's house and parked in a cul-de-sac at the end of the street.

Aguilar's neighbor on the left didn't answer the door. The neighbor on the right wasn't inclined to talk and was belligerent as well. She'd probably tell Aguilar he was being investigated. Justin walked around the block and located the house whose yard was back to back with Aguilar's.

He knocked, then backed off the small porch.

A teenaged girl wearing a ton of eyeliner, a red bikini, and earbuds opened the door. Her head nodded to the unheard beat of music on her smartphone.

Pay dirt.

She pulled out one of the earbuds. "What are *you* selling?" she asked him, fluttering her lashes. She arranged her body in what she probably thought was a sensuous pose.

Holy moly. Jail bait for sure. He stepped onto the porch. "Not selling anything. I'm a private detective. Justin Lackey." He pulled out his card and handed it to her. "I'd like to ask you some questions about your neighbor to the back, Jake Aguilar."

Her gaze flickered to his card, then back. "Sure, Justin. I'm Debi—that's with one B and an I. What do you want to know?"

"Does he live alone?"

"Right now, he does. But he had a girlfriend until about a month ago."

"Is this the girlfriend?" He pulled out his cellphone with the age-enhanced photo. "Now her hair might be different."

"Yeah, that's Kay." She smiled. "She's blond now. Wears it short."

"What else can you tell me about her? How long did she live there?"

Her dark lashes fluttered again. "Sure you don't want to come in? I've got a cold beer in the fridge."

He took a step back. "No, better not. Anything else you can tell me about her?

"Well, she was totally skinny when she moved in back in the spring, but she picked up a few pounds. Looked healthier. First off, I thought maybe she was your average tweaker. But after I met her, she wasn't like that, at all. More like she'd just been down on her luck. Like *way* down. Sometimes, we'd hang out by the city pool when I chucked school. We'd talk."

"Did she ever talk about her family?"

"Nah. Mostly *I* talked. I'm the nosy sort, but she'd get real quiet whenever I asked her anything, so I gave up."

"Any idea where she is now?"

"Nah, she took off after their last big fight. Been about a month ago."

"Did you see her leave?"

"Yeah. *I* drove her to the bus station."

"*You* drove her?" Crap. Debi didn't look old enough to have a license, in spite of her heavy-handed makeup. "Do you know where she was headed?"

"Nah. She didn't want me to come in. She made me drop her off out front."

"Thanks, Debi."

"Sure I can't tempt you...?" She twirled the loosened earbud cord.

"Sorry." He shook his head. "I've a flight to catch."

"One more thing," Debi said as he turned to walk away. "She might've—not saying she did, just *maybe*—took some of Jake's money."

He stopped. "What makes you say that?"

"Just the way she held her bag. Hugged it close to her body like it was something precious. Anyway, Jake came over the day after she left. He grilled me, but I didn't tell him nothing. Now, he never *said* she took anything, but he was awful pissed off about something."

"Thanks." Justin walked back to his rental and got inside. He beat the steering wheel with his fists.

So Aguilar had lied. He'd brought Kim home with him. And she'd stolen his money—maybe.

Now, what were the chances the bus station ticket agent would remember selling a certain bus ticket from a months ago?

Slim and none came to mind.

Jason called Special-Agent-in-Charge Chase. "I spent half the day and night with Tollison. He keeps his cards close to his chest. Plus, Oliver had more home security than expected. No luck there. Have you come up with anything?"

"As for his phone, we have surveillance in place. Nothing on Tolliver's landline. We'll be ready. You're sure this is going down tonight?"

"Definitely tonight. But Tollison has to be using burners. All he'll tell me is that I'll be notified in time to do the money transfers. I've arranged to make it appear as if

I'm bouncing the money around his designated sites, but they've all been cloned. He'll never know the difference."

"What about security?"

"His butler is the one bodyguard I've seen. I've yet to see any additional security guards at his house, but that doesn't mean he won't employ extra security for this deal. I'd be surprised if he doesn't. What about possible sites?"

"Tollison owns two warehouses in the area Oliver mentioned. Zero activity at either location. But we have surveillance set up on both sites until we pick up an increase at one or the other."

"I won't be given much notice. Just a call. Then I'll call you." One nagging thought came to mind. "There's a possibility that he'll insist on my accompanying him, rather than just meeting at the site."

"Surveillance will catch any sign of increased activity."

"Good." He added, "Expect a call if I'm in a position to make one."

"We've got your back."

Jason thanked Chase and ended the call.

Jason's future career hinged on a successful result. Screw this operation up and his career path would be flat-lined. His father would be proved right. On the other hand, his old man would deem any success as a fluke. Why bother? He would never convince him of his worthiness, much less impress him. But knowing didn't keep him from seeking—no, needing—approval from the man who reared him. Human nature was a funny thing. Until his mother's death, he'd idolized his albeit distant father. But after being on the receiving end of years of scorn after she passed, the luster of his father's sterling character had dimmed considerably.

***

Late Monday afternoon

Carrie frowned over the figures on the spreadsheet. Flights to and from Texas. Rental car fees. For what?

The office door opened. Justin. She glanced up and pinned him with a focused glare. "It's about damn time you showed up."

"You *missed* me. Well, I'm back." He perched on the corner of her desk, grinning like a Cheshire cat.

"Now, are you going to tell me what the hell you've been up to?"

His expression turned solemn. "Don't get too excited, but I found a trace to Kim."

"What?" She half-rose from her seat. "Why didn't you tell me?"

He gave her a rueful smile. "Didn't want to get your hopes up in case it didn't pan out."

"Well, did it?" She stood, wishing she could wring his neck.

"Not so much." He launched into his tale of tracing her vehicle, the casino, Aguilar, and the teenage neighbor who thought Kim had taken off with Aguilar's money, ending with, "I went to the bus station, and I'm guessing she paid cash. The ticket agent didn't remember her, so we're back where we started. I'll see if I can get into their CCTV system for that general time frame. It's a long shot."

"Yeah, maybe." She sank into her chair. "At least we still know she's still alive."

"Doesn't sound as if she's in very good shape, though."

"Definitely down on her luck. But if she took that guy's money, why doesn't she just come on home?" she wailed in frustration. "She's been gone so long, and it's my fault. I should never have been so hard on her."

"*Not* your fault. None of us blamed you. Kim needed rules. Who knew she'd up and run away?"

"I shouldn't have grounded her. I should've been more understanding. She's just a kid."

"She *was* a kid. She's a damn grown woman now. She's made her choices. You weren't to blame at the time, and you're not to blame now."

"I can't just wash my hands of her. I keep thinking of what she's gone through." She hid her face in her hands.

"I'm not washing my hands. She was my baby sister, too. But you have to face facts. If she wants to come home, she will."

"Or she won't," she said flatly and sniffed. "You're right. I've blamed myself long enough." Her voice broke, but she swallowed her grief and her guilt. "Time to move on."

As if...she ever could.

Uncertainly weighed on Tamsyn's mind as she knocked on Scott's door, then opened it. "Have a minute?" Would he laugh at her idea or take her seriously?

"Sure, anytime." Leaning forward, his expression curious, he motioned for her to be seated. "What's on your mind?"

She eased into the guest chair. "If I were to stop taking honey trap clients, just what would you see as my role here in the agency?"

Scott's jaw dropped. He leaned forward. "Are you serious?"

"Just mulling things over. This whole business with Bree's murder has me thinking I might've just taken my last new client."

A flicker of a smile played about his mouth. "I was hoping you would come to that conclusion, sooner or later."

"Heaven knows I'm not a computer whiz like Justin. And I'm not bodyguard material like Nick or any of those big burly guys you're so busy interviewing and hiring. Frankly, without those clients, I don't see a place for me here."

"Why don't you take some time off?" Scott said with a wide smile. "Give it some serious thought. You haven't taken a vacation since coming to work here."

"Have any of us?" she scoffed. "Vacations don't really fit well with our business model. Or at least it didn't before the expansion plans." She laughed. "And I'll be the first to admit I'm shit at managing the office, so don't suggest that."

His dark brows drew together as he considered. "What about going back to school for another degree?"

"I don't have Allison's medical background, but we got to talking about her legal nurse consultant courses. The legal aspect appeals to me."

Scott's eyes widened. "I could see you as an attorney, a dynamic litigator holding a jury spellbound." His expression grew wistful.

Damn. Guilt flooded through her. Being an attorney had been Scott's dream before reality slammed into their blended family with the deaths of their father and stepmother. "Hm." She placed a manicured nail between her teeth. "I have no right to ask. You're the one who should go back to school."

"No." He shook his head. "That ship sailed. I'm too busy with the expansion to go back to school."

"But I have to complete my BA first. I've already taken a lot of the prelaw curriculum, so that's all to the good. Then there's the prep to take the LSATs, and after that, there are another three years of law school. We're talking at least another five years." She let out a muffled groan.

"What else have you got to do?" He winked. "It's something to think about. We could afford to pay your salary anyway."

"No way. I'm good for the undergrad tuition. I *do* have some money saved. I don't spend it *all* on clothes. But law school—that's a huge expense."

"The agency can write it off if you agree to become our in-house counsel."

"Really?" She leaned forward. "You'd do that?" How unselfish. Just like when he'd given up *his* dream of becoming a lawyer to keep the family and the business together. "No. It's too much. Why don't you go back? This was your dream."

"Asked and answered, counselor. I'm too involved with the business side of the agency." His expression grew solemn. "Now, you'll have to commit to acting as our in-house counsel for say ten years to make it worth the agency's while. There'll be a contract."

"Of course. So I'm committing the next ten years of my life to the agency." Smiling, she shrugged. "You're right. What else is there to do? Work is work." She stood. "Prepare the contract. I'll sign it."

Scott stood, a smile wreathing his face. He offered his hand. "I'm so pleased. You'll be an even greater asset to the agency."

She took his hand. "That's a nice way to put it. Much better than saying you've come up with the solution to a problem, which is what you probably intended to say in the first place."

"Now, Tam..." He ran a finger around his collar as if it were too tight. "I've always valued your healthy additions to our bottom line. It's just time—"

"Time to adapt to a changing business model," she offered with a smile.

"You already sound like a lawyer. I have every faith you'll do well."

"Cool." She smiled at her brother. "Suddenly, I'm so excited. I *will* take a week off. I can't start school until the winter semester, but I need to start the application process. Obtain my transcripts from MTSU. I'm thinking of transferring to Vandy for the rest of undergrad."

"You thinking of Vandy for law school, too?"

"Yeah, if I can get in. I'd hate to have to leave Nashville for law school."

"You wouldn't have to. There's Nashville School of Law. Night classes. Takes four years if I remember correctly since it's geared toward working professionals. Just a suggestion. I checked into it several years ago when I was thinking about finishing my degree."

"You still could. Less expensive?"

"Assuredly. But less prestigious. You'd only be licensed to practice in Tennessee. You might want to consider which school has better percentages when it comes to passing the state bar exam."

"I don't have any plans to leave Tennessee. You've given me a lot to think about. I need to get busy and investigate further. Weigh the pros and cons."

"You have a family who will support you wherever you choose to go."

"I know. You've always supported all of us. I couldn't ask for a better brother." She winked. "Besides, I'm glad I could make your day."

He shook his head and gave an eye roll. "Get out of here."

Tamsyn closed the door behind her, able to feel the ever-so-happy smile stealing across her face.

Carrie came toward her with a questioning look. "Where'd you go? I came back with your coffee, and you were nowhere to be found. What's the deal with that shit-eating grin?" she asked. She pushed her glasses up on her nose. "Come on. Spill."

Tamsyn motioned for her sister to follow.

Once inside her office, Tamsyn sat, then smiled up at her sister. "I have a plan."

Carrie sat her hands on her hips. "All right. Let's hear it."

"I'm gonna finish my undergrad degree and apply to law school."

"Whoa! Seriously? That's fantastic and out of the damn blue."

"I know. I've been doing some thinking. After what happened with Bree, I don't have the heart for it anymore."

"But you just added a new client."

"I know, but she's the last one. My last honey trap. One and done. After that, I'm taking a week off to see what all I have to do to make my plan a reality."

"You told Scott."

"Yeah. He made me the most amazing offer." Ready to do a happy dance and let out a squee, she said, "Anyway, he's—shall we say—happy about the situation."

"I guess so." Carrie's expression grew thoughtful. "What about St. John?"

"Momentary insanity." She gestured washing her hands. "Don't know what I was thinking."

"Are you sure?"

"Sure. Nothing more than a booty call."

Chapter Twenty-two

For some reason, the bullpen was quieter than usual this evening. The acrid reek of burnt coffee hung in the air. Tess glanced over the list of objects taken from Ames's living quarters. A cell phone? "Ron, what's the deal with this cell phone? His mother said he always carried it."

"Boss, Crime Scene found it in the bottom drawer of his bedside table." Irby checked his notepad. "Checked with his mother. She didn't recognize it."

She read further. "Description says it has a red rhinestone case. Doesn't sound like any guy's phone." Could it be Brianna Tollison's cell phone?" Could they be that lucky? "Can we get inside it?"

Seth ambled over to Tess's desk. "When I interviewed her business partner, she said the victim had a red cell phone, and that as far as she knew, she only had the one. Sorry, I didn't put two and two together before now. She used it for work and personal calls both."

Tess tapped a manicured nail on the desktop. "I want to know who that last call was from."

So far, the phone at the other end hadn't been turned on. "If we're lucky, that phone number belongs to Brianna's killer. But if that's the case, it's entirely possible he ditched his phone, and that'll be the end of it."

"Yeah," Seth said with a grin. "But we'll keep trying."

Tess nodded. "Sounds like a plan."

***

The sun was low in the western sky. Jason paced his small office. Anticipation to get the deal done had built up until it seemed as if every cell in his body was tensed for action. He should've heard from Tollison before now. What was he waiting for?

Come on. Ring.

This was getting nowhere fast. Stopping, he walked around the desk and sat, leaning back in the comfortable desk chair. In his mind's eye, he could still see Tamsyn's lush body arranged across his desktop.

Another vision of her straddling his lap in his SUV. Her full breasts in his face. God.

Just thinking about her gave him a hard-on.

Another place. Another time. Why here? Why now?

Had she been sent to drive him absolutely nuts, or did the very fact that he couldn't keep his mind on business mean his father was right: he had no business being an agent, especially in an operation as important as this one.

He slammed his fist on the desk.

Ms. Buntin opened the door to his office. With a quizzical expression, she asked, "Are you all right?"

"I'm fine. Why don't you take the rest of the day off?"

"Sure thing." She glanced at her watch, frowned and shrugged.

Rest of the day off? How absurd. It was already a quarter after four. "Sorry, why don't you come in late tomorrow."

"Ten?"

"Fine." Would he even be around tomorrow? If the deal didn't come off as planned, he might be in a ditch somewhere. If it did, and the principals were in federal custody, he'd be dealing with the debrief and tons of paperwork.

While he waited for Tollison's call, maybe he had time to stop by Tamsyn's just to say... Hell, what was there to say? *Thanks for the booty call.*

Nah. Not gonna happen.

Focus.

His phone signaled a text. **Come out now. I'm waiting.**

Damn! Not a location. Using his encrypted phone, he texted Chase. **Meet's on. No location. I'm to go with him.**

Make or break. This was it.

Tollison's limo was at the curb, along with two black Mercedes. The limo's rear door opened and Tollison leaned forward. "Took you long enough. Get in."

Jason complied, noting that Hughes was the driver. "Versatile fellow," He nodded toward Hughes.

Tollison leaned back and chuckled. "You have no idea."

All sorts of ideas came to mind. None of them pleasant. "Where're we headed?"

"Relax. Hughes has to make sure we're not followed."

"What about the two Mercedes behind us?"

"Rest of my security team."

Great. An additional eight to ten men.

When the limo headed over the Cumberland toward East Nashville, Jason's stomach gave an uneasy flip-flop. East Nashville was nowhere near where his backup and the takedown teams were waiting.

Was it too much to hope that Chase had ordered surveillance on him? Someone who could communicate that neither warehouse in north Nashville was the buy site.

Tollison leaned forward tapping on the glass. "We're good."

Hughes maneuvered the limo into the left-hand lane

and turned. Another block, another turn and so on, until they were headed back over the river. His heart rate leaped ahead when they turned onto Centennial Boulevard. He swallowed the lump in his throat.

Okay. Let's roll.

"Will Oliver meet us at the buy?"

Tollison shook his head. "His presence isn't necessary."

Just like a lawyer, keeping his hands clean.

By the time Tollison's limo reached the warehouse, the sun was a mere sliver over the horizon. Jason breathed a sigh of relief. The Bureau's intel had proved correct. This warehouse was one of the two they had staked out.

All he had to do now was keep his cool, perform the fake money transfers, and not get shot during the takedown.

Piece of cake.

Bored beyond belief, Tamsyn closed her laptop. Might as well take the rest of the day off. What would it hurt to drive by Jason's office?

No. She wouldn't stop.

Well, maybe she would.

She turned down Market Street toward his office building. Just in time to see him enter a limo. The limo pulled out along with two black Mercedes. What was he up to? Was this his operation or was he in trouble?

Damn, her red Boxter wasn't the best vehicle to use to shadow someone.

"Call Tess," she instructed the phone app on her car.

Voice mail. Damn.

"Tess, I just saw Jason St. John get into a limo, and they're being followed by two black Mercedes. I think he's in trouble. What should I do?"

Hell, she knew what she should do.

Go home. Don't interfere. This had to be part of his op. If she followed she could blow the whole deal. And the Feds wouldn't thank her for that. Not one little bit.

Her phone pinged. "Tess?"

"Go home. Don't get involved. I don't know what his mission is, but you don't want to endanger him or yourself. Go *home*."

God, how she hated to be told what to do.

Still, Tess was right. Dammit.

When the limo and two Mercedes turned right, she turned left.

Doing the smart, sensible thing might be the right thing, but she didn't have to like it. Not one little bit.

One of the delivery bays opened, and Hughes drove the limo inside. The cavernous warehouse was empty. Jason scanned the overhead catwalks. Was the team already inside? "What time will they be here?" he asked.

"We're early," Tollison admitted with a grunt. "They should be here in ten minutes or so. They have a reputation for being prompt. "

"Who are *they*?"

"Need to know, son. You don't. Just be ready to do your financial magic when they get here."

Jason gave a quick nod. "Agreed."

Ten minutes later the oncoming headlights of a semi-trailer shown through the open bay. The semi pulled inside and stopped. A silver stretch limo followed the semi into the warehouse.

Tollison's security emerged from the Mercs. Make that eight burly guards armed with automatic machine guns. A *lot* of firepower.

Being naked without a weapon didn't suit him, but going armed didn't tally with his cover as a financial whiz. Against automatic weapons, his ankle backup piece was of little to no use, but it was all he dared to bring.

Hughes exited the limo first and opened Tollison's door. Tollison motioned toward the truck. "Let's go. I wanna check the merchandise."

The semi driver stayed put, but six well-armed men emerged from the rear of the truck.

Dying to get a load of the merchandise, Jason followed Tollison. What was the man selling? Arms of some sort. Whatever the cargo was, it spelled disaster.

Instead of a multitude of crates, there was only one. One large crate, heavily strapped and secured. The rest of the rig was empty.

Crap. A bomb? A fucking bomb.

One of the seller's guards spoke. "Inspect away."

Russian accent. So Tollison was dealing with the Russian mob or possible an ex-SVR agent. And somehow they'd managed to get a nuclear device into the U.S.

Holy shit.

"Open it. I want to see more than a damn crate."

The passenger door of the stretch limo opened. The long trim legs of a woman emerged. Then the rest of her. Red designer suit. Pale skin. Dark-winged brows over glinting gray eyes. A mature beauty. And if eyes were truly the windows to the soul...deadly. "You may verify, and then I want money. Much money." So this was the Russians' boss. Not mob. From the looks of her, more likely a former Russian Foreign Intelligence Service (SVR) operative.

"Patience, Marina. You'll be paid as soon as I have a look at what I've purchased." Tollison inclined his head.

"You will like merchandise. Exactly what you ordered,

Randall."

So Tollison was buying, not selling. Not how things were supposed to go. Jason had expected to be moving Tolliver's money around. "I thought you were selling," he said low under his breath.

Tollison grunted. "I am. Later."

Two deals, not one. Okay. Would the takedown team hold off until the second deal was done? The more bad guys they could take down the better. What about the Russians? Were they just supposed to get away with Tollison's money?

"Give me a hand." Tollison was hauled into the back of the truck. "Open it."

One of the Russian minions pried open the crate.

"Uh-huh." Tollison nodded to Hughes. "Pay her."

Hughes opened the limo's trunk, then pulled out two steel briefcases. He set the cases on the hood of the limo and then opened them. Marina inspected the contents with a nod. "Good doing business with you, Randall." She nodded at her security team. "We're done." Marina, her entire team, including the semi driver, piled into the stretch limo. And they were gone.

Jason waited. No sign of the take-down team. Had something gone wrong? "Okay. You've bought a bomb. Now what?"

"Now we sell it to the highest bidder." Randall smiled. "Open this link on that old school computer of yours. Go through the VPN you set up earlier."

Nodding, Jason set his laptop onto the hood of the limo and opened it. His stomach danced the cha-cha-cha while his fingers moved over the keyboard. Thankfully, he'd considered an auction as a possible contingency.

Tollison sent Jason's phone a link full of numbers. Ah, an auction on the darknet. Tollison was full of surprises.

What the hell are you up to, Randall? A nuclear bomb on American soil, unthinkable. "Randall, any second thoughts?" he asked softly.

"I'm playing the long game, son. Just mind the financial dealings and leave the difficult questions to me."

But an auction? On the darknet? "Just on the side of caution, there's no telling who'll meet your price and what they plan on doing with it."

Tollison eyeballed with laser intensity. "You're starting to piss me off, son. If you want to play with the big boys, you have to take some risks."

"A risk is dealing in pork belly futures." He was careful to keep his tone good-natured, even if his gut was more than uneasy. "A nuclear bomb is a quantum leap of risk."

"You have one alternative." Tollison shot Jason a look full of meaning. "Actually two."

Jason swallowed hard. Tollison had eight armed security men, not to mention, Hughes at his immediate disposal. He nodded, then gave a casual shrug. "Right." He made the VPN connection and followed through a standard protocol to protect his identity and location on the darknet. His mind spun with the ramifications. Was Tollison was actually going to auction off a nuclear weapon to some kind of terrorist group? Who else would want a bomb? Why? Money?

Had to be more than money. What could he want more than money?

Power?

Chapter Twenty-three

Jason's gut roiled with unease. He shifted his stance. What good was one measly backup weapon against the firepower of Tollison's security team? To cover his discomfort, he asked calmly, "So what's next? Are you leaving it here?"

"My warehouse, Jason," Tollison said archly. "I can do whatever the hell I want with it. You're asking too many questions. If you must know, my security team will move it to another site and guard it there. Wouldn't want Marina, now that she has my money, to double-cross me and come back for the merchandise. Not unheard of."

"Nice people you're doing business with."

"Hmph." Tollison leveled his beady-eyed gaze at Jason. "The kind of deals I make aren't always with those found in the social register. That's not where the real money is."

But a bomb? He'd expected a major stash of weapons or even a possible bio-weapon, but a freaking nuclear device... "Have you considered you might get caught in the havoc caused by a weapon of mass destruction?"

Tollison scoffed, "Nothing ventured. Nothing gained, son."

"But what do you hope to gain by selling a bomb to who-the-hell-knows-what kind of nut job?"

"It'll be a nut job with *lots* of money. It'll explode. Chaos will reign. Someone will step to the fore and lead." He let out a bark of laughter.

"Will that be you, or do you have someone else in mind?"

"When I sell this bomb," he paused with a self-satisfied smile, "I'll have the funds to mount a presidential campaign."

"As I said, you or some other megalomaniac?"

"I guess we'll have to see how it plays out, Jason." He gave a rueful smile. "Pity you won't be around to find out."

"What? I'm not going anywhere." Hell. Was Tollison onto him? What had he done wrong? Too many questions. Too many objections. His father was right. Too inexperienced.

"You think I didn't know you were a Fed all along. Maybe I didn't at first, but I have resources you know nothing about. You're blown, son." He gestured to his security team. "Bury him. Make it deep."

Jason barely had time to register that he'd been betrayed. Was it his inexperience? Had he been too eager, or had Oliver become suspicious of Tamsyn's presence in his office? Two of Tollison's security men grabbed him. One placed a weapon to Jason's temple. His heart pounded until he thought it might explode. His hands shook.

Tollison grunted. "Not here. I'd rather not have his federal agent DNA splattered all over my warehouse. I don't want him found...ever. Get me."

The behemoth holding the gun nodded. "Got it, boss."

Focus. He'd been in tight spots before. Never like this. "You're nuts, Randall. Losing your daughter has affected your frigging mind."

"You can't talk your way out of it, son. I liked you, but I kept you under surveillance. You think you could keep your involvement with that little P.I. quiet? So much for my daughter's devoted fiancé." He snorted his disgust.

Oliver. That smarmy bastard had to be Tollison's

source, at least as far as Tamsyn was concerned.

"I can explain that. She tried to set me up for your daughter. Yeah, Bree didn't trust me, so she sicced that P.I. onto me. I didn't take the bait, but the P.I.—man, she wouldn't leave me alone, man. That's the only reason I had anything to do with her. You gotta admit she's one tidy little package. You can't blame me for tapping that. Any red-blooded man would."

Tollison jammed his knee into Jason's groin. "Get him out of here before I lose it."

An explosion of exquisite pain. Stars danced before his eyes. He collapsed in a fetal ball of agony, trying not to whimper. And failed.

So much for talking his way out of a tight spot.

Before he could regain his sense of self-preservation, another vehicle entered the warehouse. The sound of doors opening and boots on the ground. Shots fired.

Backup. Finally.

A clearly accented voice rang out, "So Randall, I think I want more money, or I will take back my merchandise." To the sound of boots on the ground, add the click of stiletto heels on concrete.

Crap. The Russians. Tollison was right.

"What's this?" she asked, nudging his knee with a pointed toe. "Your pretty-boy financial guy is on the ground. Looks like he's in pain. Did you hurt him? What did he do?"

From his position, all Jason could see were stilettoes and long, long legs. He tried to squirm away.

"Traitor. He's a Fed."

"Oh, what a bad boy." She leered down at him. "Can I have him? Pretty please. I have issues of my own with the Feds. We could have such fun, pretty boy." She ran the toe of her stiletto pump along his thigh. He flinched, assuming her idea of "fun" and his were polar opposites.

"You can have him," Tollison growled, "but you leave my merchandise alone." He aimed another kick into Jason's side.

"No. I don't think so." She walked over to Tollison and shoved a weapon into his ample midsection. "I take back my bomb. *Now*."

Then he heard, "FBI. You're surrounded. Drop your weapons."

His heart sped even faster. Would they drop their weapons? Of course, they'd have to.

But no.

Automatic gunfire erupted. His groin still dancing with fiery pain of Tollison's knee, he crawled to get out of range.

Too late.

"Where you going, *pretty boy?*" Hughes mocked, looming over him. "Randall might've liked you once. I never did."

Chapter Twenty-four

The evening air had a definite fall chill when Tamsyn stepped from the car. Shivering she ran into the house. A comfortable warmth and the spicy aroma of beef stew drifted through the house. Yum.

"What can I do?" she asked Carrie who stood stirring the pot with a wooden spoon.

"I thought we'd have salad and French bread. You can make the salad. All I have to do is stick the French bread into the oven. The stew needs another hour to simmer, though."

"Sounds perfect." Tamsyn slung her bag over the back of a bar stool. She slipped off her jacket and took it to the front closet, hanging it up with a sigh.

"What's wrong?" Carrie called from the kitchen.

Tamsyn ambled back to the kitchen. "Nothing. Why?"

"You have a worried expression. And I heard you sigh all the way in here. Something's bugging you. What is it?"

Tamsyn opened the fridge and leaned over to pull out the veg drawer. "I think whatever Jason's up to is going down tonight. I saw him get into a limo with a laptop. They were being followed by two Mercedes. I have to say he looked a little tense."

Carrie stopped stirring, her green eyes wide. "What? Are you stalking *him* now?"

"No!" she protested. "I was just driving by. His office is just up the street from ours—like you don't know that." She pulled out a package of romaine, another of baby spinach, and a single cucumber, and then carried the veggies over to the cutting board.

"Maybe that means he'll be leaving town soon? Is that why you're upset?"

"Maybe." She shrugged, pulling a knife from the drawer. Gingerly she tested its sharpness with the tip of her finger. Yeah, sharp.

"You wouldn't like that would you?"

"Nothing to do with me." Wishing Carrie would drop the subject of Jason St. John, Tamsyn opened the packages of romaine and spinach. "Where's the salad spinner?"

"Under the right cabinet on the end...where it always is."

"Okay, then. Snark much?" Hunkering down, she removed the salad spinner from beneath the counter. Adding the greens to the container, she turned on the water to rinse.

"If only that were true." Carrie's tone was a little too smug.

Frowning, Tamsyn turned the water off. "I'm not in the habit of lying."

"Then you're lying to yourself." Carrie arched one brow.

"Okay, maybe I'm just worried he could get hurt if things don't turn out like they're supposed to." Tamsyn placed the lid and began pulling on the spinner.

"That's more like it. Besides, he's a trained agent. Give him some credit."

Tamsyn wrinkled her nose and stuck her tongue at her sister. "How about a taste of the stew?"

"Nope, not yet. The spices need more time to mingle." Carrie took a taste instead, then nodded. "I was right. Needs more oregano. Have you thought any more about your plan to finish your degree?"

She nodded. "I'm going to get started on it tomorrow. I'll request my transcripts and apply to Vandy to complete my BA."

"Good." Carrie poured a handful of spice into the palm of her hand and then rubbed her hands together over the pot of stew. "I hope you'll stick to it."

"I will. Why wouldn't I? Anyway, I've taken my last honey trap, and then I'm done. And speaking of which, I need to go over my case notes for this one."

"Husband, boyfriend, or fiancé?"

"Husband. Those are the ones I hate." She took the cucumber and began slicing away.

"That's understandable. Wrecking a marriage is a big responsibility."

"But I don't see it that way. If a man's willing to cheat, *he's* the one wrecking his marriage. Not me."

"Careful with that knife. You could do some serious damage."

"Not my style. I let their wives and significant others do the dirty work."

A few minutes later, Tamsyn heard Scott and Justin come home. Scott breezed into the kitchen, followed by Justin. "Tess says she won't be too late."

"Why don't one of you set the table?" Tamsyn said, smiling. "I've already made a salad. "

"I know what a chore that was." Justin ruffled the top of her hair.

"Be gentle," Carrie cautioned. "She's worried about our FBI friend. "

Scott frowned. "Still? What's he done now?"

"Nothing, but I think his op, or whatever you call it, is going down tonight. So I'm worried." Fighting tears, she turned, ready to run upstairs.

"Hold on." Scott stopped her in the doorway. "Does

Tess know?"

"I called her."

"Then there's nothing you can do. He's a big boy. He knows what he's doing."

"Intellectually, I know that." Of course, he knew what he was doing, but that fact wouldn't stop her from worrying until she heard he was safe.

Tamsyn set the table, and Carrie was ladling out bowls of stew when Scott's phone signaled a text. He stopped and read it. "Crap. Tess won't be here, after all. Some big shootout in north Nashville."

"A shootout?" Her heart pounded. Had something gone wrong with Jason's deal?

"That's all she said. She didn't volunteer any more than that. Too busy."

"Jason—"

"That doesn't mean it has anything to do with him or his mission."

"But it *could*."

"Calm down," Scott cautioned. "Nashville's a big city. There's a shootout somewhere, all the time."

"Sure." Right. Calm down. "What would you be doing if the love of your life was in danger?"

Scott's jaw dropped. "Whoa! 'Love of your life?'"

"Did I say that out loud?" Tamsyn gave herself a mental dope-slap. "I mean—I just— Fuck! I care about him. All right?" Cheeks flaming, she rushed from the kitchen.

"Let her go," she heard Carrie say.

Tamsyn stopped in the hall. She turned to face Carrie. "So I exaggerated a bit. I didn't really mean he's the love of my life."

"But he might be," Carrie said gently. "Come on. Dinner's ready. Have a glass of wine. No one's going to think less of you if you care about the guy. We understand.

We love you."

Care about the guy. Right. It was more than that, even if it made no sense.

No sense at all.

After dinner, Tamsyn pushed back from the table. "I'll clean up. You take a break," she told Carrie.

"I don't mind."

"No. I'm too nervous. I can't explain it, but I need something to do." Her skin—creepy crawly. She rubbed her arms to rid herself of the sensation. If she could just hear from him, she could relax. Finally, she gave in and texted him. **What's going on?**

No response.

Okay, so she was weak and needy. The booty call was supposed to be a one-off. But not seeing or hearing from him was driving her crazy. How could she have let things go this far? What made him so different from the other men she'd been with?

Face it. He'd gotten under her skin, into her pants, and worked his way into her heart.

No. No. He had to be a player. Hadn't he romanced Bree to make his cover convincing? Absolutely. He had.

So, where was he? What was happening?

Tamsyn rolled over, then pounded her pillow. Still, she still couldn't shake the feeling that Jason was in trouble. Something *had* gone wrong. She just knew it.

She rolled back over and reached for her phone. Still no response to her text. Maybe he had more than one phone. Maybe he didn't carry both while he was undercover.

What if he had and her text had blown his cover?

With a groan, she set it back on the bedside table and tried to get comfortable enough to sleep. Her phone beeped. Her heart pounding, she snatched it from the table. "Jason?"

"No, Tess. Jason's in the E.R. Vandy. Figured you'd want to know."

"What happened?" Her stomach sank. Her breath came in gasps.

"I can't go into detail. Actually, all I know is he's on his way to surgery."

"I'm coming over there."

"No. You won't be allowed to see him. He'll be guarded."

"But—"

"No buts about it. Stay home. I'll let you know something as soon as I know something."

"Okay. Thanks." Stay home and wait by the phone to find out if he was going to live? Like hell, she'd stay home. Not in a million years.

Hurriedly she pulled on a pair of jeans and a sweatshirt, then ran downstairs.

Justin was still up. "What's going on?" he called from the den. "Where're you going this time of night?"

She stuck her head into the den. "Vandy. Tess called. Jason's hurt. On his way to surgery."

He sprang from his recliner. "I'll go with you." He grabbed his jacket from the hall tree.

"How will we ever find him?" Tamsyn asked. The entire Vanderbilt University campus was enormous. The hospital proper had grown by leaps and bounds over the last decade.

"We can park here in the emergency area," Justin said. "When we find out where he is, I'll move your car to the parking garage. Sound like a plan?"

Still troubled, Tamsyn nodded "Will he be here under his real name? I don't know what it is."

"I doubt it. We'll be on the lookout for agents. They're unmistakable."

"Suits, ties, earbuds. Like on TV?"

"Pretty much."

"Fine." Tamsyn opened the car door and raced across the well-lit parking lot. Breathless, she blew through the automatic doors and stopped at the window. "A friend of mine has just been admitted." She lowered her tone. "He's an FBI agent."

The E.R. receptionist gave an eye roll. "What's his name?"

"Jason St. John."

"Sure, honey. Take a seat in the waiting area. I'll be sure to notify you if any federal agents are admitted." The receptionist's snide tone, a sure indication that notifying Tamsyn would be the last thing she did.

"You don't have to be rude," Tamsyn said with some snark.

Justin placed a calming hand on her shoulder. "She's just doing her job."

"Whatever." She shrugged his hand away and started to stalk toward the waiting area.

Tamsyn spied Tess's partner as he stopped to talk to the receptionist. Tamsyn stopped and ran over to his side. "Detective Foyle. It's Tamsyn Holt. I'm Detective Holt's—"

He nodded. "I remember you. What're you doing here?"

"Tess called me about Jason. How is he?"

He shook his head and pulled her to a quiet corner.

"He's in surgery. That's all I know." His dark brows drew together. "Didn't Detective Holt instruct you to stay home?"

"Maybe..." She batted her lashes. So what if she was using her feminine wiles on the unsuspecting detective. She needed to know if Jason was all right.

He raised one brow. "You're just cluttering up the waiting room. It may be a couple of hours before he's out of surgery. After that, you still won't be allowed to see him. He and the other agent, who was shot, will both have guards. You might as well go home and try to get some sleep."

So much for using her feminine wiles. Apparently, Tess's handsome partner was immune. "I want to be *here*."

Careful, don't whine.

He turned to Justin. "Make her see sense. Take her home."

Great. Just like the guys to join forces.

Justin nodded. "Come on, Tam. "

"Traitor," she muttered.

Reluctantly, she allowed him to lead her from the hospital. "You'd better never pull that *us guys got to stick together and protect the little woman* routine on me again."

"You should see yourself. Red eyes. Slumped shoulders. Hell, you're so tired, your ass is dragging."

She shot Justin a growl. "If I weren't so tired, I wouldn't let you get by with a remark like that." Truth be told, curling up on her bed, or anywhere, seemed a delightful prospect.

Tess was right. Detective Foyle was right. And as much as she hated to admit it, Justin was right too.

Chapter Twenty-five

Tess yawned and downed another slug of coffee. Tuesday morning, already. What a cluster-fuck last night was. Cleaning up after the three-way shootout with the feds, Tollison's henchmen, and the Russian mob had taken until the early hours. The final result was two of Tollison's men down for the count. Ditto three Russians. And two FBI agents in the hospital. One large suspicious crate, holding who the hell knew what, in federal hands. By the time her report was done, there wasn't any point in going home. She'd showered and changed into a clean blouse at the station.

With no sleep, she still had two murders on her books. No rest for the wicked so she must've been very naughty in a previous life.

And since Brad Oliver had come up with more excuses to avoid a formal interview than a teenager late for curfew, it was time to rattle his cage.

Bright lights. The soft rasping whir of some machine. Had he been hit by a truck? And his head—why was he wearing a cap in bed? And something in his throat. Something choking him. He yanked on the humongous tube.

"Number two is awake." He heard the distant sound of a nurse's voice. "Hold on Mr. Stone. That tube is to help you breathe."

Someone knew his true surname? Trying to speak, he gagged. He'd wanted to tell her he'd be able to breathe just fine if it weren't for the damned tube. He grunted and would've pulled it out except for the meaty hand of a male nurse. "We'll get that ET tube out. Give us a sec to check your oxygen level."

Finally, the tube was out. And he could breathe, for real this time. "Thanks," he croaked. "How bad?"

"Oh, just a couple of gunshot wounds, resulting in a collapsed lung and a dangling ear." The nurse delivering these bits of news with a smile had to be a weightlifter from the look of his massive arms and thick neck. "The surgeons fixed both of those. You have another tube in your chest. That one isn't ready to come out, so don't go messing with it. And you have a dressing on your head. And if you want to continue looking like a normal human being, I wouldn't screw around with that, either. You have an I.V. in your arm. You shouldn't mind that one too much because that's delivering your pain meds."

"What else?"

"The surgeon will be in shortly. He'll go over everything."

"There's more?" he groaned.

"I hit the high points."

"Okay." So, he'd survived, no mean feat since the last thing he remembered was Hughes and his gun. Jason's lids grew heavy. He blinked.

Good drugs. And drifted to sleep.

Tess and Seth strode into the law offices of Oliver, James, Smithfield, and Oliver. So Oliver had joined a family firm. The offices were plush with old world elegance. And that took a helluva lot of money. Just how dirty was the firm's money, anyway?

The firm's receptionist looked up, her blue eyes widening when Tess produced her badge. "Since Mr. Bradford Oliver, Esq. was too busy to come to us."

"You'll need to make an appointment."

"No, we don't. We'll see him *now*."

The receptionist's cheeks flushed a deep red. She hurriedly made a call. "He'll see you, but his time is short. You really should've—"

Tess blew past her. "Come on, Seth. We don't want to waste too many of Mr. Oliver's billable hours."

She opened the door the receptionist indicated to a corner office. "Mr. Oliver. I'm Detective Holt." She nodded toward Seth. "This is my partner Detective Foyle. Thank you for fitting us into your busy schedule." Even seated, Oliver was a big man, defensive end big, in an expensively tailored charcoal gray silk suit. His red-veined cheeks were full, his dark eyes deep-set, giving him a heavy and sullen appearance.

He snorted. "Make it quick. I'm busy."

Hm. He ought to be since one of his clients was in federal custody. But Randall Tollison notwithstanding, she still had his daughter's murder to solve. "So are we, Mr. Oliver. We're investigating the brutal murder of Brianna Tollison."

"I'm well aware. I attended her funeral. I assume that's why you're wasting your time questioning me."

"How well did you know Ms. Tollison?"

"I met her briefly when we were teenagers, but the reason I attended her funeral was to pay my respects to her father. Randall Tollison is one of my clients and a friend, as well."

Very aware of that fact. "So you hadn't seen Ms. Tollison recently."

"I took her to a high school dance, so at least twelve years ago. No contact since." He glared from beneath heavy brows.

Seth cleared his throat. "Our records tell us you're a man with a temper. There've been numerous calls to your residence. Altercations with your wife, loud enough that your neighbors grew alarmed and called the police."

With an obvious eye roll, Oliver glanced at Seth. "You know how it is. My wife's a hysterical bitch—at times." He chuckled. "Whose wife isn't? That's what I want to know."

"Where were you between 1:45 and 4:45 last Tuesday?"

"That when she bought it?" Jutting his chin, he leaned back in his plush leather chair. He smirked. "Seriously? You're asking for my alibi?"

"Seriously, I am," Tess replied. "As an attorney, you should understand we have to ask these questions." She leaned forward, placing both palms on his desk. "So, where were you?"

So he hadn't expected to provide an alibi. What an arrogant asshole. Or he was innocent.

Oliver tapped on the keyboard. Peered at the screen, his eyebrows arched. "I had back-to-back appointments Tuesday afternoon. My office staff will tell you I was here the entire time." He leaned back, assuming an arch expression.

Tess couldn't resist imitating his smug demeanor. "I need a list of the clients you met with."

"You'll need a warrant for that."

As expected. "We *will* be interviewing your staff."

"Go ahead." He stood. "We're through. You can show yourselves out."

Tess nodded, then said to Seth, "Interview his staff."

She headed for the door, then stopped. She turned.

"I'm surprised you're not downtown, given Ms. Tollison's father is in federal custody.

Oliver's gaze narrowed. "I'll be seeing him as soon as you haul your officious ass out of here. I told you I was busy."

She held back a smile. Good. She'd gotten his goat. Her phone beeped with a text from the M.E. **Ames autopsy report ready.** "I'll be seeing you, then."

As she drove back to the stationhouse, Tess reviewed Oliver's interview. If his staff verified his alibi, then she was barking up the wrong tree. Even if he'd raped Brianna years ago as Tamsyn had asserted—and there was no reason to doubt her word—it didn't mean he'd murdered Brianna. Given his professional and personal relationship with her father, could Brianna have made threats? Definitely couldn't count him out. Not yet.

Tamsyn awoke with a start. Jason? She sat up and reached for her phone. Dammit. She'd slept until almost noon. And not a call, a text, or even a smoke signal from Tess about his condition. Enough of this crap. She hit speed dial for her sister-in-law. She should know something by now.

Afraid to breathe, she waited for Tess to answer. No. Straight to voice mail. Dammit. It must be bad if Tess was ignoring her calls.

Maybe she was just busy.

Well, whatever...it was time to haul her carcass out of bed and go back to the hospital. If she couldn't see Jason... Well, as they said, there was more than one way to skin a cat.

***

"Okay, we have Ames's autopsy report." Standing in front of the murder board, Tess scanned the last page with the conclusions. "Let's see. Blunt force trauma from a smooth cylindrical object like a pipe. No recreational drugs in his system. Water in his lungs. So someone hit him with a pipe or something similar, fracturing his skull. The blow was sufficient to kill him, but not immediately, so he was dumped into the Cumberland where he drowned. Trace and other tox reports are pending."

"Not much to go on, boss," Malik said. "Crime scene searched both sides of the river for two miles each way. No sign of the murder weapon."

"Boss," Ron Irby interjected. "What evidence do we have that the Tollison and Ames's murders are connected?"

"None yet," Tess admitted, "but he worked at Ms. Tollison's design firm. I don't like coincidences. He was definitely stalking her. We have evidence of that from all the photos he took, many where she didn't seem to be aware of his presence. So he might've seen something or someone. Go over those photos with a fine-tooth comb. There might be something or someone in the background. You never know."

Irby nodded. "So we find Ames's killer and we might find Ms. Tollison's."

"Bingo. Breanna Tollison was killed in a rage, but Ames's killer was more controlled."

"But doesn't that mean two killers?" Irby argued.

"You might think that, and many times you'd be correct, but in this instance, I disagree. If Ames saw or even thought he saw something, Tollison's killer might've seen him too. Ames was a loose end. His murder was one of expediency. We really need to find his phone—like yesterday."

This case was dragging on too long. The longer the

final resolution eluded them, the longer Tamsyn remained in danger. "Seth, where are we on getting Eric Chapman's fiancée, Megan Hastings, in here for an interview?"

Seth stretched. "She's been out of town, *coincidentally* ever since we interviewed Chapman."

"Coincidence. I hate that word. When is she due back?" Her phone signaled a call. She glanced at the screen. Tamsyn. Frowning, Tess hit the button, sending the call to voice mail. Tamsyn could just hold her horses. She'd learn soon enough the extent of St. John's injuries.

"The maid says she's not sure when she's due back."

"Where is she?"

"Megan and her mother are off to The Big Apple. Shopping for her wedding gown and trousseau. So I insisted the maid give me the number of their hotel. I spoke with Ms. Hastings briefly. She confirmed she was with Chapman during the hours in question. I told her we still needed a formal statement." He gave a casual shrug. "I guess I could—"

"Go to New York? Not a chance." Tess shot him a smirk. "You're my right-hand man, Seth. You're far too valuable to let you out of my sight," she said with an eye roll. "Call her again. Use your considerable charm. I want her back for a formal statement, ASAP."

"Valuable. Charming. Yeah, that's me." He made a show of buffing his nails on his lapel.

"Okay. I still like either Chapman or Oliver for this. Frankly, they both give off some weird-ass vibes. We need to keep digging."

Sampson "Why don't I go deep on Oliver? I could go back to the time he was in college. Check on assaults reported, but dropped."

"No need," Seth spoke up. "I've already done that. It took some digging and a threat or two, but there were several rape complaints made, while he was in school, but dropped. It'll take a warrant to get names and details."

"Then keep working on a warrant." Tess wrote *Warrant pending* beside Oliver's photo.

Sampson frowned. "Oliver's a rapist? There's nothing in—" He fumbled through a sheaf of papers on his desk.

"Right." Tess wrote on the whiteboard beside Oliver's name. *Rapist?* "That's my fault. I haven't written up the witness report yet. It's from one of Bree Tollison's friends from school. A complaint was never filed, but I know that friend. I trust her."

"Got it." Sampson smiled. "Wouldn't be an in-law, would it?"

Tess sighed, "It would. So I'd like to keep her name out of things, as long as possible." Keeping Tamsyn out of the case and away from harm, not an easy task.

Tamsyn showered, dressed and headed out to the hospital. Maybe she could convince the ICU nurses how important it for her to see Jason's file. If he was still under guard, it probably wouldn't make any difference what the nurses said. Maybe her sister-in-law Alison could help. She spoke nurse fluently.

Still in the parking lot, Tamsyn stopped and called Allie. She'd been a case manager at Centennial before leaving for her legal nurse studies. Maybe she had a contact at Vandy, someone who owed her a favor.

"I can't help you, "Allison said. "If he's under federal guard, no one, who isn't a doctor or a nurse, is getting into that unit."

"But—"

"No buts about it. No Vandy ID. No visit."

"Thanks for nothing." Disgusted, Tamsyn let out a

frustrated sigh. Hell, she was a detective. There had to be some way to get in to see him.

One visit to a nearby uniform shop and one lab coat later, she was ready. All she needed was an ID badge. Surely Justin could whip one up in no time.

Another phone call. "Justin, darlin'. I need a favor." She told him what she wanted.

"Oh no, you don't. You're asking to get arrested."

"No, I won't." She let out a huff. She'd just have to pull out all the ammunition. "Justin Michael Lackey, all you need to do is make me an official Vanderbilt University Medical Center ID badge. I *know* we have the equipment. This isn't the first time we've used forged ID's to get around hospital ICU protocol."

"This is different. This is a federal matter, and I don't like messing with the Feds. Must I remind you that St. John is an FBI agent?"

"And I'm your sister. I *need* to see him. Get crackin'. I'll be there in ten minutes, and you'd better have it done." She punched the disconnect button and backed out of her parking spot.

Tamsyn waited, her toe tapping. "Well...?"

Groaning, Justin slid the badge across his desk. "Don't call me when you get arrested."

"I won't. And if I do, I'll call Tess." She smiled. "Look, this is a no-brainer. I'll be in and out, five minutes or less. No one will be the wiser."

Justin rolled his eyes. "Scott will kill you."

"Pfft," she scoffed. "He might *want* to kill me, but he *can't* fire me."

She glanced down at the ID. Disbelief swept over her. "You made me a housekeeper? You should have made me a nurse or a lab tech. I already bought a lab coat."

"It's a known fact. No one pays any attention to housekeeping," he said with a smirk. "Buy a set of gray scrubs and voila: you're invisible. Then wrangle a mop bucket and you're all set." He stretched and shot her a smug smile.

"Wrangle a mop bucket? You're nuts."

"All part of my charm." He let out a low, evil chuckle. "Besides, you have less chance to screw up than you would if you're part of the professional staff. You might actually be expected to be able to do something."

"You have a point. Mop bucket it is."

Back to a different uniform store to purchase a set of scrubs. "Damn it, Justin," she swore under her breath. The smallest size of scrubs the store had in stock was a size large, and she was most definitely a size small. Still, no one would be paying her any undue attention in these things. She paid for the scrubs and headed back to the hospital.

Attired in the world's worst fitting scrubs and armed with a fake ID badge, Tamsyn headed up to the SICU, keeping an eye out for an abandoned mop bucket or housekeeping cart.

It didn't take long to find an unattended cart. While one of the housekeepers was standing in front of a vending machine and chatting with one of her coworkers, Tamsyn grabbed the opportunity and eased the cart down the hallway. She breathed a sigh of relief when no one challenged her at the ICU entrance.

All she had to do was spot the agents who were guarding Jason's cubicle. Her gaze swept around the SICU. Sure enough, there they were. Who could miss two tall men in dark suits with tell-tale earbuds? One seemed so young, he probably only shaved once a week.

Tucking her head she, maneuvered the cart over to the second cubicle. She picked up a bottle of cleaning spray and sailed between the agents.

So far. So good. She could see Jason had an oxygen tube, and there was another tube connected to some kind of apparatus where the fluid fluctuated. He appeared to be asleep. Anxious for contact, she reached to touch his hand.

"Hold it!" A heavy hand clapped on her shoulder.

She jerked away. "I was just going to cover his hand. It looked cold."

Jason's eyes opened. "Tamsyn, what—"

The older agent grabbed her arm. "You have no business here. How'd you get in?"

"I walked in. I just needed to see if he was all right."

"*No* visitors."

"She's okay," Jason protested hoarsely. "I know her."

"No matter." He turned to the younger agent. "Call Metro. Get her out of here."

Glaring at the older agent, Tamsyn squared her shoulders. "I'll have you know. I'm a private detective."

"Then you should know what you're doing could be construed as tampering with a witness in a federal investigation. And against the law."

"But—"

The agent propelled her from the cubicle. She tried a sweet smile. "Just call Detective Tess Holt. She's my sister-in-law."

The younger agent managed to keep a straight face. "I'll take her down to Security. They'll hold her until Metro picks her up."

"Fine. Just get her out of here."

Tamsyn turned back long enough to give Jason a quick wave and a smile. At least she'd seen for herself that Jason would recover. And that was enough for now.

Tess stood outside the interrogation room. In their usual heavy-handed way, federal agents had swanned in and taken over interviewing Tollison. All she could do was watch. Tollison sat silent and stone-faced while his attorney, Brad Oliver, did the talking. Obviously, the feds would charge Tollison under terrorism statutes. Home Land Security or some other federal entity would arrive any minute to remove Tollison to an undisclosed location.

Good riddance.

Her cell phone beeped. Suspect being held at Vandy security office. Possible attempt on Agent Stone.

Stone? Was that St. John's real name? Or was that the other injured agent?

On my way, she texted.

Suspect claims to know you.

Crap. Who else could it be but Tamsyn?

I'll kill her. Sometimes, being a member of a large and bustling family, who happened to be private detectives, was more than any homicide detective ought to have to handle.

Not to mention inconvenient.

Chapter Twenty-six

Jason adjusted his position in the bed, wincing when his chest tube jerked against his skin. Still, he had to smile. Imagine the nerve: Tamsyn's bluffing her way into the ICU and wearing a pair of baggy scrubs. Going to all that trouble for what—a ten-second visit. Just imagine.

And the little wave and smile she gave him before being removed by his fellow agents. Yeah, she was something else. She'd certainly made his stay in Nashville more interesting. Speaking of his position in Nashville, would the local office keep him, or would he be reassigned to outer Montana in disgrace for compromising his cover and almost getting himself killed?

Maybe not. His mission had been accomplished. Randall Tollison was in custody and a weapon of mass destruction was safely in federal hands. No matter, his father still wouldn't be impressed.

The best scenario would be remaining assigned to the Nashville office. And even better, he'd have more time to figure out one feisty P.I. and decide where they were headed—if anywhere. One thing for sure, there was a connection. A pull. Whatever you called it, it was powerful and like nothing else, he'd ever experienced.

Cooling her heels, Tamsyn sat in Security while one of the guards scowled and tried to watch the monitors. "Look, I wasn't going to hurt the agent," she said. "I just wanted to make sure he was going to be okay." She fluttered her lashes, hoping to soften his expression. "You see, I'm sort of in love with him. You *could* just release me. That way, Detective Holt won't have to come down here. She's my sister-in-law, and let's say she won't be pleased. Letting me go *could* go a long way to promote peace in my family. I just needed to see if my fella was all right." She gave him an encouraging smile.

The guard narrowed his gaze, his expression clearly saying he wasn't buying her BS. "Agent Tighe said to hold you," he said evenly. "That's what I'm doing."

"Fine." She tugged on the shoulder of her scrub suit. Damn thing kept sliding down.

She glanced at her phone. She'd already been waiting fifteen minutes. "Detective Holt is in the middle of a huge murder investigation. She might be *hours*." She lifted her shoulders in a shrug. "Hours."

The security guard gave an eye roll. "Great."

"So I can go?" She half rose from the chair.

"Sit," he growled.

She sat.

A buzzer sounded. Tamsyn heard, "Detective Holt." A rush of relief swept through her body. Finally, she could get out of here. And if Tess wasn't too upset, maybe she would talk to the agents and get her some alone time with Jason.

The guard buzzed Tess into the office. Frowning, she strode to the desk. "I'll take charge of her. Accept my apologies for the disruption." Her tone was curt and no-nonsense.

No, she wasn't happy. Not at all. "Tess, I'm so sorry."

"No, you're not. Not one bit. We'll talk later. Let's go."

Tess ushered her from the office and down the hall.

"Uh, my car is in the parking garage across the street."

"No matter. I'm taking you home. Someone can pick

up your car later. I'm not letting you out of my sight until you're home and out of my hair." Tess's face flushed pink, then reddened the longer she spoke. "I was in the middle of observing an important interview. And I had to leave for *this*. Seriously, you need to grow up. St. John is an FBI agent, and if you hadn't been my sister-in-law, you would've been arrested and placed in federal custody."

"But—" What was the point in trying to explain? But Tess would understand if anyone could. "Tess, I'm sorry. Really. There's something about Jason that makes me want to throw caution to the wind. I don't know why I get so reckless sometimes. I haven't jeopardized your job, have I?"

"We can talk about it later."

They reached Tess's vehicle. She opened the back door. "Watch your head."

Tamsyn ducked and entered the SUV. "You're making me ride in the back like a perp?"

"You got it. Act like a perp. Ride like one."

"I'm sorry. I just wanted to see Jason. I needed—"

"Don't start. I don't want to hear it now. Later."

Tamsyn sniffed. "It smells funny back here. Did some drunk puke?"

"I don't normally pick up drunks. Is that your excuse? Were you drunk when you bluffed your way into the ICU?" She slammed the door, then walked around the SUV to the driver's door, opened it, and sat behind the steering wheel.

"No." Tamsyn huffed. "It was a plan—not a very good one I'll admit—but Justin should've made me a nurse's ID, instead of a housekeeper's."

Tess's head whipped around, her blue eyes flashing. "Justin made your fake ID? Of course, he did. I'll be talking to him next." She turned on the ignition and backed from the parking space.

"Dammit, Tess. We're a detective agency. It's part of the job."

"And Scott approved this screwball plan of yours?"

"Well..." Tamsyn hesitated. "...time was of the essence."

Tess let out a loud sigh of exasperation. "Translation: Scott had no freaking idea what you were up to."

Tamsyn shook her head. "You know me. I'd rather ask for forgiveness than permission."

"Perfect," Tess scoffed. "That might just go on your tombstone someday."

"That's harsh." No matter what her homicide detective sister-in-law thought, Tamsyn wasn't about to sit idly by while Jason was in the hospital. Now at least, she knew he was going to live. But his injury had brought home, like nothing else could, just how dangerous being a federal agent was. In spite of how P.Is. were routinely portrayed on TV, she'd never carried a firearm, although, at Scot's insistence, she had taken weapons training.

She really ought to give Justin a head's up so that he could smooth things over with Scott. "I'd rather you take me to the office."

"No. I need to get back to the station. I'm dumping you at the house. The sooner I get back, the better."

So much for smoothing things over. "So what all went down last night? There wasn't anything in the news. Or very little anyway."

"Nothing you need to worry about. It's way above my pay grade and definitely above yours.

Tamsyn smiled. "No problem. I'll worm it out of Jason—that is if I ever get to see him alone again."

"Pfft," Tess scoffed. "You can try."

"I *do* have powers of persuasion."

"No doubt. And I'm not interested."

Tess pulled into a spot in front of the house and parked. She emerged and opened the rear passenger side door. "I don't want to see you anywhere near this case. Leave St. John alone. Let him heal. If he seeks you out, then well and good. Otherwise, keep your nose on this side of West End. If I have to haul you out of there again, I'll arrest you myself."

"Sheesh." Tamsyn shuddered. "Why don't you tell me how you really feel?"

"Don't you have anything to keep you busy and out of my hair? Aren't you supposed to be applying for law school?"

"Yeah. Right. Guess I could work on getting my transcripts ready."

"Thank you!" Tess slammed the car door.

"Sorry—no, I really am. It's just he—"

"I know." Tess gave an exaggerated eye roll. "He makes you *reckless*. Now, I gotta go."

Tamsyn watched her pissed off sister-in-law pull a U-ey and drive away.

I went too far this time.

Before she could make it to the porch, her cell phone chimed. She glanced at the caller ID. "Justin, what's up?"

"How'd your mission go?"

"I'll tell you later. Just know that Tess is on the warpath."

"Oops."

"Oops is right. Better warn Scott."

"Will do. By the way, Carrie's already left the office, so I added a new client for you."

"No! I'm not taking any more clients."

"Come on. One more won't hurt. She'll be in first thing in the morning. Nine sharp."

"Geez. She's eager. Okay, I'll see this one, but no more.

I already have one set up for tomorrow night. Are you available? Shouldn't take too long. I'll give you the 411 tonight."

"Gotcha."

Later that afternoon, Jason leaned back against the cool pillowcase. Now that his chest tube was out—thank heaven—he'd been moved to a private room. Two agents were still in place outside his door.

The door opened. SAC Chase walked into the room. "I see you're much improved."

He straightened. "Yes, sir."

Chase took a spot at the foot of the bed. "Thought you'd like an update."

"Most definitely, sir."

"We have control of one large weapon of mass destruction. Any idea what Tollison was planning?"

"Just speculating here from what I know of the man: sell it, and after an attack on the U.S., step into the chaos with a bid for high public office."

"Tollison will be moved to a black ops site. We'll find out everything. Sooner or later."

"My impression—it won't take long. He's soft." Jason considered, then asked, "What about his lawyer, Brad Oliver?"

"He's trickier. Other than what you know personally, we have no evidence on him. Currently, he's acting as Tollison's attorney of record, but where Tollison's going, a lawyer won't help. We're keeping a close eye on Oliver though."

"What about the Russians?"

"They're a tougher lot than Tollison and his crew, especially the woman. I wouldn't be surprised if she isn't ex-SVR."

Jason nodded his agreement. "So in spite of nearly getting myself killed, the operation was a success."

"It was." Chase nodded sharply. "Formal debrief in a day or two. When you're stronger."

"Yes, sir." Jason resisted the urge to salute.

Chase's gaze grew focused. "You'll be able to pick and choose your next assignment. There's a spot in New York for one, leading a task force. It would be a promotion."

"Or I could stay here? In Nashville?"

Chase's brow furrowed. "Sure that's your next best move? Staying here wouldn't be a promotion. Anything but."

"Career-wise, probably not. Personally, maybe." Nervously, he smoothed wrinkles from the bedsheet.

"I see." Chase's expression grew inward. "Think about it long and hard before you decide."

"I will, sir."

After Chase left, Jason leaned back. 'Pick and choose?' All things considered, a surprise. He needed time to think, all right. Tamsyn Holt was special. Beyond the undeniable strong sensual connection, she was unpredictable. Life with Tamsyn would never be boring.

That evening, Tamsyn paced from one end of the kitchen to the other. Tonight was her turn to cook or provide takeout. Definitely not in the mood to cook. Too cold to grill out. Not in the mood for Chinese or Thai. Pizza and salads—now that would work. She called Castrillo's. One veggie and one meat lovers, extra-large, and seven Greek salads should do it, in case everyone showed up.

Otherwise leftover pizza for breakfast. She smiled as she disconnected.

Right away, her cell phone rang. "Hm." She didn't recognize the number, but it was local. "Hello?"

"Tamsyn?"

"Jason." He called! "You must be a lot better if they're letting you use the phone."

"I'm out of ICU, still have the guards though, so I thought I'd call and thank you for your visit." He chuckled. "You went to a lot of trouble, but you didn't bring flowers."

"Cute. I think they might've looked out of character on the housekeeper's cart. Are you really better?"

"Yeah. The chest tube is out. I never knew when they put it in, but I don't mind saying it hurt like hell coming out."

"Ouch."

"The surgeon says I'll be here another day or two, just to make sure my lung stays expanded."

"Let me know when you're discharged. I'll give you a ride home."

"No need. I can call an Uber."

"Really. But I want to. Besides, I'd like to see you without your fellow agents hanging around."

"All right." He let out what sounded like a sigh of resignation. "I'll give you a call."

After Jason ended the call, Tamsyn couldn't help but smile. He was in a room, his chest tube was out, and he'd called. Apparently, being stalked by a crazy woman in oversized scrubs hadn't turned him off.

The sound of the French doors opening caused her to turn around.

Justin tromped inside. "Brr. I think the rest of the leaves will go tonight. It's supposed to be rainy and windy."

"I know. I hate it when the leaves are all gone. We've had such beautiful autumn weather."

"Yeah, autumn-smautumn, screw that. What's for dinner?" He leaned his elbows on the countertop.

"Castrillo's pizza and salads."

"You ordered a meat lover's, right?" He thumped his chest. "Man needs meat."

Tamsyn let out a giggle. "Doofus. Of course."

"Okay." He fished his mobile phone from his pocket. "I took the details for your new client."

She let out an exasperated sigh. "I really like to meet my clients first. Talk about expectations and that kind of stuff."

"Yeah, I know. That's why I told her to come in at nine."

"What's she like?" She took Justin's phone, skimming his notes. "I really need more than what you have here. For one thing, I need a photo of the mark."

"No worries. You can get that tomorrow."

"Couldn't you have just referred her to another agency? Now that I've made up my mind, I don't want to do any more of these cases."

"It's just one. No biggie." Justin shook his head. "She seemed desperate, so I took made the appointment."

With the impromptu client's info in hand, Tamsyn nodded. "All right. Good thing this is the very, very, *very* last one."

Outside, the sky unleashed a torrent of rain. The wind blew, at times so hard the sturdy Craftsman Style house, built in 1914, seemed to shake. The Holt-Lackeys gathered around the oak table for a casual dinner.

"There won't be a leaf left by tomorrow morning." Tamsyn ate the last bite of her salad. "Who's up for a raking party this weekend?"

Carrie glanced out the French doors over her shoulder and shivered. "As long as it's not raining."

"I vote we hire it done," Justin volunteered with a jaunty smile, snagging another slice of pizza.

"Hah!" Tamsyn scoffed. She wadded her napkin into a ball and tossed it at her brother. "You would." She leaned an elbow on the table and sighed.

"Why so glum, Tam?" Justin asked.

"This time of year. Everything is dead. It just gets to me. I prefer spring and summer."

"I don't mind yard work," Nick said eagerly. "Allie and I will help." He shot his newlywed wife a hopeful smile. "Plus, we have Ben this weekend, so he can have fun rolling in the leaves."

Allie cast a warning eye at Nick. "I can help...for a while, but I have homework."

"That's right," Scott commented. "How're your studies going?"

"I love it. The law side is so interesting. I get to use my nursing knowledge without having to empty bedpans."

Justin gave a snort. "And just how long has it been since you actually emptied a bedpan?"

Allie flashed a snarky smile. "Several years, but you know what I mean."

"Ew!" Carrie scoffed. "Puh-leeze, enough! Not while there's still pizza on the table."

Ready to clear the table, Tamsyn pushed back her chair and stood. "Any word from Tess?"

"She'll be late," Scott said. "I have it on good authority she's closing in on a couple of suspects."

Now that was progress. "Who?" Tamsyn asked, her excitement growing. Knowing who actually killed Bree would remove at least one load of stress.

Scott shook his head. "You know Tess. I'm lucky she told me that much."

Tamsyn snagged another piece of veggie pizza. "I think I'll go to bed early tonight."

"You've had a busy day," Carrie said with a smirk.

"Really." She stood then circled the table, picking up the remains of the salads. "Tell Tess her salad is in the fridge if I've already gone up."

Scott nodded. "I'll tell her."

After clearing the table, she set the remaining pizza in the warming oven. "Night all."

She loved her family, but sometimes all the togetherness was a little too much. Peace and quiet were what she needed now.

Whether it was the weather or the time of year, the fact that Jason could've died was finally starting to hit her. He really could've just been gone. No warning. Without a good-bye. Like when her father and step-mother died. Her own mom had died of cancer after a long illness. She'd been so young she could barely remember the pretty mother who seemed to fade away until one day, she was no longer there.

Chapter Twenty-seven

Wednesday morning

Tamsyn glanced at her watch. Her client was late. A whole ten minutes. Maybe she would be a no-show. Even better. That would be a very satisfactory way to end her career as a honey trap specialist. Yes, indeed.

Her phone buzzed. "Your nine-o'clock is here," Carrie said.

Bummer. She sighed. "Send her in."

She rose and opened the door for her absolutely very last client. "Ms. Sullivan. I'm Tamsyn Holt."

"It's Missus," she corrected. "Oh, he'll like you all right." Elizabeth Sullivan was wiry, thin and reeked of cigarette smoke. Her gray eyes were bloodshot, and her frizzy brown 90s hairstyle needed an appointment with a good stylist.

Good thing she paid cash up front. She gestured toward the guest chair. "Have a seat and tell me about your significant other."

Sullivan sniffed. "Just call me Lizzie."

Tamsyn smiled. "When you talked to my brother yesterday, he said you had concerns about Mr. Sullivan."

"Damn right I do." She leaned forward, her elbows on the desk, her expression intense. "I know the bastard's cheating on me. Stays at that place down close to the Gulch every night, then comes home late smelling of other women's perfume."

"If you're that sure he's cheating, why don't you just leave him and save your money?"

And my time.

Leaning back, Lizzie balanced her purse on her knees. "I wanna know for certain. He's a good provider. Don't wanna give that up if he's just drinking." She frowned. "It will be *you*, won't it? You won't assign someone else? 'Cause you're exactly his type. If anyone will make him want to cheat, it'll be you."

"If you're certain you want to proceed, yes, I'll be the agent. I'm the only one in our office who deals with cases of this type."

Lizzie sniffed, then fumbled in her purse for a tissue. "Good deal. Can you do it tonight? I can't go another night not knowing what he's up to."

"I'm sorry, but I already have a case on for tonight. It'll have to be tomorrow night. Is that all right?"

Lizzie frowned, the smoker's lines deepening around her mouth. "I guess it'll have to be."

"You have a recent photo?"

Once more, Lizzie rummaged in her purse. "Here he is."

"Good," she said with a nod, scanning the photo. The mark was ginger-haired cowboy, who wore all black with a white cowboy hat sporting an eagle feather and a bolo tie adorned with a large turquoise stone set in silver. He wouldn't be difficult to find. Good. The sooner she finished, the better. "I just need to know the exact bar and what time he usually gets off work."

Lizzie gave Tamsyn the specifics and then stood. "Thanks a bunch. Better to know—right?"

"Right."

"You can expect a call from me, Friday morning, one way or another."

Tamsyn waited until her client left and retrieved the can of room deodorizer she kept in the bottom desk drawer. "Whew!" She sprayed the room and the chair where her client had sat.

Finished and done.

The last one. Scott would probably throw a party.

She smiled. Her new life beckoned, and she was more than ready.

Tess returned from lunch with Scott, a lunch cut short by her partner's text. She plopped down at her desk. "All right, Detective Foyle, since you interrupted lunch with my husband, tell me you have good news. Anything will do. But it better be good. Just sayin'."

"Sorry about your lunch date with hubby," Foyle said, not appearing very sorry at all by giving her a two-thumbs-up sign. "But I'd say it's very good news, boss. Chapman's fiancée, one Miss Megan Hastings, is sitting in our interview room."

"I thought she was in the Big Apple."

"It seems the perfect wedding dress has been purchased, and she is anxious to assist us in our inquiries. That is, she was *after* I convinced her mother that obstructing our investigation wouldn't read well in the society pages. They concluded their shopping spree, hopped the red-eye, and arrived early this morning." He leaned forward in a conspiratorial manner, lowering his tone. "I even arranged a patrol car to pick up Miss Hastings without her domineering mother."

Tess smiled. "Good work. No, make that amazing work. You've been busy."

Seth beamed. "I aim to please."

Jason unlocked the door to his rental condo, hoping he'd not left dirty socks strewn around. "I appreciate your picking me up from the hospital. You didn't have to."

Tamsyn gave him a quick wink. "I thought it might be the only time I'd get to see you."

He smiled. Seeing more of her was definitely in his plans.

"So this is how an FBI agent lives. " She gazed around his Spartan surroundings. "Gray walls, charcoal carpet. I see you went with minimal."

"Typical bachelor pad," he said with a nod. "It's a rental. I'm never sure how long I'll be in any one place."

"I'm not sure I could live like this. I'm too accustomed to having my things."

"*Things* aren't high on an agent's agenda. Having a go-bag packed is." He smiled, then asked, "Wine?"

"Please."

Gingerly, he walked over to the bar, still favoring his right side where the chest tube had been removed. "White okay?" He opened a bottle of Chablis, then poured a glass.

"Aren't you having any? "

"Not while I'm on pain meds. Better not mix."

"You're still in pain?" She took the wine glass and walked over to the leather sofa, kicked off her shoes and sat with her feet tucked under. "Comfy sofa."

"Just twinges," he said. "It's not too bad." He positioned himself opposite her at the far end. "Tell me about the real Tamsyn Holt. We really haven't done much talking before."

"I guess we haven't, at that." Her mouth twisted up at the corner. "You probably know most of it if you've done your research. I'm part of a blended family. When our parents died in a car crash, Scott gave up law school and took over our dad's agency. Carrie broke off her engagement and did the mom bit and managed the office. They kept us together as a family: body and soul."

"They made big sacrifices."

"They did." She took a sip of wine, then her dark eyes focused on him with laser intensity. "What about you?" She set the wine glass on the side table and scooted closer. "What about the real Jason St. John." She gave him a cheeky grin. "Or is it Stone?"

"Yes," he admitted, pausing. She was getting too close. Needed distance. "Stone is my surname. Being called St. John never suited me."

"Tell me about the real you. Not the cover story version."

He shifted, uncomfortable both physically and reluctant to discuss his load of personal baggage. "My father's an agent, a profiler, close to retirement. My mother's dead. My old man blames me for her death, and I haven't done anything right since she died. That's about it."

"Wow, your bio in three sentences. There must be more. Why—?" She scooted closer, her expression curious.

Again closer. He let out a deep breath. As much as he hated rehashing his history with his father, he decided to let her in. "Why does my father blame me for my mother's death? She was killed in a car crash—something, unhappily, you and I share—after she dropped me off at boarding school."

"That's a tragedy you and your father share, as well. What I don't understand is why it didn't bring you closer?"

"You don't know my father, the esteemed SSA Marcus Stone. He and my mother were a true love match. He adored her. I always felt I was more or less in the way. My mother was the only loving presence in my life. He always resented me, or so it seemed when I was a child."

Tamsyn let out a huff of disapproval. "He sounds selfish and arrogant, and he doesn't deserve a son like you. He should be proud of what you've accomplished."

"I've given up on wanting or needing his approval," he said through gritted teeth. Take a breath, man. Things getting too intense. Forcing himself to relax, he said, "Tell me your plans. Are you going to keep doing vile honey traps?"

"Not so judgy, please. You sound just like Scott." She wiggled closer until she was sitting beside him, thigh to thigh.

He nodded. "Maybe I should've said risky honey traps?"

"As a matter of fact, no. I only have one more client left—no, make that two. Then I'm finishing my degree and then law school, full steam ahead."

"Tell me more." He listened while she talked about her future plans, his admiration for her energy growing. Her eyes sparkled. Her skin glowed. With Tamsyn's passion, he could envision her holding courtrooms spellbound in the palm of her hand. If only he could stay in Nashville long enough to see her dreams come to fruition. "You're going to be extremely busy."

"For the next five years at least. Scott gave up his dream, but he's willing to use some of the agency's resources to support my going to law school. I'm not sure I deserve his support, but I'll take it. Of course, I'll be locked to a ten-year contract to work for the agency. "

"Your family is unlike any I've ever known." He'd seen firsthand how they interacted. The warmth. The genuine caring for one another...even the inclusion of the in-laws, Tess and Nick. A man could do worse. A lot worse, if he were so inclined.

"We sink or swim together—that's for sure." Her gaze grew heated. She inched closer. "I suppose you're not exactly in *fighting* condition."

"Fighting condition?" He chuckled. "You're not far off in your description." True, their session in the rain had been more like a battle for supremacy than lovemaking. Even with his injuries, the sensual pull was there, gathering in the pit of his groin.

"I can be gentle," she murmured, her words falling as softly as a caress.

Need grew, spiking through him. He shuddered. "Can you?" He took a ragged breath.

On her knees she faced him, touching his cheek. Her pupils had dilated until her eyes were black, the flowery fragrance of her shampoo filling his senses. "Bedroom?"

"Hallway," he managed with a jerk of his head. What was he thinking? Disappointing her was not an option.

Tamsyn smiled, knowing she was in the driver's seat. "I'll help you," she said with a smile.

"Ahem," he cleared his throat, adding with a wry smile, "I'm not sure the doctor's instructions included anything about..."

"You didn't ask? How short-sighted of you." She swung her feet to the floor, reaching for him. "Easy does it." She pulled him to his feet.

He frowned. "I'm not an invalid."

"I guess we'll see, won't we?"

Her arm around his waist, they reached the bedroom— more bachelor chic. "Now let's get these clothes off." She unbuttoned his shirt. He still had a small dressing on his right chest. She touched it gently.

"You should leave that on, I believe."

"Right. Let's not bother with the dressing. Any other boo-boos?" She unsnapped his jeans.

"My ear seems to still be attached, and I'm still able to undress."

"My. My. I see *something* still functions well."

"Around you?" He gave an eye roll. "I'd have to be dead."

"Around me, huh."

"You have an effect on me—like no one else."

"I *really* like that sound of that. Just so you know, cowboy. Ditto." She allowed him to step out of his jeans. "Now just let me do the rest."

"Where's the fun in that?"

"I don't want you to re-injure yourself." In spite of her sassy attitude, she had doubts about whether he would be able to make love. Did he have the strength? Time would tell. Sooner rather than later. No matter. All she wanted was to be close to him. Closer than ever before.

"You're smiling. What's so funny?" He slipped the sweater over her head, then removed her bra.

"I'm happy." She offered him her breasts. Her nipples peaked as he leaned down and fastened on one. She trembled. She skimmed her jeans down over her hips and stepped from her scrap of lace panties.

"You're beautiful." Jason's ran his hand over her waist and buttocks. "Skin so smooth."

Her breathing grew rapid. Taking his hand, she guided it between her thighs. She was already wet for him. Hot. He inserted a finger, deep inside. Heat pooled in the pit of her belly, her knees weakening. "If you keep that up, I'm going to need to lie down. My legs feel like overdone spaghetti."

"By all means."

***

Tamsyn lay spooned in the warmth of Jason's strong arms. Never had she felt so well-loved and content with his gentle breathing against her neck. This time, their lovemaking hadn't been a desperate and fierce battle, instead gentle and tender by necessity, but oh-so-sweet. If only they could stay like this forever.

"I have a choice to make, too," he murmured, his breath warm against her neck.

She squirmed around to face him. "Really?"

"If I remain in the Nashville field office, I'll remain in an entry-level position. If I take the position offered in New York, I'll be leading a task force. Success there would mean the first of more promotions."

Oh, no. Truly nothing ever stayed the same. This one moment of sublime happiness dashed with a few words. She caressed his cheek. "Y-you have to do what's best for your career." Her words sounded noble, but the mere utterance of them, devastating. How could she be so selfish? Of course, she wanted him to stay here. But she had her own career path to pursue. Law school, for one. She took a ragged breath. "I'll never forget you," she offered, swallowing the humongous lump in her throat.

"I'm tempted to stay." His hand traveled down the curves of her body.

Tears welled in her eyes. She blinked furiously to keep them from spilling. "And I'm tempted to let you, but you can't turn down this opportunity. New York, then who knows—eventually DC. You could end up being the director."

He chuckled. "Not with my politics and the present administration."

"The present administration can't last forever." She

warmed to the task of encouraging him to do what was best—for him. "Besides, New York is a wonderful city. It has everything a person could want."

"Except you." He pressed a kiss to her forehead, then her mouth, her breasts. He nudged her thighs apart. She reached for him, guiding him home. Passion once more buoyed her to the heights of joy...and then, despair.

"When will you decide?" she whispered, no longer able to stem the trickle of tears.

"Soon." He pulled away from her, swinging his legs over the side of the bed. "It has to be soon."

Sitting up, she sniffed. "Go to New York. That's where the action is. Besides, I'll be so busy finishing up my BA, then law school. I won't have time...to screw around like this." She'd chosen her words deliberately to underplay what she really felt. What she really meant was she'd be so busy she wouldn't have time to miss him, but that sounded so weak.

So needy. So female.

"I see. Decision made." His tone grew brittle. His body rigid, he swung his feet to the floor, then stood. "I'm hitting the shower."

"Good." Her words had the desired effect. "You won't regret it." But *she* would. Hell, yes, she would. She gathered her clothes and dressed, determined to be long gone before he finished his shower.

After making a very hasty retreat from Jason's apartment, Tamsyn popped by the office. She tapped on Scott's door. "Can we talk?"

Her brother smiled up at her, motioning for her to take a seat. "Sure thing. What's on your mind?"

Quickly she told him how matters lay between her and

Jason. "Did I say the wrong thing?"

He leaned back, eyeballing her. "You mean did you royally screw things up by not following your heart? You're the only one who can answer that."

"I have at least five years of school ahead. He'll wither away here in Nashville, especially when he could be in New York, leading a task force and forging a career that could take him to the top of the Bureau. He'd grow to resent me for keeping him here."

He leaned forward. "Did you tell him any of that?"

"No."

"So he's supposed to read your mind." He shook his head. "Women."

"No. He needs to take that position in New York City. I'm committed to staying here and following my plan. That's all there is to it."

"Nothing is written in stone. You're free to do whatever you want. Go where you want."

"I've made a commitment to myself. And to the firm."

Scott shrugged. "So feelings be damned? Sounds to me as if you've made up your mind." He threw his hands up in surrender. "Why ask my opinion?"

"Because I think I'll die without him." She hid her face in her hands.

"And you definitely didn't tell him that."

She raised her head. "Of course not! I'm not some weak sob sister who can't get along without a man." Yet maybe she was, or else why was she here?

"No. But you may end up being a *lonely* sister, though."

"I knew you wouldn't be any help." She sprang from her seat. "Thanks for nothing."

"Hold on." Scott frowned. "There might be another solution."

"What?"

He pushed away from the desk, his expression growing solemn. "I need to give this idea some further thought before I say more."

Tamsyn groaned with frustration. "What?"

"Later." He gave her a mysterious smile. "Go home. You're supposed to be taking some time off. Get out of here."

"Agh! Just give me a hint."

"Not yet."

"You are *so* irritating." She stood, ready to leave.

He flashed a wide smile. "Part of my job description as your boss and big brother."

She couldn't help but return the smile. "All right. You're the boss. See ya!" She gave a quick wave.

As she left the office, she couldn't help but wonder what his idea was. Would he offer Jason a job with the agency? Would Jason even consider such a step-down? Granted, having a former FBI agent on staff would add to the agency's street cred, but what would it do for Jason?

Jason took a long hot shower, more to give himself time to think before he said something he regretted. He stepped from the shower, dried off, then wrapped a towel around his waist. He emerged from the bathroom to an empty bedroom.

"Tamsyn?" He sighed. Dammit. Of course, she'd taken off. That *was* her final answer.

What the hell was wrong with her? Was what they just shared nothing more than a booty call? Were the closeness and tenderness all in his mind?

No woman had ever affected him the way she did. From the first moment he'd mistaken her for a working girl, the attraction had been intense. In spite of his first impression, he found her to be smart. Sexy. Aggressive. And ambitious.

Conversely, it was ambition keeping them apart. His and hers. Sixty years ago there wouldn't have been any question about his choice. Or hers.

But the good old days of male chauvinism were gone. Not that they'd been good for anyone but male chauvinists.

A long distance relationship wouldn't be any kind of solution because law school was no joke. Besides, she'd made it clear all she had time for was a casual romp.

His father. He could just hear his father's derision if Jason elected to stay in Nashville in order to pursue a relationship with Tamsyn. Even though his father had adored his mother, he'd never understand Jason's sacrificing a promising career move to be with a woman who wouldn't give up *her* dreams. But what he felt when Tamsyn was in his arms made his resolve to rise in the Bureau weaken. Was impressing his father worth the risk of losing the woman who could turn out to be the love of his life?

Before he could answer this life-altering question, his cell phone rang. "Agent Stone."

"Scott Holt here. I understand you might be leaving Nashville now that your mission is completed."

How had Tamsyn's brother gotten his number— Tamsyn? Probably. "That's certainly a possibility. I haven't made my decision yet."

"Am I to understand my sister has an issue with that?"

"No issue. Your sister has her plans. I have mine."

"There could be another solution."

"I'm listening."

***

Tess observed Eric Chapman's fiancée through the two-way mirror. Megan Hastings didn't appear to be a day over eighteen. Blond. Very petite. She sat, her arms hugging her chest.

What are you afraid of, Megan? Afraid you'll drop your fiancé in it? Does he already have you under his thumb?

Questions that needed an answer. Might as well get on with it.

She opened the door. Gentle. Be gentle. "Ms. Hastings, I'm Detective Holt. Call me Tess."

The blonde's lashes fluttered shyly. "Okay."

"I need you to verify something for me. Can you tell me where you were on Tuesday the twentieth from 1:45 until 4:45 in the afternoon?"

"Yes, I was at my fiancé's house." She reiterated the address, her voice tremulous, her head bobbing. "We were making wedding plans."

Word for word. Chapman had her well-rehearsed. "How are they?"

Megan's blue eyes widened. "What?"

"The plans? Big wedding?" Smiling, Tess leaned forward, encouraging.

"Oh, yes." Her shoulders relaxed, probably thankful the hard questions were over. "We're getting married at Christ Church Cathedral."

Megan might've relaxed a bit, but there was still a certain hesitance in her manner. "Did you find your perfect wedding gown in New York?"

"Oh yes!" Her eyes sparkled, showing the first real signs of life.

"What style?"

"It's a ball gown." She shook her head. "My mother wants to see me like a princess. I don't really care, but I wanted to make her happy."

Eager to please. Poor sap. A big ball gown would wear her, rather than the other way around.

"Which designer did you choose?"

"LaSalle. That's the one my mother liked best." Megan kept her gaze cast down as her forefinger traced small circles on the top of the table.

"What about you? Which designer was *your* favorite?"

"Oh, Felicia Martine. More restrained. You know, elegant and not so showy. But my mother *really* had her heart set on a ball gown."

"You like to please those you love, don't you."

"Of course." Megan met Tess's gaze. "Doesn't everyone?

"What if someone you loved asked you to do something you believed was wrong?"

Megan averted her gaze. "I guess it would depend on their reasons."

"You'd even lie for someone you loved, wouldn't you...if you thought there was a really good reason?"

Almost imperceptibly, Megan nodded yes, but she replied, "No. No, I wouldn't lie."

"You certainly wouldn't lie to the police, would you?"

"N-no."

"But you have. You've lied to me, haven't you?" Of course, it was an educated guess. Everyone lied to the police.

Tears welled up in her eyes. "No-o-o," she wailed. "I didn't lie."

As much as Tess hated browbeating this young woman, the job meant getting to the truth. "Believe me, I understand how it is. After all, Eric is your fiancé, and you love him. Are you sure he loves you, Megan, or are you just easier to manage than his last fiancée?"

Red blotches appeared on Megan's neck. "I-I don't know what you mean." She clasped her hands as if to keep them from shaking.

"If you tell the truth, Megan, we can protect you."

"Tell the truth? You'll protect me?" She hid her face in her hands.

"Eric wasn't with you that day. Was he? Did he tell you to say he was?"

She straightened, jutting her chin. "Yes, but he has a secret job, and he can't tell anyone. He's an agent for the government. His work is hush-hush."

So little Megan had fallen for one of the oldest lies in the book. "I'm sorry, Megan, but Eric Chapman has lied to you. He's not a secret agent. He needed an alibi for the time of Brianna Tollison's murder. He beat her to a bloody pulp. If you keep protecting him, sooner or later, he could very well do the same to you. He doesn't care if you get into trouble for lying to the police. All he cares about is himself." Pile on the pressure. It wouldn't take any longer than thirty seconds for her to break.

"No! He wouldn't lie to me. He *loves* me."

"Where were *you* from 1:45 until 4:45 on the day Brianna Tollison was murdered?"

"I-I don't remember."

"Of course, you do."

"All right!" Her blue eyes sparked with anger. "I was at Eric's house, waiting for him. We were supposed to be working on our guest lists. But when he came home, he had blood all over the front of his shirt. That's when he told me about an op that went wrong, and that since we were about to be married, it was okay for me to know he was a secret agent. I-I washed his shirt and took his suit to the cleaners. The blood didn't all come out of his shirt, because I forgot to use bleach. I didn't dare let him know that, so I just ripped it up to use for dusting."

Bingo! Be still my heart. Tess turned to Seth. "With Megan's testimony, we can get a search warrant for Chapman's house. I'll start on that."

After Megan signed her statement, Tess turned to her partner. "Seth, let's arrange a safe house. We don't want anything to happen to her."

"On it, boss." Foyle rose and left the room.

"A safe house?" Megan's tremulous voice caught Tess's attention. "H-how long?"

"Your fiancé has already killed one woman. It's just until we can arrest him. If he's not granted bail, you should be able to go home."

"If he's granted bail, you're saying I could be in danger."

"Yes. You'll be testifying against him."

"I-I don't know if I could do that—I mean, in a courtroom in front of everyone. Can't they just use my statement?"

Tess tamped down the rush of exasperation, continuing gently. "Your statement is enough to get him brought in for questioning and for charges, but unless he pleads guilty, you'll have to testify in court. That's the law. Otherwise..."

"He'll go free." Megan's body trembled, the shudder clearly visible. "He'll be *so* mad."

"Yes. That's why you need to be in a safe house."

"I need to call my mother, tell her where I am."

"No. That's the last thing you're going to do."

At that moment, a cell phone chimed. Megan gasped. "It's Eric. I have to answer."

Tess held up a hand. "Wait. If you talk to him, can you

keep it together?"

Megan took a ragged breath. "I-I don't know."

"Turn it off. Right now." She extended her hand, palm upward. "Give it to me."

"He won't like that." Gingerly, the young woman shoved it toward Tess.

"Tough." Tess took the phone, turned it off, and removed the SIM card. "In case he placed some kind of a tracking app," she explained.

Megan's chin dropped. "He might've. He always seems to know where I am."

"That settles it." Tess stood. "I'll see how my partner is doing on that safe house. We'll have your fiancé in custody as soon as we can get a warrant."

Closing the door behind her, she instructed a female officer to remain with Miss Hastings. "No phone contact. She's headed for a safe house."

Chapter Twenty-eight

Jason listened to Scott Holt's proposal, shaking his head. Unexpected. But doable? "I think you've misunderstood my relationship with your sister. Tamsyn made it clear this afternoon that she's not interested in anything serious. She won't have time. If I accepted your generous offer of a partnership in the agency, it could place undue pressure on her. First and foremost, you have a family agency. But Tamsyn, or maybe even the rest of your family, could object."

"I know my sister pretty well. I can't speak for her, but the way I see it is she may have been trying to do the right thing where your career is concerned."

"So you're saying she basically dumped me for my own good?"

"That's one way to look at it."

"Here's another way. If she—and only she—asks me to stay, I will consider it."

"Dude. You're as stubborn as she is."

"Such a situation is fraught with pitfalls. Suppose I accept. We get together for a while, and then we break up. You'll have family board members who are at odds...or worse, at war."

"What about a trial period—say a year—you can opt out. Your buy-in will be held in an interest-earning escrow account. If after a year, it's not working, you can take your money and run. You'll be no worse off."

"Except I will have trashed my career with the

Bureau."

"With your credentials, you'll be an asset to any venture you choose. Hell, you could open a competing firm—not that I would like that to happen."

"You've definitely given me something to think about. But I won't pressure Tamsyn to change her mind."

"Let me handle my sister."

Jason agreed. *His sister.* What a family. Here was a brother who was going the distance to ensure his sister's happiness. But so many things could go wrong. Given Jason had his mother's inheritance, as well as a healthy savings account, he could manage the buy-in. But if Scott was wrong about Tamsyn's intentions, and she truly didn't want anything more than a casual relationship, he might as well pack his bags and head for New York.

Tess reviewed the list of evidence seized from Eric Chandler's house. Several items intrigued her: four mobile phones—two of which were burners—red-stained rags, washed, but apparently not bleached. Hallelujah!

Her phone rang. "Detective Holt."

"Boss, you're never going to believe this." It was Seth. "Eric Chandler's downtown in Missing Persons. He wants to file an MP on his fiancée."

Life was good. "Bring him over. I'd just love to talk to him about his missing fiancée." A missing fiancée who was safely tucked away in a Connor Inn suite with two officers keeping tabs on her. "I'll talk to Sgt. Byrnes in MP. He's an old pal of my dad's."

While there weren't any forensics back yet on any of the evidence, she had enough to hold him based on Megan's signed statement. "We need to get warrants on these phones, so we can dump the calls. One of them might just be Jerry Ames's missing phone."

"On it, boss."

With any luck at all, the last call on Brianna's phone might be to one of the burners found in Chapman's house.

Tess watched Eric Chapman through the glass. He sat with arms crossed, his body tensed. Pasting on a smile, she entered the interview room.

Chapman sprang from his chair. "Why was I brought over to another station? Why am I in homicide? Has something happened to Megan? It's not like her to just disappear. We're in the middle of planning our wedding. Her mother said she left early this morning, and she hasn't seen or heard from her since. Why were they called back to Nashville? They were supposed to be in New York for the rest of the week."

"Calm down, Mr. Chapman," Tess said firmly. "Have a seat and I'll answer your questions as best I can. First, I need to get this formality out of the way. You have a right to remain silent."

His jaw dropped. "You're reading me my rights. Am I under arrest?"

"Anything you say can and will be used against you in a court of law. You have a right to an attorney—"

"I—"

She held up a hand. "Let me finish. If you can't afford an attorney, one will be provided for you by the state."

"I'm confused. Is Megan dead? Tell me! I'm not saying another word."

"Megan isn't dead, as far as I know."

"You haven't called me over here to identify her body?"

"No. Did you understand your rights as I read them?"

"Yes. Now, where's my fiancée?"

"Based on a statement Miss Hastings has given, we're holding you on suspicion for the murder of Brianna Tollison."

"Ridiculous!" Chapman's face grew red. "Megan told you I killed Briana? That crazy, dumb bitch." The last he muttered under his breath. "On her best days, Megan is a bit ditzy. Why would you listen to anything she says?"

She could see the wheels spinning as Chapman continued, his face growing redder.

"You see, Megan's very insecure. She was always jealous of Bree. Before she and her mother left for New York, we had a little spat—nothing serious. I can't understand why she's trying to implicate me in something so absurd."

"Let me assure you that Brianna Tollison's murder was anything but absurd. It was brutal and heinous."

"Yes. It was a tragedy. I misspoke." Chapman sucked in a deep breath. "Where's Megan? I need to talk to her. Just give me a few minutes alone with her. I'll get her to see sense. She'll tell you she made up a bunch of lies to hurt me."

"Seeing how you treated your previous fiancée, I don't think you'll be seeing your current one anywhere but in a courtroom."

"Lawyer." He leaned back, his face red with rage. "Lawyer. That's all I have to say."

Tess rose. "Wise choice, Mr. Chapman." He'd said plenty. Disparaging his current fiancée told Tess exactly what kind of man he was. Evidence would tell her the rest.

She turned to the officer guarding the door. "Take him to a holding cell. We have 48 hours to go over the evidence from his house—"

"You searched my house?" Chapman sprang from the chair, his eyes wide with rage, or maybe alarm. What was he afraid they'd found?

"Your cleaner didn't call you?" Tess faced him with a smile, then added, "I guess you just can't get good help nowadays."

He leaned across the table, his expression ugly, all traces of civility washed away. Was this the face Brianna Tollison saw just before she died? "I'll have your badge, you bitch. I'm warning you. I know people in this town. For your information, I'm an agent of the federal government, and there are explanations for what you might've found at my house. But I'm sworn to secrecy."

She leaned forward, so close she smelled his acrid coffee breath and the nervous sweat his body had begun to exude. "And once I've proved how you battered Brianna Tollison to death, it won't matter how many people you know. As for being a federal agent—pfft! " she scoffed. "You might've been able to convince Megan of that, but I know better. If that were indeed true your handlers would've already contacted us. Yes, that's what they do when we apprehend one of their agents in the midst of an inquiry. If you were a government agent, you'd know that. No. What you *will* be is the new boy in general population—that is, if you're not on death row."

The color drained from Chapman's face. He sank back into the chair. His Adam's apple bobbed as he swallowed hard.

There. Just what she wanted to see. Fear. The fear that came from the realization he wasn't going to talk his way out of this.

Gray skies. Gray mood. Gray life. Tamsyn sat at the kitchen island, sipping a wine cooler. More than anything she wanted to get drunk. Damn drunk, truth be told. If

Justin hadn't screwed up, tonight would've been her last honey trap client. If only she could stay home and sulk. What was Scott up to anyway? Honestly, nothing she could think of would induce Jason to give up a promising promotion in New York City. Compared to the Big Apple, Nashville was the boondocks. Staying here would be a setback, especially now when he had a choice.

Her phone signaled a text. Scott: NEED HELP WITH FOOD. FRONT DOOR.

She slid off the stool and ran for the door. Chinese. She smiled. When Scott stopped for Chinese, he always bought enough for a buffet. Pigging out on Chinese would substitute nicely for getting drunk.

"I see you overbought as usual," she said, opening the door with a merry laugh.

"And I see your mood has improved." He bustled through the door, maneuvering two of his four bags into her arms.

"The aroma of Cashew chicken has a way of doing that."

Tamsyn set her two bags of food on the island and began removing the containers.

"Drowning your sorrows in a wine cooler?" he remarked with a grin.

"Food's better." She paused, wondering if she should plunge right in with questions.

Before she could ask her brother anything, he volunteered, "I offered Jason a partnership in the agency."

Her jaw dropped. "You did what?" A slew of condiment packages slid to the floor. She grabbed for them but missed. "Are you trying to ruin my life?" she huffed, retrieving the packages and setting them back on the counter.

Scott's dark brows drew together in a puzzled expression. "Not the response I expected."

"You thought bribing him was the way to go? Well, way to go!" Wait a minute. It could be the ideal solution...maybe. She took a breath. "What did he say?"

"He'll think about it." Scott unpacked the rest of the food.

"*Think* about it? Not exactly a ringing endorsement, is it?"

"It's a thoughtful response," Scott said. "As he pointed out, there could be pitfalls."

"Already looking for problems? If he can't even be bribed to stay in Nashville, then he's made up his mind to go to New York." She made a handwashing gesture. "Well, that's that."

Scott gazed at her intently. "Hold on. I think he'll take me up on the offer if you tell him you want him to stay."

"No way." She shook her head. "I'm not begging him. If he takes you up on your offer, it's because that's what he wants." Tears sprang to her eyes. "Dammit. I've got a mark for tonight. When Justin gets home, tell him I've gone to shower and change. And you'd better save me some of the cashew chicken. I'll eat when I get back home."

Hopefully, tonight's mark would be cut and dried. If he didn't take the bait, she could be home before the food got too cold. She would be more than happy to inform her client if her husband was true blue.

Wiping away the tears, she ran for the stairs. Damn her interfering brother. And damn Jason for not jumping at the chance to stay in Nashville.

Chapter Twenty-nine

Thursday morning

Tess stood eyeing the murder board. "Time's running out. Let's recap. Sampson?"

Malik leaned back in his chair, a wide smile across his face. "Forensics were able to obtain a DNA profile off Chapman's shirt, now in rags that Ms. Hastings washed, but—hallelujah—didn't bleach." He stood and bowed, giving a powerful Elvis imitation. "Thank you. Thank you very much. Elvis has left the building."

Smiling at her co-worker's irrepressible good spirits, Tess nodded. "All right, we have a DNA match. What else do we have? Irby?"

"Yes, ma'am," Ron replied, his southern drawl a bit exaggerated. "We've been going over the phones retrieved both from Chapman's house and the one at Jerry Ames's home. Thanks to an assist from the FBI, we've unlocked Chapman's iPhone, and the one found at Ames's which we've determined belonged to Brianna Tollison. The last call on Ms. Tollison's was to one of the burners we retrieved from Chapman's house. Also, one of those phones we retrieved was Jerry Ames's own phone. Ames had a video of Chapman meeting with Brianna just an hour or so before she died. It was a heated argument by all appearances. Technical is still working on enhancing the audio. Lots of street noise," he added by way of explanation. "Coincidentally the last call on Ames's phone is to Chapman's office."

"Good work. Okay, we've connected Ames to both Eric Chapman and Brianna Tollison."

Tess drew lines on the murder board from Ames to Chapman and Tollison. "Seth, how are we on the financials?"

Seth finger-combed back a strand of dark hair. "After the time of Jerry Ames's phone call to Chapman's office, it appears Chapman made a cash withdrawal of $100,000 from his stock account on the afternoon before Ames's death. The cash was redeposited the same day Ames's body was found. Looks like Chapman *was* going to pay him, but changed his mind and killed him, instead."

"While I don't doubt your conclusion, it's pretty speculative, and he might be able to explain it away. The video, not so much. What we need is a motive. Why would Chapman pick now to kill Brianna more than a year after she dumped him?"

"This may be speculative too, but I found a connection between Chapman and Brianna's father, Randall Tollison, through one of his shell companies. Apparently, her father used Chapman's software company as resources for his dealings."

"Okay." Tess drew a new line connecting Chapman and Randall Tollison. "Go on. I need more."

Seth smiled. "You ask and you shall receive, boss. It appears Brianna was extorting Chapman. I can trace regular monthly deposits of $10,000 over the last year from his personal account to hers."

"That coincides with about the time he broke her jaw." She drew a second line between Chapman and Brianna. "But what did she need the money for?"

"Maybe she needed the money for her design business," Seth suggested. "Why don't we bring in her business partner and see what she has to say about their financials? Maybe the firm isn't as successful as they appear."

"Okay, bring her in."

Jason walked into Holt Investigations. He nodded to Carrie. "Good morning, Carrie. Scott is expecting me," he said, feeling moderately uncomfortable under her fixed scrutiny.

"I know," she said, shoving her glasses over the bridge of her nose. "And I'm very curious, but I'm not supposed to admit that." She smiled, then asked with a note of concern, "How are you feeling? It hasn't been that long since you were in ICU. Tamsyn was very worried, to say the least."

He nodded. "Almost normal." Now that might be fudging the truth a bit, but he'd recovered faster than he would've ever believed possible. After facing death, even a collapsed lung seemed a minor inconvenience.

"Scott said to go on back. Third door on the right. I'll let him know you're on the way." She reached for the phone.

"Thanks." He walked down the hallway and knocked.

Scott must have been waiting; he opened the door right away. "Come on in. I'm glad you decided to at least come by and see what we're up to. We're expanding pretty rapidly." He led the way to an area obviously under construction. Stacks of architectural plans and workmen in coveralls going about their tasks being the giveaway.

"Don't mind the mess. We've taken over the entire floor of this building as we maneuver our clientele toward an upscale security-based firm."

Surveying the wide area for expansion, Jason nodded. "How do you see my role?"

"As a full partner in Holt Investigations, you would head the security division. Justin is head of IT and IT forensics. More and more, I'm involved in business growth management. My main responsibility lies in keeping Holt Investigations at the forefront of the business community in Nashville."

"I'm impressed with what you've done. How long have you been in business?" Due to prior research, Jason knew the answers to his questions, but he was enjoying Scott's spiel. Tamsyn's brother was a born salesman.

"Let's go back to my office," Scott said. Turning, he continued his presentation. "Ever since my father died. He and his partner retired from the police force and opened the agency a year or so before that happened, going on almost twenty years." Scott shook his head. "I have to tell you the first few years were mainly devoted to keeping our heads above water, paying the rent, and keeping food on the table, but the last ten years or so, we've been growing steadily." Scott opened the door to his office and stood aside for Jason. Gesturing, he said, "Have a seat."

Jason nodded and sat. "And you honestly see a place for me here?"

"You'll be a tremendous asset." Scott patted Jason's shoulder. "Assuming you decide to join us." Scott sat on the corner of his desk.

"The buy-in figure you mentioned is doable." Money wasn't the issue. Doubts. Questions. Could he stand to be around Tamsyn when she'd made it clear all she had time for was a casual relationship? Jason shook his head. "Still, some sticky personal issues."

"None of which will be resolved if you take the position in New York."

"True." New York would be running away. But his father would never understand Jason's leaving the Bureau to stay in Nashville.

"Once the remodeling is completed, I envision room for growth in all the departments: Security, IT, Business Management. Carrie will take over Human Resources, but you'll have the final say on hiring and firing in your division."

Scott talked a good game. More than a game. He had a clear vision of the firm's future. "I need more time. It's a big decision. My career with the Bureau is ready to take off."

"That's why I had to get my offer in," Scott said with a chuckle. "Holt Investigations needs a man of your know-how, Jason. My sister will be tied up in school for the next five years. She won't be around the office. You won't have to see each other unless you want to. And that's all I'm going to say about that."

"But she'll be the firm's attorney once she passes the bar."

"Five *years* from now—" Scott shrugged. "Who knows where we'll be. A lot can happen."

Plenty of time to know if he and Tamsyn had a viable relationship or not. Plenty of time to resolve the doubts and questions.

Tamsyn spent the morning requesting her transcript from MTSU. Then she pored over the Vanderbilt website, checking the requirements for transferring her credits. She called the university admissions office and learned she was too late to apply for the spring semester, but could apply to enter in the fall. Not enroll until the fall semester of the next year. What the hell was she supposed to do for the next eleven months?

She pulled her cell phone from her pocket and called

Carrie. "Can you believe it? I can't start until fall."

"I'm sure that sucks for you," Carrie responded rather unsympathetically. "But guess who's being given the grand tour—*right now?*"

"Oh, please. I don't know. Some big country music singer? Why should I care?"

"Well, you *ought* to care. None other than a certain Special Agent Jason Stone."

"What?" Her heart revved up. "Jason's there?" Why was he taking a tour? Had he decided to take Scott up on his offer, after all?

"Yeah, baby, first thing this morning, Scott told me your fella was coming in and to send him back straightaway."

"I don't understand."

"I don't either. But something is definitely up. Scott only does the tour for prospective clients and big ones at that."

Tamsyn hesitated. Should she mention Scott's offer? He hadn't said anything about keeping it quiet. "Can you keep a secret?"

"Sure. You know me. I'm the soul of discretion. Have to be around here."

"Scott made Jason an offer to buy into the firm. I was furious at first. As if bribing him to stay in Nashville was the way to go. But maybe..."

"Holy mama! That's the solution."

"Not really. I told Jason I was going to be too busy for anything except casual sex. That was so he would make the right decision for his career."

"How uncharacteristically unselfish of you, as well as the exact opposite of what you really want. On the other hand, maybe *casual* is all he wants, too."

That would be even worse. Imagine his being fully

involved in the family business and all he wanted from her was the occasional booty call. "Who the hell knows? I don't."

"You'd better get busy and find out. Gotta go." Carrie disconnected.

Tamsyn huffed, setting her phone on the counter. She still had her last honey trap tonight. Once that was over, how was she going to occupy her time until the fall semester started? No answer in sight. And now she had an even bigger question: what to do about Jason?

Tess followed Brianna Tollison's business partner into the interview room. Everything about Sophie Nunley said *successful*, from her camel wool suit to her geometric silk scarf in shades of brown, orange, and olive green, down to her dark tan Louboutin stilettoes.

The designer sat nervously on the edge of the chair. "Are you any closer to finding Brianna's killer?"

Tess sat across from Nunley. "We're questioning someone, but he hasn't been officially charged yet."

Sophie gripped her bag, her knuckles whitening. "How can I help?"

"I need to know how your business was doing?"

Her dark eyes widened with alarm. Her body tensed. "You don't think her murder had anything to do with our design studio, do you?"

"Possibly. But mainly, I need more background. Is there any reason Brianna would need a regular influx of outside cash? Her father's a wealthy businessman, and her mother comes from an old Belle Meade family. Did she gamble? Use drugs? Is your business sound financially?"

Nunley sighed. "No to the first two. A definite no. But we're a young firm. We struggle. We have a good roster of clients, but it's always a struggle to keep building our brand. We constantly have to put ourselves out there in the community. Other than our clothes, which *is* part of our brand, we lived fairly frugally. We both put our personal money into the business whenever there was a shortfall. Bree always seemed to have plenty of money. I always assumed it came from her family."

"Do you know anything about her former fiancé Eric and her father being in business together?"

"She mentioned once in passing that they had some business dealings, and she bet her father would kill him if he knew how he'd treated her. I thought she was over exaggerating and said so. But she said, no, her father could be quite ruthless in business, and even more so when it came to his little girl."

"Yet Chapman beat her up and he's still alive."

"She always took care to hide the bruises... Except for the *last* time, he never touched her face."

"And that last time?"

"Bree lied when he broke her jaw. She told her father she was mugged and told the police she fell. I wanted her to report Eric as her abuser, but she wouldn't. I guess she didn't want her father to find out and possibly end up arrested for killing Eric." Sophie brought her hand went to her mouth. "It has just dawned on me that Bree had more ready money to put into the firm after that. Do you think maybe—?"

"Thank you for coming in, Ms. Nunley," Tess said, cutting her off. "You've helped a great deal."

She motioned for a uniformed officer to see Bree's partner out. Tess walked down the hall back to the bullpen and to the murder board. "Now we have a motive: evidence of blackmail. We can take this case to the DA. With Megan Hastings's statement, DNA evidence, motive, and the

phone evidence, we have enough evidence to charge Eric
Chapman with both Brianna Tolliver's and Jerry Ames's
murders."

It had taken more than a week, but she and the best
damn team of investigators around had nailed the bastard.

"Good work, guys!"

Thursday evening

Sitting in the den, Justin signed out of his laptop and
closed the lid. Any minute now, Tamsyn would be heading
off for her last case. Good news for him. No more dogging
her steps. Keeping her backside out of trouble. While it was
true that one of the agency's other PIs could cover her butt
just as well, he wanted her last case to go well.

She tapped on the doorjamb. "I'm heading out.
Ready?"

Justin looked up and grinned. "Right behind you.
Don't worry, if I get caught in traffic, I can still track your
phone and your shoes. You are wearing the insoles, aren't
you?"

"Yeah, I like those thingies." She wiggled her foot. "I
can't tell they're there. Besides, if tonight goes like last
night, I'll be in and out before you get parked."

Following Tamsyn was always a little precarious. His
sister drove as if she were a NASCAR driver. Having more
than one way to track her was the way to go. Her current
target frequented a country-western bar in the Gulch. Busy
night. Lots of traffic.

He followed her down West End until it turned into
Broadway. Great. Her red Boxter just blew through the
intersection ahead as the light turned red. He stopped. The
Silver Buckle was only a couple of blocks away on the outer
edge of the Gulch. He could catch up with her in plenty of

time.

Bam! He was thrown forward.

Damn. He'd been rear-ended.

If this honey trap went as well as last night's, she'd be on her way back home in an hour. Last night's mark had been true blue, and despite her best efforts, Tamsyn had been delighted to let her client know that her husband hadn't taken the bait. Maybe there were some men who were faithful to their wives, even if they needed a beer or two before heading home. Now, this was the very last one, and she wasn't looking forward to it, at all.

For one thing, the venue was decidedly low end. Ditto the clientele. The Silver Buckle was nothing like Gatsby's or like the majority of the upscale area. The dance floor was crowded, ass- to-elbow. She glanced over her shoulder. Justin should be coming along any minute. In the meantime, she'd use the time to scope out her target. She'd memorized the photo the client had provided. Ginger-haired cowboy in black. White hat and feather. Bolo tie with turquoise stone. Shouldn't be too hard to find.

Staying on the alert for the cowboy, she sipped her club soda and lime.

"Don't turn around."

Something hard nudged her side. She straightened. "What?"

"Yes, that's a gun in your ribs. I'm *not* happy to see you. You're coming with me."

"The hell I am." She twisted around trying to see her attacker. She knew that voice. Had to be none other than Brad Oliver's sweaty lips next to her ear, his icky warm breath on her neck. Her stomach grew queasy. Did he seriously think he could get away with dragging her out of the Buckle without someone noticing?

He jammed the gun harder. "I said. Don't move."

"If I can't move, then I guess I won't be coming with you. Will I?" she said through gritted teeth.

He dragged her off the barstool. "Move, bitch."

It was so crowded. The music so loud. No one was paying any attention.

Leaning forward, she pretended to stumble, then drew up her knee and rammed one of her stiletto heels into his arch. At the same time, she fumbled in her bag for her handy dandy canister of pepper spray.

"Bitch," he hissed, hopping on one foot. "You'll have to do better than that."

Found it. "Give me time," she said, stalling. Her fingers circled the small canister, then pulled it from her purse, holding her hand close to her side. Waiting...for him to loosen his grip just enough...for the right moment. "Can't blame a girl for trying."

Where the hell was Justin?

Jason sat in his rented condo staring at the TV without really seeing. After the tour, Scott had invited him to join the family for dinner, but given the situation with Tamsyn, he'd declined. Now he had a long boring evening ahead. Maybe he'd just turn in early and allow his battered body more time to recuperate. More than anything, his reattached ear itched like crazy.

His cell phone rang. Justin Lackey, the caller ID read. What did he want? Maybe he objected to the possibility of an outside partner? Reluctantly, he answered, "What is it?"

"Don't ask questions. Just listen. You've got to get to Tamsyn. She's at the Silver Buckle meeting one of her honey traps. I'm supposed to be her backup, but I've had a fender bender. So she's on her own. You live in the Gulch. You're the closest."

"A block away. I'm on it." Without another word, he ended the call, then grabbed a jacket and headed for the door. Should he stop long enough to take his SUV or race down there on foot? A twinge of pain caught him mid-stride. Hang on. He might need to follow her vehicle. The twinge also told him he wasn't in fighting condition if her mark was uncooperative.

Oliver's iron fingers bore into Tamsyn's upper arm. She'd have bruises tomorrow...if she was still alive. He jammed his weapon firmly into her flank. What vital organ was located there? Kidney—well, she had two of them. So she could live without one. "Just shoot me now and get it over with."

"Nah. I intend to introduce you to the *Brad Special*." His voice was raspy and his breath sour with whiskey. "Like the one I gave your friend back in the day. Think you can handle it, bitch?"

"I really hate that word." The heated atmosphere of the club almost suffocated her.

Inexorably, he dragged her toward the door. Where was Justin? How would he ever find her in this crowd of drunken cowboy wannabes?

When they reached the door, a cold blast of air hit her as if someone had dropped an ice cube down her back.

Now or never. Before he could get her into his car. She gripped the can of pepper spray, managing to align the push button and sprayer. Only once chance to get it right. No point in spraying herself in the face. She let her bag slip to the sidewalk and aimed the spray over her shoulder.

A gust of wind blew the spray in her direction. Her

eyes burned, watered. Crap. Damn. Hell. It hurt.

"Shit." Oliver hesitated, stopped. His grip loosened just a bit.

Good. Some of the spray had gotten him too. She yanked her arm away. Or tried to.

"Not so fast." His hold tightened, his free arm going around her neck. "Pull another stunt like that, and I'll break your stupid neck."

Knocking the canister from her hand, he swept his arm around her waist and literally dragged her like a sack of potatoes toward the parking lot.

"No!" She tried to shout, scream, whatever, but his arm was cutting off her air.

Stars danced before her eyes, then blackness enveloped her.

After renting a condo in The Gulch for several months, it hadn't taken him long to learn the downtown area was the place to go for food and entertainment. Tonight it was packed. How would he ever find her? Car lots were full. He double parked and jumped out. Located on the far perimeter of the Gulch, The Silver Buckle was decidedly lower-end. Throngs of people streamed in and out of the popular club. Likewise, the sidewalks were crowded.

"Hey!" he heard a woman's yell. "Someone lost her purse. Anyone know who this belongs to?" She held it aloft.

He craned his neck to see. Hell, he'd know the huge red leather shoulder bag Tamsyn always carried. "Here!" He waved to get the woman's attention. "It's my girlfriend's bag."

Dubious, the woman, looked him up and down. She pulled out the wallet. "What's her name?"

"Tamysn Holt," he replied.

"Winner. Winner. She owes you a chicken dinner." The woman handed it over with a smile.

If Tamsyn's bag was outside the club, she must've already left. Where could she be? He scanned the crowd. No one even bearing a resemblance to Tam.

Hold on. He recognized a tall, lumbering figure clad a black overcoat, heading for the parking lot.

Brad Oliver. What the hell was he doing down here? Not exactly the cowboy-bar type.

Bracing his ribs, he ran toward Oliver who was just slamming the rear door of his Cadillac Escalade. "Brad, wait a sec!"

Oliver stopped. Shaking his head, he stared. "This doesn't concern you, pretty boy." He ran for the driver's side. "Fucking Fed."

"Have you seen Tamsyn Holt?" he yelled, as he caught up with Oliver.

"Who?" He yanked open the door just as Jason clapped hands on him.

"I said wait." He couldn't see inside the vehicle. Dark windows. Maybe he was making the wrong call. *Nah.*

Oliver spun around and rammed a vicious back fist into Jason's ribs. Nausea and pain threatened to overwhelm him. *No. Can't give up. He has Tamsyn. Know it in my gut.*

By the time he recovered from the blow, Oliver was inside the vehicle and revving the engine. Suddenly the Caddy reversed. Jason jumped out of the way, barely. Catching his breath, he sprinted for his vehicle. He couldn't afford to lose Oliver in traffic. Upon reaching the Range Rover, he craned his neck to catch a glimpse of the Escalade.

There. It was heading up 1st Avenue S. ready to turn onto Union.

A plan. He needed a plan. He didn't want to ram Oliver's vehicle and risk Tamsyn's life. No way had Oliver bothered to belt her in. Where was he taking her?

Consciousness returned with a flash. Tamsyn sucked in a deep breath. Damn the man. Now that Brad's meaty arm wasn't crushing her ribs, her thinking powers returned. "Where are you taking me? You won't get away with this. My brother is right behind us."

"There's someone behind us, bitch, but I don't think he's your brother." He laughed an evil sound that sent a chill up her spine. "It won't do him any good. I know this town like the palm of my hand. Your FBI lover doesn't have a chance."

FBI lover? So Jason was chasing them? How did that happen? With his injuries, he might just need some help. Feeling around the backseat, she tried to find something to slow down the pursuit. Too bad she'd lost her purse. She could've used the strap to choke the bastard. "You'd better slow down. There's a lot of traffic tonight."

"Fuck the traffic." He whipped the steering wheel sharply careening around a corner, fishtailing as they went. She slid across the seat into the opposite side. "Whoa! You're trying to kill me. I won't get to see the Brad Special if you keep this up." Like never, if she had anything to say about it.

He whipped into a parking garage, crashing through the barrier. The car sped around level after level. "I'll show you the Brad Special right now. I've lost your boyfriend, and I'll find us a nice dark corner. Feel free to struggle all you want. I like it when women fight. Makes me hot."

Her mouth dried. Sick bastard. All he needed was mustache to twirl. She'd show him *hot*.

He braked, then jammed the lever into park.

She positioned herself on her back and raised her knees. Fight hell. She was going to run. He yanked open the door and leaned in, his fat face with an expectant expression. She aimed her stilettos at that fat face and rammed him good. Perfect.

"Ugh!" Grabbing his eyes, he stumbled back. "Bitch! Blinded me. Kill you!"

Grabbing the second's opening, she sprang from the car.

She kicked off her shoes, stopping only long enough to bend down and grab one. She might need a weapon. And Justin could still track her.

Barefoot, she ran and screamed, "Fire! Fire!" And ran. Ran like the devil.

Behind her, she could hear him beginning to recover. Footsteps, faltering, but all the same, he was still behind her. He wouldn't give up so easily. And once he got going, he'd be fast. She remembered that much from the first time he'd tried to grab her.

He'd lost them. Jason braked, slowing the SUV down to a crawl. Okay. Oliver had turned on Union. Where could he have gone? No sign of the Escalade on Union. Panic rose in his chest, his heart threatening to explode. He had to find her. Grabbing his cell phone, he called Justin. "I've lost her."

"No problem. I installed trackers on her phone."

"She dropped her purse, and I have her phone."

"Good thing I put trackers in those crazy shoes she likes to wear. I'll send you the app I use to track her."

Jason's phone pinged, signaling the arrival of Justin's handy app. A loud blast of a car horn spurred him to turn left on Third. Still, no sign. How could they have disappeared so quickly?

He stopped, and again, double parked. The app downloaded quickly. Right away, a flashing red dot appeared. Just off to his right. Close.

Oliver must've pulled into the parking garage. Then he heard a woman screaming, "Fire."

Smart. Better than yelling, "Rape."

Movement caught his eye. There—in the periphery of his vision—a woman struggling with a man in the entrance to the parking garage. Tamsyn and Oliver.

He turned off the motor, pulled his SIG Sauer from the locked compartment, then sprang from the SUV. Oliver was dragging her farther back into the dark recesses of the garage. She was struggling and stabbing at her attacker's body with a stiletto-heeled shoe.

He ran toward them. "Let her go! Federal agent! Let her go!" He grabbed Oliver's shoulders and jerked, loosening his hold on Tamsyn.

Freed, she let go with a stream of creative obscenities—some of which Jason had never heard, but seemed appropriate to the occasion.

Oliver turned, lowered his head and charged. Oliver caught Jason on his left side. Thankfully, not the right.

Jason rocked back but somehow managed to stay on his feet, his hand on his weapon.

Tamsyn leaped onto Oliver's back, drew back, and stabbed the heel of her shoe into his shoulder.

"Agh!" He turned, glared, ripped the shoe from his shoulder, and flung it to the garage floor.

Tamsyn's distraction gave Jason time to draw his SIG Sauer. "You're done, Oliver. Give it up."

His face contorted, Oliver roared and aimed a Magnum .357.

Jason fired. Oliver dropped in place.

"Is he dead?" Tamsyn asked, her voice barely above a whisper.

"Yeah. Three shots. Center Mass. Very dead."

"Omigod." She rushed to Jason's side. "Are you all right? Did he hurt you?"

"Me?" he scoffed, ignoring the rasping pain in his chest. "What about you?"

Her face paled. "I'm okay, but I think I need to sit down for a minute. Or two. She started to sag. "I feel kind of weird." He caught her before she could hit the ground. He slid his arm around her waist and together they limped over to his SUV. He opened the door with his free hand, so she could sit. Damn, he needed to sit too. "You're all right. It's the adrenaline. Put your head between your knees." Needing a moment to catch his breath, he gave a sigh of relief.

She smiled at him. "Yes, sir."

That brave smile warmed his heart. She was all right. He'd come so close to losing her. No telling what Oliver had in mind. He'd come armed.

By this time a small crowd had gathered. "FBI", he said holding up his ID badge. "Crime scene. Stay back." After taking photos with his cell phone, he called 911, explained the situation, asking, in addition, for Detective Holt to be dispatched since one of her family members was involved. "They'll send Tess," he told Tamsyn while keeping an eye on Oliver's weapon to prevent any onlookers from making off with it. "Now I have to call my boss."

Tamsyn sat in Jason's SUV, shivering. In a minute or so, there'd be sirens. Not yet. She rubbed her arms to stop the tremors. How much was due to adrenaline and how much was due to coming within a hair's breadth of seeing Jason die? Her heart had nearly stopped.

How had he found her? She'd dropped her purse, forgetting in the confusion that her phone had Justin's tracking app on it. Somehow Jason had just shown up when she needed him most. She'd made it to the entrance when Brad had latched on and started dragging her away.

She'd come way too close to finding out about the Brad Special. Way too close. Her body shuddered at the memory. The stink of his nervous sweat. Sour whiskey breath.

Someone rapped on her window. She jumped, but quickly recovered and opened the car door. "Justin! What happened to you?"

"Fender bender." His blue gaze checked her for damage. "You okay?"

"Shaken, but not stirred." Okay, she was both shaken and stirred. Who wouldn't be after being dragged off by a rapist? "And how did Jason find me?"

"I sent him the tracking app."

"But I didn't have my phone on me."

"Your shoes." Justin reached over and tussled her hair.

"Right. Good thing I kept one handy." She let out a sigh of relief. "You're a genius. Thank heaven."

The wail of multiple sirens blasted into her consciousness. "We're going to be here all night."

"It'll take as long as it takes, Tam."

"Thank you for sending Jason." She slipped her arms around her brother's neck and gave him a bear hug. "If he hadn't come when he did…"

"I know. I know. But you're safe now."

She gazed over Justin's shoulder. Jason was performing crowd control. Any second, MNPD would take over the crime scene. There was so much she wanted to say. To do.

But all that could wait. It would have to. Two large black SUVs had just pulled in behind Justin's SUV. The Feds had arrived.

Chapter Thirty

Friday Morning

Outside their First Avenue N. condo, the sky was dark with thunderclouds. Tess sat across from Scott at the breakfast bar, inhaling the always fragrant aroma of her coffee. "I really need this," she said, then took a sip.

Scott reached across the granite counter and stroked her hand. "You haven't been to bed yet. Have time to tell me what happened?"

She smiled at the tenderness of his touch. What she wouldn't give to spend the morning curled up in the bed with her husband. "Long story, but I do have time. I'm not going in until this afternoon."

She spent the next fifteen minutes relating the details of Tamsyn's abduction by Brad Oliver and his subsequent death at the hands of one FBI Special Agent Jason Stone. "Plus, we've closed the case on two murders—well, Brianna Tollison's murder for certain. The DA is still a bit iffy on Jerry Ames. She wants me to come up with more evidence connecting Chapman and Ames but given enough time, we'll find it."

Scott sipped his coffee. "I don't suppose you want to share the nitty-gritty."

"You know I can't, but I will tell you this much. The DA is charging Eric Chapman with first-degree murder in Brianna Tollison's case. We have everything: DNA; video of an argument they had less than an hour before her time of death, and a statement from his fiancée blowing apart his alibi, solidly implicating him in the murder."

"So a slam-dunk." Scott leaned back with a smile. "You must be thrilled."

She shook her head. "Stop it. That's bad luck. No case is ever a slam dunk; however, I feel certain she'll ask for the death penalty unless he makes some kind of deal."

"Congratulations." He took a sip of coffee. "By the way, I offered Stone a partnership in the firm."

She straightened. "You did?" Just when she thought her husband could never surprise her. "What brought that on?"

"Tamsyn, but of course she's halfway pissed off, anyway. Called it a bribe. Even said she doesn't want anything to do with his staying unless he tells her he really wants to."

"Will he take your offer?"

"Don't know. He said he won't unless she asks him to stay."

"Well, crap. Aren't they a pair?"

"You said it."

She stood, walked around the counter and massaged his shoulders. "I don't suppose you could go into the office a little late this morning?"

He turned around and slipped his arms around her waist. "Thought you'd never ask." He swept her into his arms and carried her to the bedroom.

Her heart filled with love for this man. Her man. Forever.

His future still undecided, Jason strode into SAC Michael Chase's office for the formal debriefing on Brad

Oliver's shooting. He'd spent the majority of the night with MNPD's homicide unit. With Tamsyn's statement on record, he wouldn't be charged. Still, whether his superior would bust his chops or not was another matter.

Chase glanced up from the papers on his desk. "Right on time. Good." He leaned back, gesturing for Jason to have a seat. "You look rough. Get any sleep?"

"Not much." He sat, willing his body to relax. "After I gave my formal statement to Metro, I got home in time to shower and change and come in here."

"Before we start, the Special Agent in Charge in New York called. He's pressing for a decision."

"That's still on offer?"

"It is."

Jason sucked in a breath and blew it out. "I'm on the verge of deciding."

Chase leaned back. "Look, you can stay here. You're a good agent, and you can definitely handle yourself. The downside is it may be two or three years before an opportunity for promotion opens up. The task force position in New York is guaranteed. They want you."

Jason nodded. "You should know I have another offer to consider, as well."

An expression of consternation crossed Chase's face. "That–uh, P.I. asked you to stay? Not that your personal life is my concern."

"Actually, Scott Holt of Holt Investigations asked—no, he offered to make me a partner in the family firm. If I buy in, I'll head their Security division."

"You can afford that?" Chase chuckled. "Should I be going over your financials?"

He felt his face heat. Uncomfortable under Chase's scrutiny, Jason shifted in his seat. Talking about his inheritance gave the impression he was some kind of trust fund brat. "It's family money, sir. There's enough."

"As for New York, you have until the end of the day to decide. Otherwise, they'll go with their second choice." Chase's expression grew firm. "Now, how the hell did you get involved in a shootout in downtown Nashville?"

Jason cleared his throat. "Sir, it was like this..."

After the debrief, Jason sat in the parking lot and called his father. Might as well get it over with. At the very least, he owed the man an explanation of what he was up to. He'd put it off way too long.

His father answered, his tone, as always, impatient.

"Dad."

"I've heard good things. I've been meaning to check in. But I've been in Minnesota on a serial case. I take it you weren't too injured?"

Like he cared. "No. I'm healing. Just thought I'd touch base. I have a decision to make. I've been offered a task force position in New York or I can stay here"

"Easy choice. New York."

"Not so easy."

"Why? Why on God's green earth would you turn down a promotion?"

"There's this woman."

"Right. A woman." Jason could hear Marcus Stone's disgust clearly through the line.

"Not just any woman, Dad. *The* woman. I love her."

"She can't move to New York? What's wrong with her?"

Jason clenched his jaw. "Nothing. She's finishing her degree. After that, law school."

"Sounds too young for you."

"Not true. She's older. She's already had one career as

a private investigator. Her family owns a firm here in Nashville."

"The woman of your dreams, then?" His father's tone softened. "I adored your mother. She was the woman of my dreams until..."

"Until I killed her. That's what you meant to say. Say it."

"I've said it too often." His father quietly added, "And I regret it."

That was as close to forgiveness as his father could come. "Thank you. Losing mom was hard for both of us." And this was as close as Jason could come to forgive his father for years of dismissive criticism and emotional abuse. "By the way, I've been offered a partnership in her family's firm. It's a great offer, Dad."

"I know I've given you hell over the years, but maybe you have to go with your heart. I never regretted going with mine."

"I'll let you know what I decide."

"Do that," his father said, then disconnected.

Typical. Too much time spent on emotion and feelings already. But it was a step forward, at least.

Tamsyn awoke with a groan. She stretched—yes, every single muscle in her body was stiff. Reaching for her phone, she checked the time: one o'clock. Yikes!

Hurriedly, she showered and dressed in a fresh nightshirt and robe. Coffee. She definitely needed coffee. As she descended the stairs, she caught a whiff of what had to be fresh coffee. Someone must've come home for lunch and left it for her. That someone could only be Carrie. Only Carrie would be thoughtful enough to come home to brew a fresh pot of coffee. Bless her. She rushed to the kitchen but stopped at the doorway.

Jason sat at the island, smiling. "Good morning, sleepyhead."

The very sight of him revved her heart. *Keep cool. He's come to say good-bye. That's it.*

Why hadn't she bothered to dress in something besides a sleep shirt and robe? Frowning she set her hands on her hips. "What are you doing here? How'd you get in?"

"After I left the bureau office this morning, I stopped by your office. Carrie was kind enough to give me her key and the passcode to the alarm."

"I see. So you thought you'd just come in here and make yourself comfortable. Great." She entered the kitchen. The aroma of fresh coffee was irresistible.

"I brought bagels." He nodded toward a bag. "And I made coffee."

"Still—"

"I saved your freaking life last night. You could cut me some slack."

"Well, there is that," she said, churlishly. Why couldn't he just get the goodbye over with and leave her in her misery?

Avoiding his gaze, she busied herself with spreading strawberry cream cheese on her whole wheat bagel. How did he know she liked whole wheat? Carrie probably. Oh-so-helpful Carrie.

"Thank you for the coffee and bagels."

"And," he prompted.

"For saving my life. I'm not sure he was going to kill me, but he definitely had something else on his mind." At that, her body trembled. She crumpled. Her eyes running, worse her nose. Jason pulled her into his arms.

"H-he was going to r-rape me, for sure," she sniffed.

"No doubt about it. Why would he leave you alive to

accuse him in court? He had a gun. I'm very afraid he would've used it."

"He was going to kill you," she sobbed. "Y-you shot him in self-defense."

He caressed her hair, soothing her. "Yes, the detectives agreed. They pulled CCTV footage from the parking garage. The whole incident was caught on tape."

"Good. So you won't get in trouble." She gazed into his icy blue eyes.

"No." He pulled a tissue from the box on the island. "Here. Blow your nose."

She blew. "You've seen me at my worst, snotty nose and all."

He smiled down at her. "*And* I've seen you at your best."

"When was that?" She blew again.

"Without going into lurid details..." His voice dropped into that sexy range she loved. "It would have to be during a certain rainy Sunday morning in Brentwood. You invaded my personal space," he said, favoring her with a sexy grin.

"You! Of all the nerve. Surely I've had better moments than that."

"Not with me," he said lazily, then took a sip of coffee. "Eat your bagel."

She took a bite, savoring the creamy cheese. "You never said why you're here. If you're here to say good-bye, say it. Get it over with."

"I'm still undecided. But I have to tell them by the end of the day whether I'll take the New York spot or not."

"It's your career." She shrugged as if it made no difference to her when it the thought of his leaving was killing her.

"Come with me. Carrie said you didn't start school

until next fall. Come with me. You would love New York City."

"And that idea makes no sense at all. Not one bit. I can't just up and leave. I still have things to do in preparation for going back to school."

"Need to buy new pencils and a backpack? A supply of legal pads?" he gently mocked.

"T-there's paperwork. Applications. All sorts of stuff."

"*Stuff* you can do online. I'm sure you've heard of it. There's this wonderful thing called the Internet."

"Pfft," she scoffed. "So what. My spending a few months in New York won't solve anything."

"What's to be solved?"

"For one thing, you'd never be around. I'm not going to New York to sit in some tiny apartment while you're having the time of your life chasing bad guys. My father was in law enforcement. He wasn't around a lot. I'm sure the FBI will have plenty for you to do." She shook her head. "No. I'll stay here and proceed with my plan." And what about his other choice: Scott's offer? Not one blessed word about that.

"I could stay here." He added with a wry smile, "It would only put my career back two or three years."

"I won't be responsible for ruining your career or delaying it or whatever."

"It would be *my* choice."

Was he wavering? Was he playing her? Torturing her with the possibility he might stay? "Why on earth would you want to stay here and pass up a great opportunity in New York? Career-wise it doesn't make sense. None at all."

He took her face in his hands, his gaze warm and tender. "I'm not just my job, Tamsyn. I'm a man, too. If I stay, it'll be because of you. I've fallen in love with you."

The words. He said the *words*.

"I won't be the one who holds you back," she protested, feebly this time. Her heartbeat surged with excitement she didn't dare show.

An expression of consternation flickered across his handsome face. "Tamsyn, did you hear me? I said 'I love you.' Are you so set on your future plans that you won't have time for our relationship? So all you're interested in is an occasional hookup? Is that truly all you want from me?"

"Don't act like you don't have another choice."

"Another choice?" He gave her a mischievous grin. "Oh, you mean the partnership in your family's business. That?"

"Yes, that!" She poked his chest with a finger. "You're torturing me and enjoying it."

Jason shook his head slowly. "Not so. I won't take his offer unless you agree. I don't want to be a thorn in your side. A constant reminder of how I feel and you don't."

"Scott said you saw obstacles," she said with a pout. "Don't you want to stay here? You say you're in love with me."

"Oh, I am."

"Why should that be an obstacle?"

"Contrary to what you might think, I'm not a stalker. I won't stay where I'm not wanted."

Unable to hold her tears back, they began to spill down her cheeks. "I-I want you to stay. I just don't want to ruin your career. I don't want you to hate me."

"Silly woman. I could never hate you." He inclined his head and kissed her forehead. "And I'll never be bored."

"Then stay." She swiped away her tears. No man had ever made her cry before. "Take Scott up on his offer. I may be swamped with school work for the foreseeable future, but I'll still have time to love you."

A broad smile wreathed his face, his gaze growing

warm and tender. "Tamsyn, am I hearing you correctly?"

"I love you. I don't understand it, but I love you. I've never felt this way before. Please stay. I love you. I really, really love you." There. Words she'd never said to any man. Feelings she'd never felt. A future she'd never thought she could have.

"And I'm really, *really* glad." Hesitating, he bit his bottom lip.

"What?" Why the change in expression. What was he holding back? "Okay, what is it? Tell me now, or I'll never give you any peace until you do."

He gave a little chuckle. "Now don't be mad. After the debriefing, when I went by the office, I accepted Scott's offer."

"So you *were* torturing me and enjoying it." She gave a pout.

"Maybe a little."

"Now it's my turn." Her hands went to his belt buckle, unfastening it until she had the free end firmly in her grasp. She gave a tug and headed for the stairs. "Come on. You're mine and don't you ever forget it."

He stopped, immovable, and pulled her into his arms. "Some room for discussion about who belongs to whom."

"Maybe—" He stopped her onslaught of words with his mouth. He kissed her, thoroughly too, his tongue probing the inner recesses of her mouth, then hitched her body upward, her legs around him, his erection nudging through his trousers.

"Not here," she said, giving him a lazy smile. "My room."

"Your room, it is."

Unbelievably, injuries and all, he carried her up the stairs. He laid her gently on her bed. Dizzy with love and lust, her mind soared.

This man of her dreams. This man who filled her heart with love and swept her body to heights of passion, before unknown, undreamt.

And so freaking hot.

The End

About the Author

Marie-Nicole Ryan was born in a small western Kentucky town, but aftercollege and marriage, she said "Good bye" to small town life. After spending three years as an army wife, she landed in Nashville, TN, where she spent several decades working as an R.N. and case manager. Finally in 2002, she achieved her dream of becoming a published author.

She loves writing about lawmen and detectives. She writes contemporary romantic suspense, as well as erotic historical western romance. TOO GOOD TO BE TRUE, won a 2008 EPPIE for erotic romantic suspense. In addition, her mystery/suspense novel, ONE TOO MANY, was a 2009 EPPIE Finalist.

She was an active member of RWA® for many years, as well as PAN, MCRW, and PASIC. Currently she lives in western Kentucky. When she's not slaving away at her current work in progress, you might find her walking her dog Kelsea, a Sheltie rescue, or at the Y. But you won't ever find her in an airplane. No, not ever.

Also by Marie-Nicole Ryan

Music City Heat Series
Measure of a Man, 3
Because of You, 2
Love Me if You Can, 1
Beginnings, Prequel Short Story

Hill Country Lawmen
Hunted, 1

FBI Guys
Broken Promises, 2
Holding Her Own, 3

Love the Lawman Series
Mastering the Marshal, 3
Pleasuring the Pinkerton, 2
Seducing the Sheriff, 1

Stand-alone Romantic Suspense
Too Good to be True
The Man for the Job
See You in My Dreams

David & Miranda French Mysteries
One Too Many
Love on the Run

Holiday Interludes Short Stories
Valentine's Gift, 3
Pillow Talk, 2
Mistletoe & Mario, 1